Rough Diamonds

ALSO BY KURT JOHNSON

The Outlaw Shuffle

Las Vegas Turnaround

The Barrens (with Ellie Johnson)

Rough Diamonds

KURT JOHNSON

First Published by Street Level Press

Copyright © 2025 Kurt Johnson

All rights reserved.

ISBN: 979-8-9900350-1-0

Street Level Press
www.StreetLevelPress.com

For Cecil – He'd fit right in.

CHAPTER 1 – THE SWEDE
May 1991, Chicago

The old folks in Oak Ridge were dying off like poisoned roaches. Most homes in that suburb were built when Karol was just a baby, and those first owners were now living in decaying skins—if still alive. They'd raised their kiddies, saw them off to college, saved their pennies, retired from clean desk jobs, and now undertook the process of getting dead; their life cycles coordinated like a German waltz. About every weekend, he'd driven out to the suburb in his Buick to paw through estate sales, eyeballing the cast-off antiques and collectibles that the now-educated offspring thought too antiquated or unfashionable for their own paint-by-numbers domiciles. Those kiddies were all foggy on dollar values.

Chester and Hines ran nearly all the top-dollar estate sales. As far as Karol understood, neither Chester nor Hines still managed the business day-to-day, and the job belonged to a fuddy-duddy woman, Dawn, who coincidentally woke up at dawn each weekend to open a decedent's doors to the wolfpack of deal seekers: collectors like himself, snoopy neighborhood homeowners, antique peddlers, junk dealers, and grubby hoarders. Karol mailed Dawn a newly minted one-hundred-dollar bill each month for inside information and the sole privilege of getting first pick. She'd phoned him earlier to let him know this coming sale had a glass cabinet full of the porcelain figurines Karol collected. He was there before the doors opened.

He needed to be careful, shifty. Another collector he knew from antiques shows and swap meets, Hazel Smooth, was wise to his setup. She stood on the concrete sidewalk in tight designer jeans, waiting for the doors to unlock. She'd make a scene if she saw him enter the home before others. She'd done it before, yelling like a lady whose purse was snatched, "He's cheating!" The outburst had sent Dawn into a convulsive fit, and he'd had to smooth things over with an extra C-note.

Karol crept through the neighbor's yard and jumped the dividing five-foot fence, barely scuffing his brogues. He rapped on the back door of the sunroom. Dawn let him in a minute later, looking on like some annoyed schoolteacher whose snot-nosed student wanted a changed grade. She stood momentarily, her arms crossed, then walked away without a polite howdy-doo. All this to show Karol that their little exchange was somehow beneath her. Dawn could think whatever she wanted.

He stepped in and silently closed the door.

His eyes searched out pre-war figurines from Lladro, Dresden, or Meissen. Karol couldn't say why he'd started collecting the dusty knick-knacks. The when was simple enough. His grandmother had died, and he purchased her two-bedroom bungalow in Andersonville. The tiny house came with a glass cabinet filled with figurines. All had been post-war

Hummels, innocent German and Swiss children at play. His dead grandfather, whom Karol never knew, had been a G.I. stationed in Bonn and shipped the figurines home, probably snatched from some pathetic Nazi widow. And then maybe part of the why had to do with his father, an alcoholic bum who had died two years after his mom, leaving Karol at the age of seventeen to care for himself and a younger sister. The figurines did not shoot smack, drink booze, or fuck. The cleanliness of that appealed to him. Karol still lived in the bungalow, now lined with eighteen glass cabinets filled with his collection.

He followed Dawn at a distance through the sunroom and into the living room, where the display case stood. Like she'd said, it was filled with figurines. Right off, scattered among the Hummels and Disneys, which he had little use for, stood a Meissen Monkey Orchestra Conductor worth over a grand. He possessed others in the monkey orchestra—the bagpiper, drummer, and flutist. Dawn stood nearby and watched. Without having to be told, she stepped up and unlocked the cabinet. He fingered the price tag and saw it was marked at five hundred. Without looking at Dawn, he nodded. She slapped a SOLD sticker over the marked price.

Karol left the way he'd come and, with his lanky height of six-foot-two, easily scrambled over the fence a second time. He waited in his Buick until after the front door unlocked and the initial onslaught of deal seekers thinned. He stood by until he witnessed Hazel leaving empty-handed. Then, he collected his monkey.

◆ ◆ ◆

The doorbell rang. He was back at his grandmother's

bungalow, sitting with a tuna fish sandwich at the kitchen dinette with his new acquisition. Karol hadn't thoroughly studied the figurine at the sale, so while eating, he examined the monkey's tricorn hat, orange topcoat, monkey feet, and unbroken conductor's baton—near perfect for a hundred-year-old porcelain. To Karol, the monkey was more than just a valuable piece of clay; it was rapturous, like what he guessed a priest felt at the sight of a virgin choir boy.

He put down his sandwich and wiped his hands with a disposable napkin, then stood to answer the door.

He lived alone, had no wife, girlfriend, or children—illegitimate or otherwise—and was not expecting visitors. He walked into the front room and looked through the heavy damask curtains. He knew instantly who it was from the unmarked patrol car parked at the curb. Tommy Ryan, a Chicago detective.

He opened the door an arm's length. "Hey Tommy, what's doin'?" Karol did not put out his hand for the detective to shake—he preferred not shaking hands—and Tommy knew better than to offer his.

"Hey, Swede. Not much." Tommy and the others called him "Swede." He was only half Swedish, but he thought the "Swede" business had more to do with his girly first name, which most couldn't bring themselves to say out loud. He couldn't care less what name they used. He'd once answered to Asshole, but after that one time, not again.

He stepped aside and let Tommy in. "What brings you out?"

Karol knew what brought him out, a job—anything else and he would've called. Tommy worked as a bagman for Sam Stantuffo, a made Outfit guy everyone called Tufa. Karol had done only one job for Tufa in the past, a motel break-in. He'd known about a jeweler transporting goods to some dealers downtown. Tufa knew the day and place where the guy would be staying the night. He even had a key copied for the exact motel room door. It was an easy job that Karol did himself. Boost a car, change the plates, sit in the parking lot until the guy goes out for supper, then open the door and take the case. Of course, it had all been set up in advance. Normally, Karol did his own thing, mostly freight hijacking with a few connections he had at the Stock Yards. But it was hard to say no to Sam Stantuffo. Tufa was a word for a type of stone found in Italy, and the guy would come down rock-hard—something would get busted. He figured Tommy had a similar job lined up.

"Let's sit down and talk."

"Okay, in the kitchen." He walked toward the back, and the detective followed. Karol knew the place with all its glass cabinets looked queer for a flatfoot like Tommy, the insides cluttered with porcelain figurines, the kind old ladies hoarded. He cared about appearances up to a point, that point being the front door of his home. He didn't care at all what Tommy thought about the stuff. Karol put his plate and half-eaten sandwich in the sink and sat down. Tommy sat across, looking at the Monkey Orchestra Conductor.

Tommy nodded toward the figurine between them. "What's that?"

Karol slid the monkey to the table's edge, minimizing its distraction. "Nothin'."

Tommy smoothed back his longish hair with both hands. "Okay." He started in. "We got another job for you."

"Yeah?"

"You know Jewelers Row? Mallers Building on Wabash?

"Sure."

"Well, a guy from New York is bringing in a case full of diamonds. Two Jews on the seventh floor want us to do a stick-up on this guy once he's in the building."

"By us, you mean me?"

"Yeah, you. They'll know you're coming. You say it's Jacob from downstairs, and they'll let you in. It's an insurance deal, so you'll need to make it look like you didn't know the New York guy would be there. The two Jews will leave a few other things around the office for you to grab, like watches and stuff. Knock the three around a little to make it look good. The guy's coming next week, Tuesday, 10 a.m. That's it." Tommy raised his hands in the air and swiped them together. "Easy peasy."

"Easy."

Tommy was dirty. Not just a dirty cop, but filthy with greasy spots on his tie, his shirt collar opened and sweat-stained, and his corduroy blazer ill-fitting with the shoulders too wide and sleeves too long, which said something about Tommy's body—narrow shoulders, short arms, and bratwurst-fed belly. Tommy didn't know about easy. "It's a two-man job. What's the pay?"

"Ten grand. You split it any way you want."

"Why doesn't Tufa use his own guys? Why me?"

Tommy leaned his elbows on the table. He whispered as though someone had an ear to the walls. "He don't trust his own guys not to pocket a few stones. And you, Swede, got a nice reputation." Funny how Italians don't trust other Italians. They always want a good white boy to count their money. Swede.

Karol did have a reputation, one he was proud of. He didn't take from the top and didn't steal. If he hijacked a load, what he delivered always matched the manifest. He could've snatched a few jewels from the case he'd heisted from that motel, but he didn't. Karol said simply, "Okay." He'd learned early that words were a liability, like women and kids.

"Then we're good?"

"Write down all the details." Karol removed his squarish, black-framed glasses and cleaned the lenses with a small chamois from his back pocket.

"Great." Tommy lifted his elbows from the table and swung his arms out and up like some touchdown signal. In the process, his left hand clipped the porcelain monkey's head.

Karol dropped his glasses and instinctively reached over with outstretched hands, his chest bucking the dinette. But he was too slow. The Meissen Monkey Conductor spun to the linoleum floor. Shards of porcelain shot into all corners of the kitchen.

"Fuck! Sorry Swede. I didn't mean to do that. Fucking sorry."

Karol picked up his eyeglasses, which were not broken. He tried to remain calm. Notwithstanding, he wanted to kill the dirty, grubby cop and would've under different circumstances. He knew he couldn't—if he put up a big stink about the broken monkey, crying over a busted clay doll, he'd be sending a message that he was anything but tough. It would cost him in the end. But that monkey meant something to him. He wasn't sure exactly what, but the monkey was as real as flesh to Karol. Realer. He clamped down on his emotions and forced out the words, "Don't worry about it."

Tommy quickly lifted out written instructions from his inside coat pocket. He laid down the three sheets of paper torn from a spiral notebook directly on the spot where the figurine had just stood.

Two seconds later, the detective was out the door.

His brother-in-law came from a Canadian mining town five hundred miles north of Winnipeg called Flin Flon. Karol understood from a mostly one-sided conversation that, in addition to digging for copper and drinking beer, the working stiffs there played ice hockey. The town had sent some to the professional leagues, tough miners who'd clawed their way up from the Flin Flon Bombers using their fists more than finesse, which fit the description of his idiot brother-in-law, Dunc.

Karol dialed Dunc right after sweeping the porcelain shards off the kitchen floor. He laid out the job in easy steps that Dunc could follow and offered up a couple grand for help with the muscle work. Dunc made peanuts playing hockey with the American League Wolves, and two thousand for a half-day's work was a no-brainer. They'd done jobs together in the past, and this one was simple enough. They agreed to meet an hour before at a coffee shop near Jewelers Row to go over the details one more time. He told Dunc to dye his hair black, wear a dark suit and tie, a black fedora, and bring dark glasses and gloves.

Karol was there a half hour before Dunc, sitting in a booth and gathering his thoughts. He carried what he needed in a charcoal-gray American Tourister briefcase: two Colt Government 45s, dark glasses, gloves, a drawstring sack, and a roll of duct tape.

Dunc showed up on time, ambling in with his bowlegged gait, which his sister had explained resulted from skating on ice rather than scurvy. His hair was black, and he wore a black suit, white shirt, dark tie, and black fedora. Karol had also dyed his hair black and wore a similar outfit, both business-looking,

Jewish-looking, like they belonged at a jewelry wholesaler market. Dunc sat down and ordered coffee and a Danish from the waitress. Karol then went through each detail of the job—how they'd get into the building and past the security guard, the "Jacob" greeting, what they were after, and how they should make it appear. Karol finished by saying, "It's set up. The two Jews are in on it. All we got to do is make it look like a random robbery."

Dunc looked up. Besides being bowlegged, he had a smashed nose. It looked like a mouse was stuck inside and trying to tunnel its way out. "They know they're going to get robbed? How does that figure?"

"It's an insurance thing. They get robbed, get insurance for the stolen goods, and then get most of the goods back after the guy who hired us gets his piece."

Dunc paused, then said, "Oh yeah, sure."

Whether or not Dunc actually understood an insurance scam did not matter.

The two walked down Wabash to the Mallers Building. The day was sunny, and both wore dark glasses. At the entrance to the building, a tired guard with a clip-on tie and peaked cap sat on a stool next to a ledger. The guy carried a Billy club in a loop on his belt, and no service pistol. Karol knew the building security wasn't too tight—more about keeping bums from stumbling in off the street. He and Dunc presented fake business cards printed on a small letterpress in Karol's basement the day before. They signed the register, the reason for visiting, and the time. Dunc's alias was David Levy, a simple Jewish name that could easily be remembered and spelled, but Karol noticed that in the book he wrote, David Levis, like the jeans. How Dunc could confuse the names, he didn't know, but the security guard did not notice or even look.

They took the elevator to the 7th floor. Karol rang the doorbell. The door itself was reinforced with steel sheeting, drilled through with a peephole, and secured with double bolts. He heard from inside. "Yes? What?"

"This is Jacob from downstairs." He and Dunc had their dark glasses and gloves on, their handguns out and ready. Karol saw the light through the peephole go dim as the guy peeped through.

"Okay, okay, just a minute."

The bolts turned. When the door cracked open, Dunc pushed his shoulder through. Swede followed.

Dunc commanded, "Hands up. Now!"

The three Jews lifted their hands in unison. And to Karol, they all looked alike with dark beards, black wide-brimmed hats, dark clothes, white shirts, and funny sideburn curls. Two wore thick-rimmed black glasses. Tommy hadn't said what the two brothers looked like, and somehow, all assumed it would be obvious. But then it didn't matter; they'd all have to take a beating to make it look right.

Karol hit the closest one in the side of the face with the butt of his pistol. The glasses and hat went flying, and a gash opened up on the side of his head—all as the man dropped to the floor. Karol hit him in the head again, like driving a nail. Dunc punched the one with no glasses in the face. The nose collapsed, blood gushing, and he fell to the ground. Karol looked at the last one standing and could see the edges of his mouth quake, his lips spread in what was sure to be a prolonged sob. Karol motioned with his free hand for the man to get on the ground, and he did it quickly, falling to the floor as though he, too, was beaten. Karol kicked him hard in the gut, then again in the face, shattered glasses flying. Dunc bound each man's hands with duct tape, then stood above, watching.

Karol went through desk drawers and, like Tommy had said, found random jewelry and watches. He threw those into the sack he'd brought. He pulled out each drawer of a filing cabinet, spilling the contents onto the ground, all worthless paper except for one locked canvas deposit envelope, which he took. He did all this while eyeing the leather briefcase on a side table between two chairs. He took his time, searching through a second desk and through the pockets of the black coats hung on wall hooks. When he finally reached the case, he could see that the closure strap was locked with a three-digit tumbler. He removed his dark eyeglasses and cleaned the lenses slowly with the square of chamois from his back pocket. After lifting them back on, Karol pointed his gun at the closest man, the bloodied one he'd hit with his gun, but looked at all three. "What's the combination?" He pulled back the Colt's slide and chambered a round.

The one that had been kicked, apparently the one from New York, said, "1,2,3."

Dunc said, "Serious? I've had piggy banks more secure."

The man did not respond.

Dunc continued, "Now, if I was to keep on me a briefcase with valuable stuff inside, I'd chain it to my wrist."

The man now looked up. His shattered glasses had left cuts around his eyes. He said, "So, then you'd chop it off?"

Dunc nodded as though what the man had said made sense.

Karol ignored the imbecilic exchange and laid his pistol next to the case. He turned just the one tumbler that was out of sequence and popped the lock. Inside were little compartments like he'd seen on antique Advent calendars at estate sales. Each compartment held a single diamond; some he could tell were over five carats, and all were well over two. He collected twenty or so in his palm and tossed them into the duffel. Then, in the corner of the case was a loose velvet baggy the size of a tobacco pouch. He took that also but didn't look inside.

Dunc asked, "What do we got there, Karol?" And just as he finished, Karol could see that Dunc knew he'd fucked up, mentioning his name. He tried to correct himself, "Daryl?"

Karol shook his head. Fucking idiot. He lifted the Colt pistol from the table. He moved quickly over to the man lying on the floor, who'd given up the briefcase combination minutes before. The man from New York. He lay in a fetal position with his bloodied face turned toward the floor, his eyes closed. Karol pulled at the man's suit coat next to him, yanking until it slipped from his arms. He wrapped the coat around the New York man's head. The man lay limp and just allowed Karol to do what he wanted. He pressed the muzzle of the pistol against the coat and pulled the trigger. The sound was loud but muffled. Blood seeped through the folds.

Dunc said nothing.

Before they left, Dunc wrapped duct tape around the mouths and eyes of the surviving brothers.

Karol stuffed the bulging duffel bag, handguns, and duct tape into the Tourister briefcase.

He checked through the peephole to make sure the hallway was clear. They left the office and then rode the elevator to the lobby. Outside, the two walked the half block to the Wabash/Washington platform, both dressed in almost matching black suits, white shirts, dark ties, fedoras, and dark glasses. Just two more Jews in the Diamond District.

It was only later that evening, before Tommy stopped over to pick up the jewelry, cash, and diamonds, that Karol loosened the drawstring of the velvet pouch found in the corner of the briefcase. He shook out the contents onto his kitchen dinette. Spread over the linoleum were about twenty frosted stones the size of Juneberries. Rough, uncut diamonds, like raw clay, ready to be molded and kiln fired. He counted exactly twenty. He knew that once cut, none would be over two carats. At one carat each, medium quality, they were worth approximately thirty grand, a small fraction of the total haul. He picked up each with his pinched fingertips and slipped them back into the velvet pouch.

Karol sat at the same table where, the previous week, Detective Tommy Ryan had broken his valuable Meissen Monkey Orchestra Conductor. He was still angry. The cop had quickly half-apologized and run out the door. Karol knew Tommy and the others thought his collecting was a stupid obsession, like an old lady hoarding crumpled grocery bags. They didn't get that his collection was worth more than any of them made in a year—much more.

Then, two things collided in his mind. Tommy owed him. That, and what everyone knew—given the opportunity to steal, everybody steals.

Karol took the velvet pouch and hid it among his vast collection of porcelain on a top shelf in a rare Dresden gold-leafed urn, the kind that looked as though it could hold human remains. Then he remembered a guy he knew in Las Vegas who ran a jewelry store, and that guy owed him, too.

CHAPTER 2 – SKINNY
Friday, May 18, Las Vegas

Skinny stood out front of the Aladdin Casino near the alley that divided it from Bally's. Back in the alley was an emergency exit, his getaway, where he'd jammed a throwaway hotel keycard between the door's bolt and strike plate. The sun had risen to its peak, high above, and the tourists walked past in groups metered out by the crosswalk lights. He waited under some Arabian-looking cornice, next to a palm tree that offered some shade from the heat. He waited for the onesie-twosie tourists to pass, the slackers who couldn't keep up with the groups released by the green crosswalk light. He looked for a necklace, a gold watch with a twisty band, or a designer handbag.

He also watched people's eyes as they passed, watched to see if they saw him. None looked his direction—none could offer up a description. Skinny thought it was his superpower to become unnoticeable—invisible—and, in a way, disappear. It wasn't like the Invisible Man or anything; he couldn't actually make himself transparent; he wasn't Scotch Tape. Most people just didn't see him. He knew because he noticed. He once stood outside the Flamingo Hotel with a cardboard sign that said HOMELESS, PLEASE HELP, and after hours of standing, or often slumped with his knees tucked to his chest, he was lucky to collect five dollars. He needed twenty-five for a bag of smack just to get through the morning, fifty for a jumbo that would last the day. What was it that made him invisible to these people? The way he looked? Skin tanned to a dust color, average height, kinda skinny, dirty blond shoulder-length hair, a face that was possibly unrecognizable—in a word, non-descript. Then again, he was just another homeless junkie kid on the Strip panhandling for spare change. The tourists in their clean golf shirts and shorts did not fly all the way to Vegas to get reminded of the squalor back home that they could watch from the safety of their minivans. But Skinny figured out months ago that he didn't need to panhandle, that he could turn his one superpower into a moneymaker—just stand there on the Strip, invisible, and watch for the one unsuspecting lady or old dude or fat person with expensive stuff. Then, make his move—the snatch and dash.

Skinny looked for clues to figure out who had the good shit. He'd been burned before. He worked for a good part of one week snatching gold chains, taking a sack full down to Nuts at the jewelry store just to find out most were junk, bad plate jobs that weren't worth squat. So now he watched for the details. The shoes—were they cheap or plastic? Age—older people were more likely to wear the real thing. Guys in khaki pants didn't wear fake chains or replica Rolex watches, but guys in tracksuits did. He'd steal a purse, especially if it was handheld, not strapped to a shoulder or clutched tight to their chest like a football. He could spot a Coach purse. Anyone with a Coach might have stashed inside a stack of casino chips, wads of cash, or credit cards.

So he watched and waited. The lights on Harmon cycled through WALK and DON'T WALK, and it seemed the stragglers were nothing but nickel-slot tourists wearing Timex and tracksuits. But then he saw the perfect mark. The dude looked mid-fifties and fat, like three-bills fat. His pants were bright pink, like the kind he saw golfers wear years ago when he spent a summer toting bags at a course in Costa Mesa. And the man's hat was one of those jaunty Frank Sinatra numbers. The woman was younger, smaller, and pretty, like maybe a second wife the guy could afford. Country Club people. She wore a string of fat pearls that Skinny figured had to be the pricey real thing. Skinny knew the real ones were knotted and wouldn't slip off the string when pulled from a neck, spilling onto the sidewalk like a bag of marbles. Nuts—if he'd still let him into the store—would take a pearl necklace.

They passed him without even looking in his direction. Invisible.

Skinny silently stepped in behind to get a closer look. Gaps in the pearls, knots. He made his move. He ran the three steps as fast as a cat, slipped his middle finger under the necklace, and yanked. The gold clasp broke easily, and the strand came off in one piece—no marbles on the sidewalk.

The woman screeched, something like the sound of that chimp, Cheeta, from the old Tarzan movie.

The man turned just as Skinny ran back toward the alley. He heard, "Hey, stop." A man whose commands at his company or wherever were almost always obeyed. Then, just as Skinny turned the corner, he heard another voice, "Stop that kid." No one stood within a hundred feet, no one who would catch him before he reached the door. The fat man would certainly not give chase.

He stopped at the emergency exit. The door was spring-loaded with no outside handle. He had a little tool, one of those paint can openers you get free from the hardware store, the kind with a beer cap opener on the other end. He'd done the trick countless times, wedging the tool into the crack between the door and frame, then prying. As soon as the door passed the frame, the plastic key card fell to the ground. He caught the door's edge with his fingers.

Skinny looked back. A guy was chasing him, closing in from about fifty feet away. He hadn't seen the guy on the street and wondered whose magician's top hat he'd stepped from.

The door was open half a foot when he lost his grip, and the spring-loaded door started to shut. He quickly reached into the gap to get a new hold. But the spring was tight, and the door was sheathed in heavy steel. He had just one middle finger in the gap, the same finger used to snatch the pearls, when the door crushed it.

The guy was now almost on him, but Skinny was able to get the rest of his fingers through the gap and open the door. He slipped past and quickly pulled the crash bar. Outside, he heard the guy banging on the thick steel. Skinny was in a stairwell, safe for now, and no one was around to hear the hammering fists.

He entered the casino and walked casually toward a back entrance. His crushed finger had started bleeding, and he shoved that hand into his pants pocket to cover any drips that might attract the attention of some security dick.

In his other pocket was the necklace. His adrenaline-fueled mind quickly did the math. The pearls had to have cost the fat man a thousand or more. Nuts would give him a fraction of that, maybe two hundred. Two hundred would get him a couple jumbos plus a week at the Oasis Motel with clean sheets and air conditioning.

A nice score.

Skinny waited outside The Gold Rush jewelry store to make sure no customers were inside. He knew the place was once owned by a Chicago mob guy who did robberies all over town and eventually ended up buried in some Midwest cornfield. Back then, he'd heard that you could fence anything at The Gold Rush, not just gold chains and watches, but antiques, fur coats, hi-fi stereos, TVs … anything. Now, it was owned by another mob guy, Nuts, who was moving away from fencing stolen stuff. He'd kicked Skinny out of the shop when he'd shown up with the bag of fake gold plate chains—that was before he knew the difference. Another thing—Nuts didn't like being called Nuts, an old street name from Chicago that had somehow circulated around Vegas. His real name was Emilio, and now he wanted to be called Emmy, like the movie award or some high-roller big shot.

It was fucking blazing hot while he waited. After twenty minutes, a customer walked out. Skinny looked through the barred windows. The place looked empty. He opened the door, setting off a buzzer somewhere.

Seconds later, Nuts or Emmy walked in from the back room. The guy looked the part of a mafia gangster—dark suit, white shirt, gold chain, gold watch, and a fucking pinky ring. He stopped at the counter and looked at Skinny, said to him, "What the fuck d'you want?"

He instinctively stood up straight. It was like walking into his mom's house and seeing one of her boyfriends waiting there like some father figure expecting an answer—like *where you been motherfucker?* "I got something I know you're going to want."

Emmy moved from around the counter. "Get the fuck out of my store. I told you last time I didn't want to see your skinny ass in here ever again. You are officially eighty-sixed."

That last time, when he'd brought in the plate chains, he left the store but not before saying, "Fuck you, Nuts." He needed to back away from that somehow. "Hey man, sorry about that time before. I was like fucked up, trippin'' or something."

"Why don't you just trip your ass out of here now?"

"No, no, no. I got something you want." Emmy took another step toward him, but before being physically tossed, Skinny pulled out the necklace from a deep pocket in his cargo shorts. He held it up like some rosary to ward off Dracula. "It's real, man, fat pearls, top quality. Look at this little thingy here on the clasp; it says, Tiffany." Skinny knew Tiffany like he knew Coach and Rolex. The clasp was broken, but it was still attached.

Emmy stopped. From a distance of a few steps, he looked at the pearls. He knew better than to ask where they came from.

Skinny went on. "Look here, each pearl tied separately, each one as big as a cat's eyeball."

Emmy took another step forward, less threatening. "Big as a cat's eyeball, huh?"

Skinny knew where the comment had come from. When he was like ten, a neighbor kid they called Spade had whistled him over to look at a dead cat. Spade had killed the cat with a snare fashioned from fishing line. Skinny remembered the dead eye staring up at him. Spooky.

It took a second to get his mind organized again. He just

responded, "They're big alright."

"Give it here." Emmy took the pearls from Skinny's fingers. He looked closer at the Tiffany logo, then the pearls. He put one pearl into his mouth and nibbled it like a rabbit. Skinny guessed it was one more way to tell if they were genuine.

He went for the hard sell. "Looked it up. Those pearls are like five grand new. Ten percent is like five hundred. You could turn those around today and get like three grand easy." He was still hoping for the two hundred.

"Okay, let me see." Then Emmy went into the back room.

Skinny waited. Now, he was thinking about a fix. His whole head was dripping sweat in the air-conditioned store, his body spasming in jittery bursts, and his thoughts turning irritable. It made no sense, but he wanted to run, flee.

Then the front door opened, and the buzzer sounded. Skinny looked back and saw a FedEx man in his purple and orange uniform, shorts, and black tennis shoes. Skinny moved around behind the counter as the man walked toward him. The man put a small package on the counter and offered a clipboard and pen. He said, "Sign."

Skinny did as he was told, signed where the guy pointed, the next open line on a paper form. His real name was Leopold Skinner, and he was used to signing that signature, loopy big L and S, the rest in standard cursive. The FedEx man left with his pen and clipboard.

Skinny put the small package into the large bottom pocket of his cargo shorts, where the pearls had been.

An eternity later, Emmy came out from the back room. "Who was that?"

Skinny lied, "I don't know. Guy came in, looked at the

case of watches, then left."

Emmy had an envelope and handed it over. "That's it, not a penny more. Now seriously, get the fuck out of my shop."

He opened the envelope and peeked inside. Four crisp hundred-dollar bills. He folded the envelope in half, then pushed it into his back pocket. Skinny said nothing, certainly not, "Fuck you, Nuts." He turned and walked out the door, the buzzer buzzing like a recurring echo in his head.

In that moment on the sidewalk, he quickly planned his next moves—stock up on two jumbos, buy a week at the Oasis, eat a few tacos, then party. He'd call his friend Niven and go out.

Party like it's 1999.

The Oasis Motel was only a few blocks from The Gold Rush in an area of town near the Strip called Naked City. Skinny's best friend, Niven, had a studio apartment not far from the motel, and one night, while they were sitting around getting stoned and watching a TV show, some old-lady-sleuth mystery that neither of them could follow, he asked him why they called it Naked City. Niven was smart. He'd grown up near Baltimore and finished a year of college before dropping out and moving to Las Vegas.

Niven answered that the neighborhood was once where all the showgirls lived. The casinos didn't pay much, and this part of town had the only affordable apartments near the Strip. The girls all performed topless or nearly topless with little more than dental floss covering their shaved junk, so they couldn't have tan lines. To meet the demands of their fleshy talent, they all sunbathed out by the pool topless. Thus, Naked City. Skinny had been over to Niven's apartment about a hundred times. It was on a second story that overlooked the pool, and Skinny had watched. But he never saw any topless showgirls. Besides junkies and old couples on Social Security, a few hookers lived there. But even the hookers didn't sunbathe naked.

Skinny opened the Oasis office door and stepped up to the registration desk, caged off like a dog kennel. The woman who worked registration also lived somewhere in the back and looked a million years old but still dressed in tight-fitting clothes like she was still the hot hooker escort she once was. Everyone called her Sweet, and before he could say anything, she said, "What do you want, Skinny?"

"Well, hello to you too." Skinny gave her a look. He was flush with cash, like hot coals in his pocket, and felt he deserved a bit of service.

She pulled on her cigarette, the ash an inch long. "Again, what do you want?"

"I *want* a room with a view of the mountains, one of those bathtubs with little jets that massage my sore back, and a vibrating king-sized bed. Oh, and a bottle of your finest champagne. But since my means are somewhat limited and, in any case, you have no rooms with the shit I *want*, I'll take room number twelve if it's available." Room twelve was slightly larger than the others. It had a sought-after cushioned chair— a comfortable spot to shoot up and watch TV.

His little speech brought on a laugh. Smoke billowed from her mouth, and the cigarette ash fell onto her right breast. She brushed it off with her free hand. "How long you gonna stay?"

The quarter-hour hooker rate at the Oasis was ten bucks,

but for twenty-five, you could stay the night. Then, for a hundred dollars, you could stay the week but without any daily towel or sheet service. The monthly rate was three hundred, and a few people lived there on the monthly rate, one being the local dealer, Kitchen. From what Skinny heard, his name had to do with the fact that he sold everything but the kitchen sink. Payment for both drugs and rooms was strictly in advance. "A week, thank you." Seven days until he had to think about where he'd stay next. A whole week would feel like a month … or a year.

His dealer, Kitchen, stayed in number five, the Jungle Room. The deal was, you knocked just once on the curtained picture window that looked out over the parking lot. Skinny knocked, and Kitchen opened the curtain just an inch to see who wanted drugs. The curtain closed, and a second later, the door opened with the security swing bar still latched. "Hey, Skinny, what do you need?"

He tried to think of a jokey response, like the one he'd given Sweet minutes before. But the reality was, he was tweaking hard, his hands starting to shake, his anxiety sky-high, and that twitch in his neck like a biting fly. He wanted to do this fast and get back to room number twelve. He said, "Two jumbos."

"You want two jumbos?"

What the fuck did he just say? "Yes, two."

"Never seen you buy two before. You got the cash?"

"Yes."

"A hundred? You got a hundred?"

Fuck. "Yes."

"Show me."

He thought, *Fuck you, you fucking soup kitchen.* He wanted to say it out loud. In fact, he wanted to reach through the cracked door and twist the nose that protruded like some accusing finger. But he needed to get high fast. He reached into his pocket and pulled out the envelope. He opened it to show the two bills left over after paying for the room.

Kitchen said, "Nice," then closed the door.

Skinny heard the swing bar unlatch. The door opened, and Skinny walked inside.

It was called the Jungle Room because, once upon a time, the owner, some Italian named Nicolo, had the walls painted to look like a jungle: leopards, palm trees, tropical birds, snakes, and other jungle shit. This was back when Nicolo wanted to upscale the place and have fantasy-themed rooms for newly married couples who tied the knot just down the block at the Little White Chapel. But then the room mostly got action in fifteen-minute increments, and the Oasis didn't need jungle themes to attract street hookers for short-term fuck rooms. Now Kitchen lived there, dealing drugs for Nicolo.

He handed Kitchen a hundred. Kitchen walked into the bathroom and came out with a fat, twist-tied baggy. He knew Skinny had another hundred and said, "You want some coke?"

"No thanks." His friend, Niven, who thought he'd reached big-shot status with a waiter gig at TGI Fridays, had kicked heroin and was now into coke. A hundred dollars' worth of coke, a gram, would only last a night, and then he'd want more and more and more. And he'd still need to shoot up to ward off the shakes. Skinny was no coke player.

"Crystal?"

"Don't really need the whole kitchen sink, if you know what I mean. Kitchen."

"Hey, your party."

Skinny said, "Thanks," and then turned to leave. He was already going through how fast he could get to his room, unpack his kit, and cook up.

Then he was high. He'd learned to love the sting of the dirty needle—he guessed like a nympho learns to love a good ass slap. The high hit his head, a sensation like sinking beneath the surface of a heated pool. His anxiety dissipated, and the fly bites on his neck became little kisses.

For an hour, he watched a soap opera, *Guiding Light*, with one character, a skinny hot-chick babysitter, Elsie, then an older hot chick named Sam with big hair and long dangly earrings. He had a thing for older women, like moms, and would have jerked off if his sexy feelings weren't all lost in the smack. He looked at his finger then, the one crushed in the door at the Aladdin. It wasn't so bad, the nail black and blue. It seemed to emit a warm pressure like a tight T-shirt right from the dryer.

He then slept for what felt like a hundred hours. But when he woke, the sun still peeked past the closed curtains. He turned over on his side and adjusted the pillow, which smelled like the Tide detergent his mother had used. It was then that the box in his shorts jabbed his thigh, the small FedEx package he'd signed for at The Gold Rush. He'd almost completely forgotten.

He sat up and pulled the package from the cargo pocket. The box was glued tight, and he used his teeth to tear at the edges and open a seam, ripping the rest with his fingers. He dumped out the contents, a little velvet baggy with a drawstring closure. After fumbling with the drawstring, he emptied the contents onto the bedsheet between his legs. Little white rocks dropped out. Skinny pinched one from the bedsheet and set it in his mouth. It tasted like nothing, like a piece of rock. He didn't have a fucking clue what they were, but Nuts or Emmy wouldn't be getting a FedEx package of stones that weren't worth something. Then it came to him—uncut diamonds. He counted twenty.

◆◆◆

He ate his tacos at a stand across the street from Vegas World, paying with a hundred-dollar bill that the amigo behind the counter initially didn't think looked legit. It took the guy a few minutes to confer with another cashier, and then the two called the manager over, who eyeballed Skinny and then the bill. He held it up to the light, looking for the watermark, then twisted it back and forth, Skinny guessed to feel if the paper was genuine. He told the manager, "Why not stick it in your mouth to see if it *tastes* like a hundy?" The manager peered at him with squinty eyes, trying to decide whether to eighty-six the wiseguy. In the end, he said something in Spanish to the cashier, and Skinny was given his change along with the three carnitas tacos and orange Fanta he'd ordered seemingly hours before.

Afterward, he walked the few blocks to Niven's apartment. He had the velvet baggy in his pocket and wanted to get another opinion as to whether or not the uncut diamonds were the real thing. Niven usually had Sundays off from TGI Fridays, and at 9 p.m., he'd still be around. Later, maybe they could party with the change from his hundy.

Niven opened the door and stood there in his uniform from work—black pants, a red and white striped shirt covered in grease stains, and suspenders with enough buttons, badges, and pins to decorate a banana republic general. He smelled like greasy cheeseburgers.

Skinny asked, "I thought you had Sundays off?"

"Closed last night, then the fucking manager asked if I could work brunch. Then brunch turned into dinner. Just got off a double."

"Why didn't you just tell the manager to fuck off?"

"Asking isn't asking; it's telling. If I don't work the brunch, he takes it out on me later in the week, like I lose my closing shifts on Friday and Saturday."

"Motherfucker."

"Yeah, well, what do you want?"

"I'm flush. Thought we'd go out to Tramps and party. Also, I got these stones I want you to see."

"Okay, sure. Let me get in the shower first and wash off this stink."

Skinny had known Niven for over a year. They'd met at the Oasis. Both were hooked up with Kitchen at the time, coming and going from the Jungle Room without meeting or speaking. It was Niven who finally stepped up to him as he came from his room, number twelve. He introduced himself, Niven, like Livin' with an N—a joke Skinny didn't think was that funny. That was before Niven kicked his smack habit—before he got that first busboy job at TGI Fridays and moved out of the Oasis. Niven had always been smarter than Skinny and more ambitious. Now Niven thought of himself as a coke guy, no more of the good black tar, and Skinny knew Niven's ambitions ran more along the lines of bigger jobs, bigger payoffs. Niven had been talking about ways to get into the Friday's safe and was getting lessons from some old safecracker who lived in the same Naked City apartment.

The studio apartment was just the one room with a bath, and Niven dressed in front of him—khaki pants, a button-down collar shirt, and preppy penny loafers. Skinny wore what he always wore—shorts, a long-sleeved Corona beer T-shirt that covered his pockmarked arms, and dirty Vans Slip-Ons.

Skinny sat at the small table off the kitchenette and spilled the rocks from the velvet baggy.

Niven picked one up. "Where'd you get these?"

"Nuts, the pawnshop. FedEx guy was delivering this package while he was in the back getting cash for a necklace I snatched."

Niven looked closely at the rocks. "Nice."

"I think they're uncut diamonds. You ever seen uncut diamonds?"

"No, but you got to ask yourself what else they could be. Like they got to be gems. Emmy wouldn't get a package with like agates or some shit. They're white, gotta be diamonds."

"Fucking A. What do you think they're worth? There are like twenty rocks here. Each one looks like it could be a wedding ring for some trophy wife. Got to be worth thousands, tens of thousands."

Niven was thinking, making little twitchy movements with his nose and mouth like he'd eaten something sour. "I know a guy who could maybe tell you what they're worth, maybe know a buyer in LA."

"Who?"

"A guy I know."

"Like, let me know who it is, I'll reach out."

"This guy is connected. He won't just talk to anyone. I know him, though, and can get him to take a look. You leave these with me, and I'll make it happen."

Niven was like his best friend. Skinny had been homeless on the street plenty, and sometimes Niven had let him sleep on the floor of his apartment. He'd been hungry before, and Niven had fed him. He trusted Niven as far as it went, but

Skinny had no rosy illusions—both were street thieves. Now Niven was hunting bigger game, and this was just the score he'd be looking for. He'd fence the diamonds and give Skinny a couple hundred for his troubles. *No Fucking Way.* "I don't know, let me think on it."

"You think on it." Niven knew not to push it, not to spook his mark.

Skinny put the uncut diamonds back in the velvet baggy, then into the front pocket of his cargo shorts. He noticed Niven deliberately looking elsewhere. Like checking out a hot chick, you don't go staring at tits if you want the whole package.

From another pocket, Skinny pulled out his double jumbo baggy of smack. "You still got your kit? Mind if I top off?"

"Sure, in the kitchen drawer."

"You want?"

"No, not into that stuff anymore. You know, more of a coke guy now."

And Skinny thought to himself, *What a snob.*

At around midnight, they pulled into the parking lot of Tramps in Niven's Jetta. Already, a line snaked out the door. They waited. Twenty minutes later, they were inside and ordering drinks at the large horseshoe bar where three bartenders hustled to mix cocktails and open bottles of beer. Sundays were especially busy with half-priced drinks for service employees who showed pay stubs to prove it. Half the town of Las Vegas worked in the casinos, hotels, and restaurants, many with Sundays and Mondays off, so the place was packed. Niven had his stub from Fridays and ordered a Stoli cranberry for himself and a Bacardi Coke for Skinny.

The music was loud and danceable, and Skinny felt the smoothness of the smack he'd done in Niven's kitchen. His body was like seaweed, and the music like the swells of water that swayed him back and forth. And just that thought of swells and waves made him think about swimming naked at Wood's Cove, at the one spot only a few of his friends knew about. He'd kissed his first girl there, both naked, a hair-trigger hard-on between them. He remembered he came without being touched, just the fantasy of nakedness. He didn't think the girl knew. Later the next day, he called twice, but she never answered or returned any of the messages left on her parents' phone. But then it didn't matter because he'd had that beautiful moment in the waves of the ocean, and the thought of that day was still with him as he swayed to the music, now a little too rock and roll for his taste. He followed Niven around the dance floor, looking for a table or booth that might be open.

Niven tugged on the sleeve of Skinny's T-shirt and spoke loudly in his ear. "I got us a seat."

Two girls sat at a table for four right next to the dance floor. Niven, standing, introduced him, "This is Leo, but everyone calls him Skinny because, you guessed it, he's kind of skinny." The girls laughed at that and then said their names, Tina and Paulette. Both were waitresses from Fridays and genuinely looked pumped when he and Niven sat down with their drinks. Paulette was the one who sat next to Skinny. She had brown hair teased big and a tight-fitting neon-green dress that he surmised just barely covered her ass. She was a big girl and probably outweighed him by fifty pounds, though on the whole, she was kind of hot. Tina was all big blond hair with maybe too much makeup, but definitely the hotter one, and he knew Niven would be all about Tina. Niven played the big shot and ordered another round of half-priced drinks from a cocktail waitress.

They talked some, mostly Friday's work talk, but the music was so loud that Skinny could barely follow. Finally, Niven said, "Let's dance." Skinny knew the song, "My Prerogative." Great dance tune, and he looked at Paulette. She smiled and stood. All four slithered their way through the club and onto the dance floor.

The dancers were packed tight, bumping into each other like newborn puppies. Niven made his cool moves opposite Tina, who looked equally cool. Skinny also had some moves, but slowed it down after hitting a guy next to him with an elbow and getting a hostile look. Paulette was a larger girl, but she moved fluidly with little sexy gestures, all light as a feather. He tried to look her in the eyes and get a vibe, but the eyes stayed mostly shut, then focused down on her body, then around the dance floor at others.

The song ended, and the DJ put on some Rolling Stones crap that pretty much cleared the dance floor. The fresh drinks were waiting, the cold glass condensation like a TV commercial. Skinny was hot and sweaty and took half his rum and Coke in one long gulp. Now he felt a layer of drunk on top of his high, like waves building into steady rolling surf.

Throughout the night, they danced more and drank more. At some point, Niven whispered something to Tina, and both excused themselves. Skinny knew they were going out to the Jetta to do lines. They were back at the table a half hour later with that telltale sign of sniffles and jaw clenching.

The four of them danced to some Michael Jackson thing with fancy footwork, and then the DJ mixed the ending with that *Animal House* song, "Shout." He remembered the movie with John Belushi in a toga, the song at a frat party, and some dance thing they all did together. Skinny followed the others.

He remembered it was Otis Day and the Knights, and every time Otis yelled "Shout," everyone jumped up in the air, hands held high, and screamed along after him, "Shout." And the whole dance crowd jumped up and down, screaming and jostling, and no one cared that everyone was crashing around like bumper cars—it was fun. Skinny was sweating, and he noticed Paulette's hot neon green dress turning dark beneath her armpits as she jumped up and raised her arms, yelling, "Shout!"

Then the way the song went, Otis sang, "A little bit softer now, a little bit softer now…" and the music quieted, and everyone started bending their knees, hands in the air, sinking lower and lower to the dance floor until everyone's ass was nearly touching. Some were on the floor, squirming; Skinny was squirming. Then Otis sang, "A little bit louder now, a little bit louder now…" and everyone gradually rose, the music getting louder and louder until everyone was crazy dancing.

Then the music stopped. The DJ put on a slow thing, Madonna's "Crazy for You," and Skinny followed Paulette off the dance floor.

They sat down and watched Niven and Tina slow dancing, then necking.

Then Niven and Tina were gone. No "Let's go" or "See you later," just gone.

Skinny, on his way back from taking a piss, checked outside for the Jetta. Gone.

Then Paula said she had to go to the bathroom.

Skinny waited for like a half hour alone, conspicuous at a table for four. She never came back.

Then the check for the drinks came, the cocktail waitress standing over him like he might bolt for the door. He did think about running but knew he'd get maybe ten feet before being tackled by one of the knucklehead bouncers. Eighty dollars and some cents was all the money Skinny had on him, not even a dollar extra for a tip. The cocktail waitress gave him that look and then walked away without a word.

The Oasis was about five miles away in the direction of downtown—Fremont Street, Glitter Gulch—the lights of which he could see on the horizon. He started walking.

It wasn't too hot, the wind was calm, and he was accustomed to walking. He walked the Strip up and down almost every day. He was slightly drunk, slightly dopesick, but nothing he couldn't handle, and he knew that in two hours, he'd be back in a clean room with clean sheets, a full bathroom, and his double jumbo of smack. He stuck his hands in his pockets and walked.

He was almost to the Strip when it dawned on him that outside of a few coins and the smack, his pockets were empty—it dawned on him that the little velvet baggy with the uncut diamonds was gone.

Then he remembered the song "Shout" and the dancing and bumping. Niven split right after that, without saying a word to anyone.

Skinny was sure Niven had picked his pocket.

Motherfucker.

CHAPTER 3 – CORY
That Same Friday

He sat in the back row of his Social Studies class, slumped at his desk and staring at Mr. Tierney who droned on and on about the alliances between European nations at the onset of World War I and the assassination of Archduke Franz Ferdinand. Mr. Tierney was this tall, balding man with bad teeth. His two front beaver teeth were stained yellow, suggesting that he either smoked unfiltered cigarettes or didn't brush, and Cory knew for a fact that the man didn't smoke. Then his rumpled shirt with a quarter-size grease stain and his pants that might have shown pee stains had they not been Levi's suggested that he rarely washed. His delivery of the lecture was almost monotone, and he stood there unmoving—no gestures, inflection of speech, smiles, frowns, or laughs. Tierney couldn't tell a captivating story if he was standing on a scaffold, a noose around his neck, and his life literally depended on it. The captivating story he *could* have told was about Franz Ferdinand, the heir presumptive of Austria-Hungary. In his lifetime, Franz had killed more than a quarter of a million trophy animals from around the world—the exact number Cory knew from the school library's Encyclopedia Britannica: 272,511. The sadist had kept a detailed diary filled with every hunt and kill. Cory did the math—Franz Ferdinand was fifty when he died, so the man had killed 5,450 animals per year or fifteen per day. Assuming that he ate breakfast, lunch, and dinner, took two days off per week to travel to each kill site, slept a good eight hours each night, began killing at the age of five, and possibly took off a couple hours to fuck and defecate, the Crown Prince, then Emperor, had killed roughly three animals per hour during his active, working life. Oh, and talk about the hundred thousand heads that adorned the walls of his castle. Just picture that, a hundred thousand heads. This very real psychopath was the man whose assassination instigated World War I, which resulted in the deaths of over twenty million human beings. Talk about tragic irony. If foul-tooth Tierney knew how to tell it, *that* was a good story.

Two rows in front sat a girl, Tanya, whose head rested on arms folded over her desk, nearly or actually asleep. Cory wrote a message on a piece of paper ripped from a page of his spiral-bound notebook. After folding the paper twice, then three times, he pinched out the ink cartridge from his clear BIC pen. He ripped another edge of paper from his notebook and chewed it into a small spitball. Cory loaded the hollowed-pen blowgun, held one end to his lips, aimed, and silently shot. The spitball hit Tanya in the neck. Her head bolted up, then she turned to face him. She mouthed the word, "What?" and gave him that look of pure irritation. Cory had a slight crush on Tanya, and she knew it.

He tapped the person between them on the shoulder and passed the note up to Tanya. She unfolded the scrap of paper and read, "Give you a ride home after school?"

She didn't look back at Cory but just raised a thumbs-up.

A few things he liked about Tanya. First off, she didn't give a fuck. Everyone, including the teachers, knew she was smart. Tanya always had the answer if called upon in class, and she could elaborate. But she did not turn in homework. Cory had the feeling that Tanya actually *did* do the homework, but he imagined she torched it right after finishing the last question. She only passed her classes because she *did* complete the tests, always screaming through each answer, handing in the test before anyone else, and afterward spacing out at her desk. Then, he liked the way she dressed. He guessed it was just a costume to her (again, she didn't give a fuck), and lately she'd been all Goth. She wore black boots with two-inch platforms, a bust-revealing shirt, and baggy black pants with enough zippers to close Paul Bunyan's fly front trousers. Her hair was wrapped up with an entire package of bobby pins, her lips painted fire engine red, and her eyes peeked through gobs of black mascara. It kinda turned him on. The only thing that wasn't a costume was the fancy camera she carried around like a purse. Finally, Tanya was drop-dead beautiful, and probably the only reason she'd entertain Cory's advances was because she scared the fuck out of all the other boys at school.

They met up in the parking lot. Cory had a small, secondhand Suzuki dirt bike that he'd bought with money he earned. He'd gotten his driver's license without the help of his mom, then the motorcycle endorsement. He owned just the one helmet and gave that to Tanya. He kick-started the bike and Tanya hopped on. While he drove, she shouted directions over the motor's loud whine. The house he stopped at looked like all the others on the block, a one-story ranch with a few cactuses planted in a front yard covered with white rocks.

Tanya stepped from the bike and took off the helmet. She handed it to Cory like a gift, an offering. But when he reached over to grab the helmet, she pulled it back, smiling, then in almost the same motion, she leaned forward and kissed him on the lips. A long, sloppy kiss. She stepped away and said, "You want to come inside?"

Cory had an instant hard-on that he casually knocked to the side so that it lay flat in his jeans. He was dumbstruck, tongue-tied, and simply said, "Yes."

She reached for his hand and led him up the concrete path to the front door. She produced a house key from one of the many zippered pants pockets and reached forward to unlock the door.

Then, before she could get the key in, the door opened seemingly on its own. Inside was an adult man, whom Cory figured to be the father. He wasn't entirely sure because Tanya said, "Emmy, what are you doing home?" Probably not the right thing to say.

The adult man was dressed in a dark suit with an open-collared shirt. His black hair was gelled and combed back from his forehead like some Italian greaseball. Cory tried to remember Tanya's last name—Hansen or Johnson or Swanson or something—but definitely not Italian. The greaseball, Emmy (and what was Emmy short for?), ignored her question and looked directly at Cory. "Who's this?"

Cory stammered, "Hi, Mister," and paused there, not knowing how to finish. The man did not help him out, and Cory just continued. "My name is Cory Fresh."

"Well, Cory, I don't appreciate you taking my stepdaughter home on your minibike. I think it's dangerous. And I don't appreciate you necking with her out front where everyone on the block can see you. In fact, I don't appreciate you kissing and fondling her at all."

So much there. It wasn't a minibike, but a street-legal dirtbike. He now knew that Emmy was the stepdad. Then Cory wasn't the one who initiated the kissing or *necking*. And he had definitely not fondled her.

But before he could say anything, Tanya interjected with, "Emmy, just stop it."

"Just stop it? I haven't even started. Tanya, get to your room. I said you were grounded until you started turning in your homework." Now, he looked at Cory. "You, I don't ever want to see you again. I don't want you anywhere near my stepdaughter. Is that clear?"

"It's a dirt bike, a motorcycle, not a minibike." He knew he shouldn't have said anything, and from behind her stepdad, Tanya gave him a look, wide-eyed like Cory was acting all hostile. But then she laughed. She shouldn't have laughed.

The adult man, Emmy, stepped outside, shutting the door on Tanya. His voice began as almost a whisper but then grew in volume so that the whole neighborhood could listen in. "Let me be very clear. I am not a man to mess with. You need to turn around and get on that fucking thing, start it up, and get the fuck out of here. Don't think I won't hurt a kid if I have to, because I will if I ever see you around Tanya again. And if I see that thing, whatever you call it, on the street or under your ass, I'll run it over with my very large Cadillac. *Capisce?*"

Italian greaseball. Cory looked down at his feet, then whispered, "Capisce." It's what they said in the movies. Then he turned around and left.

Cory drove off and didn't look back. He thought the guy was an asshole and had overreacted. Cory had really done nothing—she'd kissed him, not the other way around. But he knew the guy was serious and would do exactly what was threatened.

Though it wouldn't be the first time he'd had his assed kicked. And the fact was, he and Tanya took classes together. She liked him; that was for real. And Cory was still a virgin with a hard-on that wouldn't fuck itself. He wouldn't stop, and Cory could creep around with the best. The adult man, the stepdad, Emmy, could go fuck himself.

Cory turned the corner and shifted up into second gear.

The Naked City studio apartment where he now lived came furnished with a full-sized bed, a lounge chair with cigarette burns in the armrests, and a small kitchen table with two chairs. There were no dishes or pots and pans in the kitchen, but then he wasn't much into cooking and took most of his meals on the street at fast food joints or at Tramps, where he worked three nights a week cleaning the floors and bathrooms. He also took toilet paper home from Tramps, nearly empty rolls after changing them out in each stall—he'd squirreled away a whole trash bag full. He'd left home six months ago when he was still sixteen. He turned seventeen in the apartment, and though still a minor, his mother or her new husband couldn't have cared less where he lived.

The apartment had no TV set, but Cory had his Sony stereo with a built-in turntable and cassette player. The stereo had been a gift from his mother for his sixteenth birthday when just the two of them lived together in an apartment near Sam's Town Casino. His mother worked there as a keno runner, and he figured the gift cost like a week's wages and tips. Cory had some records with music, but mostly he collected comedy albums. His dream was to become a comedian himself, and one of the reasons he'd applied for a job at Tramps was because they hosted a stand-up comedy show on Mondays and Tuesdays before the dancing started later in the evening.

Cory put on Steve Martin's *A Wild and Crazy Guy*. The first bit was "I'm feeling it," a crowd warmer to introduce himself and get them focused with a rat-a-tat of quick jokes. Cory guessed the word for his schtick was sarcasm, and Martin played it way over the top—"Nothing better for a person to come out and do the same thing over and over each night, the same jokes," then, "Because I work here, I get my drinks for half price, so that for every drink you buy, I get two." All of which is kind of funny, but it was his delivery that made it work—over-the-top, goofy, nerdy. Cory had tried to copy him in the mirror—the same bit, inflection, movements—but it just didn't feel authentic (he wondered how authentic it was to Steve Martin). In the same mirror, he'd tried out material from many of the greats: Sam Kinison (the screamer), Eddie Murphy (raunchy), Rodney Dangerfield (one-liners), Richard Pryor (character sketches), and others. He thought the comic who did feel authentic to him was George Carlin. It was *Class Clown* that he listened to over and over, tried to imitate, and then emulate. Of course, the fact that Carlin was doing bits about high school was close to Cory's circumstances, but it was the delivery itself—no one-liners, few imitations, no props, just funny storytelling. That's what Cory thought he could do, and after listening to the end of *A Wild and Crazy Guy*, he jotted some notes down in a journal about Tierney's Social Studies class and Franz Ferdinand's big game slaughter. Possible bits.

He punched in at Tramps by 9 p.m.. His title was Porter, and his job was to make sure the bathrooms were kept clean and stocked, then move throughout the club with a long-handled dustpan and mini broom to make sure the floors stayed clean of trash. He started with the bathrooms before the club got busy, changing any empty and almost empty toilet paper rolls—which he saved—filling the hand towel dispensers with c-fold towels, and topping off hand soap dispensers. In both men's and women's, he set up an extra waste bin so that he didn't need to empty one every fifteen minutes. Afterward, he checked in with his boss, Deedee, to ask about other chores needed before the club got busy. She had him help the barbacks with stocking bartender stations with ice.

Cory knew Deedee liked him and was probably grooming him for a promotion. Barback was one step away from being a bartender, and those guys could each bring in five hundred on a busy Friday. Not like he didn't make good money. The wages were only seven dollars an hour, but all the cocktail waitresses and bartenders tipped him out, like five bucks each, and there were around twenty of them each shift. Then he could keep anything swept off the floor with his dustpan and mini broom—not just coins but bills and sometimes jewelry. He'd give the jewelry to Deedee, and if no one made a claim, Deedee would sell the jewelry to a guy she knew and give him the proceeds without taking a cut. At least, that's what she said, and he believed her.

DJ Danny started the music at 11 p.m., and almost immediately, the club was packed, all the tables taken, and standing room only. By 11:30, Cory could barely move through the club, and the customers ignored him like some bum on the Strip asking for change. He moved through the club with his dustpan and mini broom, and by 1 a.m., he'd collected something like fifteen bucks.

Then Danny played "Shout." For Cory, it was a real

moneymaker, and he moved onto the dance floor. When the guy sang, "Shout," everyone jumped up, and then when the song slowed, everyone crouched down, some squirming on the floor. And with all that jumping, crouching, and squirming, coins, bills, and stuff just fell off the dancers. He'd found gold chains before, gold earrings, and once a Philippe Patek watch with a busted wristband that Deedee sold to her guy for a thousand—he'd used that payday to buy the dirt bike. He moved through the crowd and swept up anything loose on the floor. Danny transitioned from "Shout" to some slow song, and Cory moved to one of the bus stations to pick through the goodies.

Right off, he had a few singles and a five, a few quarters among lesser change, a sealed Trojan condom wrapper— which he'd save for that eventual moment—and a little vial of what he knew to be cocaine. He'd give the cocaine to the barback, Dickey, who'd given him rides home in his Buick back before he'd bought his Suzuki. Then, a little velvet baggy. He opened the baggy and dumped out a bunch of stones. The stones were white and rough and did not look like something valuable. But he didn't think someone would carry valueless rocks in a velvet baggy and cart them all the way to a nightclub. He decided to show Deedee.

Cory found her in the back office across from the bathrooms. She looked at the stones and asked, "Where did you find these?"

It should have been obvious, but he said it anyway, "On the dance floor, during 'Shout.'"

"Not off a table, right?"

He guessed she was asking if Cory stole them. "No, on the dance floor … on the floor of the dance floor."

Deedee looked up. To Cory, she looked old, like fifties,

but behind that was also something hot and sexy. She was slim with nice breasts, had long black hair in a fat braid down her back, and the complexion and eyes of someone south of the border. She was smart and tough and didn't take any shit from employees or customers.

She said, "I think they're diamonds."

He knew diamonds were super valuable. He counted twenty of them and thought maybe there'd be another payday like the Philippe Patek watch. What would he do with another five hundred or a thousand? Maybe ask Tanya to the prom and pick her up in a limousine.

He said, "Well, crap my pants."

Deedee laughed.

CHAPTER 4 – EMMY
That Same Friday

Emmy sat at his desk in the back room of The Gold Rush and inspected the Tiffany pearls he'd just bought from the kid, Skinny. With a jeweler's loupe, he saw the sharp reflection of light off the smooth surface, almost mirror-like, and the holes for the silk thread carefully crafted with an ultrasonic drill. Their size was the same as the marbles he'd played with on the streets back in Elmwood. He remembered the game where they shot marbles from outside a chalked ring with larger "shooters." They had red ones called "devils," black and yellow ones called "bumblebees," and white ones called, coincidentally, "pearls." Emmy had kept a whole tobacco can filled with the marbles he'd won, right up until the bigger kid called Swede took them. He guessed that's where they first met, Swede giving him a beating just to get the can of marbles. A lot had happened since then. Now he was in Vegas, still connected to Swede, who was sending him diamonds to fence and still buying stolen shit from street kids like Skinny.

He tried to imagine how the kid stole the pearls. It wasn't

hard since he and Swede and others had done the same—stalked Michigan Avenue looking for rich people carrying their logoed bags of expensive merchandise or fur-clad women loosely clutching a purse. Skinny likely waited on the Strip in some shadowed corner, his escape already planned, since for sure there'd be screaming and yelling and some do-gooder trying to chase him down. The clasp on the necklace was about as solid as an overcooked pasta noodle.

It was a funny thing, getting older—how he'd begun to imagine the other side, what the woman must have felt as the pearls were ripped from her neck. He guessed a kind of shock at first, not really understanding what had just happened. In a spontaneous outburst, she would've screamed and come up with some word like "thief" that she might have remembered from a movie. She'd expect someone else to run after the thief, and on the Strip, there was always someone else. Then, minutes later, she would've touched the stinging scratch across her neck from the broken clasp. She'd cry. And it wasn't so much the loss of the pearls, though they could have been sentimental like a gift, and they were certainly expensive. It was more the trauma of being assaulted. In her hotel room later, she'd make the calls, recount the scene, cry some more, and exorcise the whole incident like an evil spirit. Then maybe some lasting effects. It would've likely been her first time, and he remembered that first time Swede had given him a beating and taken his marbles. For Emmy, it'd been all anger and then retribution. He'd taken up boxing and learned to use a knife. For this lady, it would be the opposite, a wounded and frightened victim response like a turtle pulling back into its shell. She might become a different person—guarded, scared, withdrawn. If she once felt outwardly smart and sexy, all of that might be gone. That was the kind of thing he thought about nowadays.

Did the woman's trauma bother him, that he was part of it? He guessed it was beginning to.

◆ ◆ ◆

Emmy closed up early. All day he'd had a nagging headache and now just wanted none of it—kids like Skinny trying to sell him mostly crap, men shopping for quicky wedding rings, big-shot, high-roller wannabees looking for a pinky ring or Rolex-looking watch. It was all such a shit business, and now he just wanted to close up, get home, and sip a cold beer. Relax and maybe watch whatever game was on the television.

Emmy started up the Cadillac and headed east on Sahara. What was it, April? And the weather had already turned blazing hot, his AC on high. He thought about stopping to take off his suit coat but figured he'd be home in minutes. He took a right into his neighborhood of Paradise Palms, then slowed up behind some crappy Impala stopped at a four-way intersection. He waited patiently for the Chevy to move, but it just sat there, filthy exhaust, like cigar smoke, blowing his direction. Emmy pushed the heel of his palm against the horn and let out a blast. Still, the car didn't move. He shifted the Cadillac into reverse to drive around, thinking the Chevy was probably broken down. He shifted the car back into drive and turned the tires. Then the Chevy guy opened the door and stepped out, leaving the door ajar and blocking his way.

Now what? The guy stood there glaring. He looked to be in his early thirties and wore a green silk-looking jacket, though it was like a hundred out. Beneath the jacket, Emmy could tell he was beefy like a weightlifter, probably some meathead all jacked up on coke and steroids. Guy thought he was Genghis Khan, ruler of the Mongol Empire, striking fear into the hearts of men, women, and children. Emmy's headache now seemed to focus its knitting-needle pain at a spot right between his eyes. Did this guy want to kick his ass? Was that it?

Emmy opened his door slowly, stepped out, and took off his suit coat. He carefully folded it once lengthwise and laid it across the seat back. He looked up at the guy and said, "You gonna move that heap or what?"

The guy stood there with a stupid smirk on his face; the world his and there for the taking. "Fuck you, old man. Get in your car, turn it around, and go back the way you came." He folded his thick arms across his chest, showing off the meaty guns.

Emmy stepped forward.

Then the guy stepped forward.

Now they were spitting distance apart. Emmy could now see the acne scars on his Cro-Magnon forehead—steroid scars. He didn't say a thing; he knew the talking part was over. A momentum of will and violence had taken its place.

The Gold Rush was a jewelry store, but people were always trying to sell him guns and knives. He bought and sold some, and the one knife he saved for himself was an Italian handcrafted stiletto with a single-action three-inch blade, which he kept on him at all times—Vegas could be a dangerous place. Emmy put both hands in his pockets. Just the one hand would've signaled that he was reaching for a weapon; two hands signaled vulnerability.

The guy stepped forward, just one step to move within an arm's length away. He said, "Turn around, old man, before you get a beating that you'll remember for the rest of your short life."

In one quick motion, Emmy lifted the stiletto from his pocket, lurched forward, depressed the latch that released the spring-activated double-edged blade, and stuck it two inches into the guy's groin.

He screamed out, "Fuck," as he fell to the pavement.

Emmy got back into his car. He shifted into drive, then drove halfway up the curb and around the beefy guy who stood looking at the blood on his hand.

Fifteen minutes later, he was home, sitting at the kitchen table with a cold beer. Both his heart and his headache were still pounding when he heard the dirt bike pull up in front of the house and then power down. Emmy left his beer on the table and walked into the front living room to look through the drapes.

He saw the kid who wore jeans and a T-shirt with some rock and roll band emblazoned across the front. His hair was longish like that Skinny punk, and for a reason he didn't understand, the kid made him think about the steroid freak that he'd just stabbed. He touched the stiletto knife through the fabric of his suit pants. His stepdaughter was his stepdaughter—all dressed up in that silly costume of black fabric, zillions of zippers, and bad makeup. Last month, it'd been hippy shit with out-of-fashion bell-bottom jeans and braless tight shirts, accentuating her nipples, which poked unnervingly right in his face. If he'd dressed like a freak back in Chicago, his dad would've kicked his ass. In fact, he got his ass kicked for simply rolling up a pack of cigarettes in his T-shirt sleeve. But you can't go hitting girls, especially a stepdaughter who hates you just for being in her space. Really, he couldn't tell Tanya anything—she'd just tell him to fuck off, run to her bedroom, and slam the door. He didn't know what to do and was scared that by summer, she'd be into something more frightening, like the tight slutty dresses he'd seen the hookers wear down on East Fremont.

Then, like some East Fremont hooker, she kissed the kid all sloppy on the mouth, right there on the sidewalk for anyone to see. And then Emmy thought he saw the kid grab her ass, or maybe he imagined that part. For sure, that kid had a hard-on packed in his pants. Emmy went for the front door.

His daughter was dragging the kid up the front walkway, leading him into the house. She was on the stoop when he opened the door.

She said, "Emmy, what are you doing home?" Never *Dad.*

So, she had expected the house to be empty, and now he wondered how many boys she'd had up in her room while he was at work or wherever. There'd always been that sneaking suspicion she was a slut. How come all the costumes? Then he wondered if she did it in the master bedroom, soiling his bed sheets, disrespecting him. Now he was really pissed.

Then, the inevitable confrontation—slamming doors, threats, and back talk. What had the fucking kid said? "It's not a minibike, it's a motorcycle." He'd wanted to hit the kid then, make it official.

Finally, standing alone on the front lawn of the house, he suddenly felt foolish. It wasn't the neighbors peeking through their blinds to witness the whole scene. Back in Chicago, in Elmwood, Emmy would've known every family on the block and might've felt embarrassed—all the Italians talking amongst themselves, the mothers gossiping, and anything he'd done getting back to his parents, who'd give him the *what for.* In Vegas, not so much—no one knew each other, and in this neighborhood, most were childless and from other states, some from other religions and countries. He didn't think there even existed a park or playground nearby, just stretches of open desert lots filled with trash. He felt foolish because he'd pretended to be some dad who pretended to care.

Tanya wasn't so bad; she was smart and, on some level, amusing. He'd only been with her for five years and only three since her mother, his wife, had died. Her biological father was long gone and unknowable. Emmy knew he needed to leave it alone, let her do her thing, and make mistakes. He'd be there if she needed him—if she came to him. What *he* needed to do was simply be accessible. And that boy on the dirt bike was no predator like the steroid meathead in his Chevy. If anything, he knew Tanya well enough to know she could handle herself, and if she was going to be kissed, she'd instigate the kissing.

Fucking live and learn.

CHAPTER 5 – NIVEN
Sunday

That Sunday night at TGI Fridays was slow, the restaurant nearly empty, and the cock-sucking manager, Carl, wouldn't let any servers go home. Niven had just three tables in his section, the area nearest the windows and furthest from the bar, where the hostess sat anyone who shouldn't be near alcohol, namely families with little kids and senior citizens. Niven could read his customers—not that difficult—and knew none were good for more than ten percent. He'd just served the food for one family of five with two kids still in highchairs. After a few minutes, he checked back, saying, "Everything good? Anyone need anything?" They just sat there, silent and motionless, staring at their food. He thought maybe they'd seen a cook's hair in the cheese dipping sauce or a bug in the salad, and he asked again, "Everything alright?" Nothing. *Rude.* Then, like an eternity later, the father finally said, "Amen," finishing what must have been a moment of God silence. They all commenced eating like piranhas. In Niven's experience, religious nuts, along with ranchers, old people, and the British, were notoriously bad tippers. Not so coincidentally, the other family in his section wore cowboy boots and had ordered chicken-fried steaks. Then the older couple split an entrée— one hamburger—and were just fine with the water, *thank you.* Not so coincidentally, because Carl was playing hostess and had seated all three, punishment of sorts for what he'd done the night before.

On that busy Saturday night, Niven had the station five steps up from the floor that overlooked the bar—a great station because the younger crowd there loved to drink expensive cocktails, watch the action at the bar, and be seen. Big tippers. That Saturday, management was finishing up a week-long fajita contest. Fajitas had just been added to the menu, and the company was promoting them hard. And they weren't that difficult to sell because all the servers were pushing and selling them; the whole restaurant filled with the lime-smelling steam that rose from the red-hot cast iron platters. Niven was close to winning, tied with a waitress named Jill who'd worked at Fridays for like three years and, because of her seniority, was often Shift Leader, taking the best stations. That Saturday, she worked the station opposite his, also overlooking the bar.

Niven knew he'd acted rudely. He had a four-top with two couples and did his whole fajita pitch—steak, chicken, shrimp, or a combination. Comes with warm flour tortillas, guacamole, pico de gallo, and shredded cheese. He sold four fajita entrees, a real boost that could put him up over Jill, but then the one bitch had to go ahead and say that maybe she and her date should just order one, the combination, and share. That's when Niven added his joke, which got laughs, like a hundred percent of the time. "How many Mexicans does it take to eat a plate of fajitas?" They all looked at him, ready for the punchline. He said, "Just Juan!" Laughs all around, and he quickly added, "Okay, we'll make it dos fajitas," the presumptive close, and he walked away before they could say boo.

Of course, he knew he'd fucked up when he came out with the four skillets for the table. The woman said, "I'm sorry, my boyfriend and I just wanted to split ours."

Niven immediately apologized and said, "Go ahead and keep it. I'll just take the other one off the check."

But the tally was close, up by only one order over Jill, and he needed the sale, so he added insult to injury by leaving the order of fajitas on the check. He thought the worst that could happen was that the woman, the bitch, would see his mistake and make him take it off. He'd be all apologetic again, like, "Sorry, I forgot," and he'd be back, tied with Jill. But that's not what went down. The woman noticed the charge and, instead of bringing it to his attention, called the manager over. Carl.

For Niven, the impending reprimand had a silver lining of sorts. It was like management 101, where a manager should never scold an employee in front of other employees—like you shouldn't shame a person in public. So, you took them someplace private. Carl asked Niven to speak with him in the manager's office. He followed as Carl led the way to the back of the kitchen. The office door was secured with just a push-button keyless lock, and Niven watched as Carl pressed in the code. Niven had seen this done countless times and knew the code, Y0451C. Inside stood the safe, a Gardall, bolted to the concrete floor. Now, Niven got a good look at it while Carl did his thing.

Safe cracking—it was something Niven was interested in. He'd talked to a guy who lived in the same Naked City apartment. Chester was his name, an old washed-up drunk who'd done years at the state penitentiary in Carson City for a string of robberies back in the 60s. He was a safecracker among other things, and for a few pints of cheap Kamchatka vodka, gave Niven lessons. Niven even bought an old Mosler floor safe from the Dog Pawn on Main Street nearby, borrowing a two-wheeler from the shop to cart it over and up the stairs to his apartment. With the help of Chester, he became reasonably proficient and able to crack the Mosler in less than an hour. The trick without drills, explosives, or prybars was to listen for the slight imperfections in the tumblers, the gaps where the hammer barely skipped the edge of the notch, then keep track of the gaps and corresponding numbers on a piece of paper. The older the safe, the easier it was because the constant use wore down the tumblers, accentuating the imperfections. And the Gardall safe at Fridays was used often. He figured it was a Type 2 safe, which meant it was guaranteed from penetration for a minimum of fifteen minutes. Chester, in his prime, could have cracked it in fifteen minutes, but for Niven, it would take hours. He'd need to somehow sneak in after closing, then spend five hours working the tumblers.

After the three tables paid their bill, Carl cut him, allowing the remaining three servers to close. Probably for the best—the safe on a Sunday night would be nearly empty. Weekends were the ticket, and he'd likely have a closing shift the following Saturday.

When he finished his side work and punched out, the time was 10 p.m. and still early. He had sixty in tip money and decided to go by the Oasis, buy some coke, and see if Skinny was still sitting on those diamonds.

In the back lot of Fridays, he got behind the wheel of his Jetta. It was a 1984 model, four-door, with a manual four-speed transmission that, even now, four years after his father had given him the car for his high school graduation, was fun to drive. That was way back before his dad had kicked him out of the house, before he'd driven west to Vegas. The only trouble had been the license plate tags. The car was still in his dad's name, so he couldn't apply for Nevada registration. That issue was easily solved. He bought a cracked-up Jetta from a chop shop on the north side. The shop kept the salvaged Jetta but handed over the title, which he then used to register his own. The only other problem was the color. The salvaged Jetta was metallic blue while his was silver, but he'd been pulled over twice, and the cops never made the connection.

Niven started the car, a throaty sound like a Porsche, and drove north on Maryland Parkway, then west on Sahara. He pulled into the lot of the Oasis, parked in front of Kitchen's apartment, and wrapped once on his window. Ten minutes later, he was out with a quarter-gram packet that cost him twenty-five, along with a pin joint for an additional dollar. He'd split the joint with Skinny, but the quarter was not enough to share. He did a line on a mirror kept in the Jetta's glove box. Just a taste, and he folded up what was left—maybe six or seven more lines that might get him through the night.

Niven banged on Skinny's door until the kid finally said, "Wait a minute."

Niven waited five seconds, then banged some more. He heard, "Just hold on."

A couple of minutes passed before Skinny opened the door. Niven asked, "You been jerking off?"

"No." Skinny looked pissed, all stiff-shouldered and

blocking the door. "What do you want?"

"What's your problem? Let me in already. Let's blow this doobie." He held out the joint for Skinny to see.

"What's my problem? You ditched me at the club. I had to walk the whole fucking way back. That was not cool."

Niven pushed through Skinny's shoulder and walked into the room. He sat on the bed. The TV was on, playing some loud cowboy movie with horses and Indians. He lit up the joint and took a hit. "Sorry, man, I thought you had it solid with Paulette. Like, I thought you two were going back to her place. Like, what happened?"

Skinny closed the door, turned down the volume on the cowboy movie, and then sat in the one chair. "She ghosted me."

"Sorry. Like I said, I thought you were solid with that chick. Like, that's fucked up and all." He added, "So, you want to blow this or what?" He held out the pin joint, now halfway burned.

"Fuck, sure." Skinny pinched the joint in his fingers and took a hit, holding the smoke deep and long. He took another hit and passed it.

And while they smoked, Niven told him about the weekend, how Carl had fucked him over and given him the booster chair and senile section. To Niven, it was all blah-blah-blah, loosening Skinny up before he got to the point. "So, what happened to those diamonds?"

Skinny looked at him, pissed again, and stared him down like the TV cowboy gunslinger. "You should know."

"What?"

"The club. When I left Tramps, they were gone. I know you picked my pocket when we were dancing."

"No way."

"Don't fuck with me."

Niven knew it was something he would've done if it had occurred to him at the time. But he'd definitely been wrapped up with the girl, Tina, from Fridays. Coming off the dance floor, he asked her to go out to his car and do a line, and she said yes. Then, in the car, while they were listening to the new cassette stereo he'd put in the dash, *she'd* kissed *him* unprovoked. She said, "Let's get out of here." What was he supposed to do? They drove east on Flamingo, her hand on his thigh the whole time, him trying to shift over the outstretched arm. Then, just past the Strip, she said they should go for a last drink at The Steak Out, a bar where many servers went after their shifts ended. They met up with a few others from Friday's, and then the shots of Tequila started. When they finally got back in the car and drove to her apartment, she was beyond drunk, which was just fine with him, but then she threw up *in his car*. That's where Niven drew the line—he wasn't going to screw a girl who'd just thrown up in his car. Then, the next day at work, she acted like nothing had happened. Meanwhile, the diamond business had been percolating in the back of his brain.

"I did not pick your pocket. I did not take the diamonds." He paused for a second. "Then how did you fucking lose them?"

Skinny was deep in thought, no doubt going through the scenarios: Was Niven fucking with him? Could he have actually lost the diamonds? Did someone else steal them?

Before Skinny could answer, Niven said, "Did they fall out of your pocket while you were sitting down at the table or while you were dancing? That song, 'Shout,' you were squirming on the floor like a fucking worm."

"Shit, maybe."

"Well, I guess they're gone for good." So was the joint, now just a speck of cinder that threatened to burn his fingers. He flicked it onto the carpet and squashed it with his toe.

Skinny looked down at the soiled carpet, shaking his head, but didn't respond. The guy was a junky with about as much imagination and forethought as a dog waiting for his kibble. By tomorrow, he'd move on to his next fix, his next snatch and dash.

In the meantime, Niven would not move on and did not think the diamonds were gone for good. They still had to be at Tramps, most likely handed over to the manager to be placed into the non-existent lost and found.

They'd be locked in an office safe.

CHAPTER 6 – EMMY
Monday

He got a call from Swede.

A lot had happened between them since that day Swede stole the can of marbles. He was from the neighborhood and lived a few blocks over. He should have been with the other Swedes in Andersonville, but his father was a cop who married into an Italian family. Like most cops, he was connected, and in Elmwood, he did jobs for the Outfit's boss there, Joey Aiuppa.

In their early twenties, he and Swede also worked for Aiuppa, and they did robberies together. They were acquaintances, associates; Swede was a weird motherfucker and impossible to befriend. He may have been queer, no one knew for sure, but he didn't go whoring around with the rest of the gang. And he didn't drink or do drugs, which also made him an outcast. But everyone knew not to fuck with Swede, that he was to-the-bone dangerous. He was the first person on a job who'd pistol-whip a security guard, and Aiuppa had already used him for collecting debts. Then, in one late-night department store robbery, they must have set off a silent alarm. By the time Emmy and Swede started loading stuff into a van, the cops rolled up. Swede got pinched but made a show of running, then struggling, to buy Emmy time. He got away, and Swede took the rap, never snitching. Swede did two years for the robbery, and for that, Emmy owed him.

Emmy answered the call, "The Gold Rush."

"Nuts?"

He knew the voice. "Swede?"

"Yeah, you got the package?"

It took him a second, but he remembered Swede was sending him a package, some rough diamonds to fence. That Swede hadn't fenced them locally was a red flag, but then, because of what had happened between them, the request wasn't something Emmy could refuse.

He had not seen the package. "No."

"I sent the package last Thursday, overnight FedEx."

"I didn't get it."

"It's FedEx. Guaranteed. You didn't confuse it with something else?"

Emmy could hear the frustration in Swede's voice. Uncut diamonds could be worth tens of thousands. Depends. "No, Swede, I didn't confuse the package with something else. I haven't had any FedEx deliveries in the last week, not even the last month."

"Nuts, look around again. Now, okay?"

Nuts, his old neighborhood name. He wanted to correct Swede but guessed it was not the time. He said, "Okay, give me a minute." He pressed a button to put Swede on hold. There was no looking around to be done, so he just waited for the minute hand on his Omega to move five clicks. Emmy put Swede back on the line. "Nothing."

"Someone must have signed for it. You check your guy there and see who did the signing. Find my package."

"Okay."

He was ready to hang up the phone, but then Swede added, "Nuts?"

"Yeah?"

"You need to fucking find that package."

He had breakfast on the kitchen table when Tanya's bedroom door opened. He was embarrassed about the scene with the minibike kid the day before and figured the best course was to keep quiet and say nothing.

But then she stepped into the kitchen and whatever had happened the day before was now eclipsed. Tanya had changed from the black clothes with zippers costume, Goth, and this time wore tennis shoes, khaki pants, and a white polo shirt with one of those little alligators stitched on the pocket. Her hair was combed straight and not pinned up in the usual rat's nest. He knew better than to comment on the outfit, and anyway, Tanya wasn't speaking to him. She sat down and ate the eggs and toast, took her finished plate to the sink, grabbed her school bag and camera, and then stood, staring at him—her signal, *let's go*. He drove her to school with neither of them making a sound. And during that whole time, Emmy wondered if this new look was just another costume or if she had, in fact, turned normal. In the end, "normal," whatever that meant, would never be a word he'd use to describe his stepdaughter. She had just moved on to another costume. He guessed, preppy.

The local FedEx office was near the airport on Palo

Verde, and after dropping Tanya off, he drove there to figure out if the package with the diamonds had been delivered and, if so, who'd signed for it.

The woman at the customer service counter looked a little older than Tanya, but that's where the similarity ended— shorter and boxy, with dark hair shaped into a pompadour like a young Frank Sinatra. She addressed him as "Sir" and asked how she could help.

"I'm looking for confirmation that a package was delivered."

She cocked her head sideways, "You didn't receive your package? Did you check with the sender to make sure it was sent?"

It seemed like all these young women were conspiring to bust his balls. He ignored her question and said, "When I get a package, the driver always makes me sign. I assume you keep those records on file somewhere."

"Yes, sir, we do. If a sender sends a package and we deliver the package, the driver asks for a signature. That information is recorded in our central computer, and signatures are kept on file here in this office. But you say that you didn't receive your package?"

"I didn't say I didn't receive my package. I just want to see who signed for it."

"So you did receive the package?"

Emmy paused, letting his frustration hang in the air like fog before it finally cleared. He wanted to say something flippant like, "You own the company; you take this personally?"

What he did say, though, was straightforward, all business. "The sender said they shipped a package, but I haven't personally received it, so I want proof that it was delivered or proof that it wasn't. Is that okay with you?" He shouldn't have added the *okay* part, but now it was out there like an insult. Well, fuck her.

She got all officious and didn't look up as she asked in a tone reserved for DMV clerks, booking officers, and court bailiffs, "Name and address?"

He answered, and she typed that information into a green-screen computer. It took only seconds before she had the tracking number and date of delivery. She said, "Just a moment," then walked into a back room.

It took way longer before she returned with the paper logs. She thumbed through, then turned the log his direction and pointed to the signature, time, and date.

She said, "Satisfied?"

He ignored her and looked at the delivery log. "Leopold Skinner" scrawled out in very legible cursive, like a grammar school kid just learning. Who was Leopold or Leo Skinner? The date was the previous Friday, at 2:45 in the afternoon. Took him seconds—Skinner, Skinny. Fucker took the package while he was opening the safe to get the four hundred for the pearls.

He turned and left without a word.

Before the door closed behind him, he heard, "Thank you too."

Emmy needed a favor and called his guy on the Las Vegas Metro Police Department, Detective Pete Askoff. Pete had walked into The Gold Rush about two weeks after he'd taken control of the business. The detective had called the Chicago cops and knew what Emmy had been caught doing and what he was purported to do. Emmy, then Nuts, had done plenty of illegal jobs for Aiuppa before getting moved to Vegas. The Outfit theoretically still owned The Gold Rush, but now, seven years later, most of those bosses were now either six feet under, in prison, or in hiding after turning snitch. Aiuppa was in prison. The business was in Emmy's name, and no one from Chicago had ever called for a piece. But when Pete walked in that day, he made it clear he wanted his. Emmy paid for Metro protection, but also did work directly for Pete—mostly fencing stuff cops had taken in a bust. Now Emmy guessed he and Pete had what might be called a symbiotic relationship. Emmy did work for Pete but could ask favors in return, and he wanted the cops to locate Skinny.

It took him only a minute to explain the situation to Pete, who simply said, "On it."

The information came back that afternoon. Leopold Skinner, aka "Skinny," was staying at the Oasis Hotel just blocks from The Gold Rush. He'd paid in advance for a week. Room number twelve.

Then, not fifteen minutes later, he got another call—Deedee from Tramps. He'd known her for a couple of years, and she sometimes sold him stuff from the club's lost and found—usually gold chains busted loose while dancing, but once a Philippe Patek watch. As far as Emmy was concerned, it was good, honest business. They'd met through Pete, who told her where to sell the stuff. Deedee and Pete were close. In fact, Emmy had recently sold him an expensive three-carat wedding ring, substantially discounted.

She said, "Hi, Emmy."

He knew her voice, like velvet. "What's going on, Deedee?"

"You wouldn't believe what was found on the dance

floor last Friday."

"Yeah?"

"Diamonds, a whole little pouch of uncut diamonds."

Just too strange a coincidence. "You're right. That *is* hard to believe."

"I'm off tomorrow. Okay I come by?"

"Of course."

Then he remembered something his father had said to him years ago. "Sometimes a problem ignored long enough quits being a problem."

CHAPTER 7 – CORY
That Same Monday

Cory was back at Tramps on Monday night. Six months prior, Deedee had contracted with a comedy club in LA called Igby's to have four comedians fly out and do shows. Mondays and Tuesdays had slowed, and her thought was to get a crowd in before the music started. As she put it, "To shill the place." Cory guessed it had worked because Tramps Comedy Nights were still going strong six months later. He wasn't scheduled to work but was there to see the show. He wanted desperately to be a comedian.

Cory studied the show from the busboy station nearby.

The one comedian he particularly liked was a guy named Gabby Cruz. Gabby had done the show at Tramps five or six times, and his routine was almost always the same. Like George Carlin, he did stories, but instead of high school, his thing was growing up in Brooklyn. He had that accent like the guy Tony in *Saturday Night Fever*, like "How you doin'…" The stories were about the trouble he and his buddies got into—for example, stealing a car when he was ten, sitting on a phone book to see over the dashboard. Or the time his buddies distracted the owner at the corner drugstore, and Gabby stuffed so much stolen candy down his pants that he looked like Ron Jeremy. It seemed a lot of the stories were about stealing stuff. Anyway, the guy was knock-down funny, and though Cory had heard the routine a few times, it still made him laugh.

Gabby was the host and closer, meaning he introduced the other comedians and also had top billing, performing last. After the show, Cory approached him while he sat alone at the bar having a drink. He introduced himself, told Gabby his routine was great, and that he, too, wanted to be a comedian. He asked the dumb question, "How do I become one?"

Gabby didn't look as funny as his name—thinning black hair combed back over his balding head, a long pointy nose, and plastic-rimmed eyeglasses shaped like playing cards. He could have been a carpet salesman. Gabby repeated the question—twice. "How do I become one? How do I become one?" Then he answered. "Well, you've got to be funny." He paused. "Kid, you funny?"

It was like being asked if you had a big dick. If you said no, you'd be truly humiliated, but if you said yes, you'd have to prove it. If you wanted to be a porn star like Ron Jeremy, you'd better say yes. Cory hedged a little, "I think so." Now, he had to prove it.

"Okay, let me hear something." Gabby put down his drink and swiveled in his barstool to give Cory his full attention.

Cory had never thought to write out a bit; he just figured he was funny in general. But there he was in front of the big man, and now he had to whip something out. He said, "Okay," and then paused.

"Any time now."

"Okay."

"Really? You got something?"

Cory started in, pure improvisation. He cleared his throat. "Okay, so I was in my high school social studies class listening to blah, blah, blah, Red Coats and Indians, and like muskets, and I'm seriously half asleep. Then I notice this girl sitting two rows ahead. She turns around and looks me right in the eye. She turns around twice, and I'm thinking maybe she's got a crush on me or something. I know the girl; her name is something like "amnesia," maybe Ophilia or Cecilia or something. She's Goth, all dressed in black with these pants with enough zippers to close the fly on Paul Bunyan's trousers. But she's definitely hot. She turns around a third time and now has one of those clear BIC pens in her mouth. I can see there's like no ballpoint to it or ink. She quickly spits into the thing, and a little wad of chewed notebook paper shoots out and hits me right in the face. A spitball—no shit, seriously. Hits me right below the eye and sticks there. She turns around just as quickly, and I peel the spitball off my face, a gob of her saliva dripping down to my lips. Then I taste it. And now I imagine a whole tongue full of her saliva in my mouth. Then, like, I get that tingly feeling between my legs. From there on out, it was pure love."

Gabby stopped him there. "Okay, kid, heard enough."

"No, I got more," He was ready to talk about taking her home on his dirtbike, the wet kiss, and the goombah father.

"That's okay, kid. I can tell you got something. Tighten it up, put together fifteen minutes of material, write it down, and practice. I'll see you in three weeks when I'm back up here. We'll get you on stage."

"Seriously?"

CHAPTER 8 – NIVEN
That Same Monday

He waited and watched. Monday nights at Tramps after the comedy show were deadsville. A backup DJ, some kid with greasy hair and acne, spun the records while absolutely no one danced. Most of the tables were empty, and a few regulars sat at the big horseshoe bar, some feverishly dropping quarters into video poker machines. The other bar was closed, with one cocktail waitress working the few seated customers and just two bouncers lounging at the front door. The office was down a narrow hallway across from the bathrooms. He'd seen a manager use his keys to get in, and the guy hadn't come out since. Niven sat on a bar stool, sipped a Stoli cranberry, and, from time to time, slipped a quarter into the poker machine. Every hour or so, he'd go into a bathroom stall to do another line of coke. At about three in the morning, the manager came out to let the handful of customers know they'd be closing in half an hour—to drink up. Fifteen minutes later, Niven took what was left of his quarters and locked himself into a bathroom stall. He snorted the last crumbs of coke, then pulled his knees up above the toilet seat. About half an hour later, someone came in and turned off the bathroom lights. No one checked the stalls.

He waited another fifteen minutes, counting the minutes clicking by on his glow-in-the-dark wristwatch. He opened the stall door and then blindly felt his way to the bathroom exit. All the lights were off, the club pitch black. He had a lighter in his pocket and flicked on a flame. He walked around. The club had zero windows. The place was designed to keep any sunlight from entering, creating a den of sorts that, on a busy weekend night that stretched deep into the morning hours, insulated the partiers from the real waking world. Niven turned on a light and extinguished the lighter.

He searched around the office door for any security alarm sensors. None. The door lock was a joke, a spring-loaded bolt that he easily jammed back by sliding his driver's license between the edge of the door and the strike plate. He switched on the office light.

The room was small with two desks crammed together in the middle, a set of filing cabinets at one end, and the floor safe at the other. The safe was a Mosler with a simple hundred-point dial and a handle for pulling back the series of bolts that secured the door—a newer version of the one in his apartment. He sat down cross-legged in front of the safe and started the process.

He began by twisting the dial quickly to the left, six rotations to pick up all the wheels. He counted just three wheels—three numbers he had to figure out. Then he turned slower, listening for when the inside lever touched both the front and back of the gate, the contact points. When the three wheels aligned with the combination numbers, the lever would fall into the gate between the contact points, and then the safe would open. He could not only hear the movement of the lever but also feel it in his fingers, a spot on the dial between numbers 10 and 14.

Graphing. This process required graphing, and Niven hadn't brought graph paper along. Or a pencil. He stood up, stretched his legs, and went through the desk drawers. The top drawer had a few mechanical pencils, and he took one. Then, in a center drawer, he found an accounting ledger with soft green paper crisscrossed with lines. This would do, and he ripped out a page and numbered lines from 1 to 100. He sat back down at the safe.

He turned the dial to the right several rotations to pick up all three wheels, stopping at "0." Next, he turned the dial to the left until he reached the front and back ends of the gate, the contact points. He graphed those two points and then started over again; this time, instead of stopping at "0," he stopped at "97," then turned left again until reaching the contact points. He graphed those right below. He repeated this process in three-number increments until he reached "0" again. When he was done a half hour later, the graph revealed the approximate combination within a three to four-number range. Now, he'd need to do an amplified graph for each range of numbers. He stood up to get more graph paper and, while he was at it, went out into the bar and lifted a Corona from one of the coolers. He wished he had more coke.

An hour later, Niven thought he had the three numbers and now only needed to do each combination to discover the order. He looked at his watch, nearly 7 a.m.. He was close. Fifteen minutes later, the lever dropped into the open gate, and he lifted the handle to withdraw the bolts. The four-inch-thick door opened. He'd cracked his very first safe.

The bottom was piled with register trays filled with

quarters, ones, fives, and tens—ready for the next shift. He was not interested in the small bills. On a shelf above were boxes of heavy quarters that would eventually work themselves into the hoppers of the video poker machines. A box totaled five hundred dollars, but it weighed twenty pounds. On the top shelf lay a deposit envelope from the night's sales. He took the envelope, the size of a small woman's clutch, and slipped it beneath his waistband. Behind the envelope was a pistol. He slid it out and gripped the handle. It looked like a handgun from a World War II movie, an officer's sidearm.

Niven had never owned a gun. To him, they represented thugs and hacks, guys who robbed convenience stores for a few hundred bucks. Most eventually got caught and, with a gun possession, ended up doing ten years or more. And if you didn't have a gun, chances are you wouldn't shoot someone and take a murder rap or get shot yourself. Niven was smarter than that, but the gun he held felt almost magical—and oddly sexy. He thought about putting the pistol in his waistband along with the deposit envelope, but then he thought it might be loaded and possibly blow off a leg along with his testicles. He put it back on the shelf and kept searching. The velvet pouch with the diamonds sat right next to a stack of confiscated fake IDs.

Then he heard the front doors being unlocked. Niven closed the office door and turned off the lights. Someone walked in. He had nowhere to hide and just sat back on the floor in front of the safe, waiting.

A key slipped into the lock, and the office door opened. The lights switched on. A woman walked in. She saw him but did not scream.

She said, "You motherfucker."

The woman looked to be in her fifties, with jet black hair

and a dark complexion, like Mexican. Still beautiful. He didn't know what to say—no lie he could come up with on the spot. It was obvious that he'd broken in and taken the safe's contents. He said nothing.

She said, "Stay right the fuck there," then picked up the phone. Ballsy.

And there was the gun. He pulled it out. She made no movement toward him but now reached 911. She stared at him with the gun while speaking into the phone. "My name is Dolores Welch from Tramps on Flamingo and Arville. I'd like to report a robbery in progress." Ballsy.

He pointed the gun at the woman. "Hang up."

She kept talking. "Yes, he's right here in front of me." Ballsy.

He pulled back the slide thingy to chamber a round. He'd seen it done in countless movies. He said again, "Hang up."

He pulled the trigger.

The sound startled them both.

The woman lay there unmoving but still breathing, still staring at him. Blood seeped through her crimson blouse, the blood darker than the blouse, like spilled burgundy wine.

Niven didn't stay around to see if the woman would die. He took the diamonds and the deposit bag but left behind the weighty boxes of quarter rolls and the handgun.

When he neared the woman, her eyes were now closed. She made little twitchy movements. Her lungs moved small wisps of air like a sleeping child. He looked at what he'd done—a waste.

If she could have just shut the fuck up.

Then he noticed the pea-sized rock on her shaky finger. He reached for the ring and pulled. It slipped off easily.

CHAPTER 9 – DEEDEE
Previous Saturday

She ran Tramps like it was her own, like she thought her ex-husband, Frank, had run it: employee uniforms clean at the beginning of each shift, table place settings consistent with forks and knives on thick paper napkins, food orders turned in twenty minutes or less, dirty plates cleared, and water glasses topped off. Then, after the DJ music started, after the food servers were replaced by cocktailers, empty glassware signaled poor service, and a dirty restroom implied a dirty kitchen. Deedee wanted it just so, and all the employees knew her expectations. Most had worked there before she'd taken over five years ago, right after Frank had been murdered while *he* was making a bank deposit.

That Saturday, she came in at 4 p.m., an hour before the dinner rush, to have her own supper, which she'd make herself on the kitchen line. It wasn't that she didn't like what the cooks made. In fact, she usually prepared something on the menu. What she wanted was to be *in* the kitchen, see if it was clean and ready for the evening. And she wanted to show them she *could* cook and would work the line if needed—it had happened.

After finishing her meal, she walked the floor, seating people, following up to ensure customers were pleased with their meals, and coping with the complaints, inevitable as July heat. The dance floor was cleared of dinner tables at 10:30, and the music with DJ Danny started at 11. Saturdays were always packed by midnight with a line out the door and down the sidewalk. That Saturday was a little more special. Caesars Palace was hosting a boxing rematch between Sugar Ray Leonard, the local favorite, and Thomas Hearns from the Kronk Boxing Gym in Detroit. Billed as "The War," the fight would attract every big-time hustler from LA, New York, Chicago, and Detroit. After the fight, many would end up at Tramps with their entourage. The guys from Kronk would also be at the club. In anticipation, her bar manager, Ed, had ordered extra cases of Dom Pérignon, Cristal, and Courvoisier. These guys did not drink Korbel or Hennessy.

Normally, Tramps catered to the locals with no cover charge and no preferential treatment at the door for high rollers and big shots—everyone waited in line. Fight nights were the one exception, and the locals were well aware. The guys who rolled up in their rented limos, along with their entourage, did not wait in line. The Kronk guys and celebrities also did not wait. Tables were reserved. The cocktail waitresses and bartenders would make twice what they'd normally make on a Saturday, and the club would double its gross.

The fight was over by midnight, ending in a split draw— bets voided, and wagers refunded. No one was joyous, but no one was miserable and fuming, which suited Deedee just fine. The booths around the dance floor were filled by 1 a.m. By 2, they'd gone through three cases each of Dom and Cristal, a hundred a pop, which added up to around seven thousand in revenue.

The Kronk guys walked through the doors just after 2 a.m., probably right after patching up their champ. They'd come to the club after other fights, arriving as a group, six or seven, all dressed in tracksuits, gold chains, and their shamrock-green silk jackets with "Kronk Gym" spelled out across the back in white stitching. These guys were mostly other fighters in the gym who worked out and sparred with Hearn. They'd been in Vegas to train with Hearn over the last week and were jacked up to party. The Kronk guys were from the streets and had money in their pockets, but not the kind that could buy French Champagne. They came in and roamed the club, drinking their Courvoisier and Cokes and asking any attached or unattached woman if they would dance.

That's where the trouble started, with an older pimp from LA who went by the name Iceberg Slim. Deedee knew him from way back and called him Bob, his given name. As far as Deedee knew, Bob still worked women (and men) in Hollywood, but he'd also written a book, *Pimp*. The trouble started when a Kronk guy asked one of Bob's girls, one sitting on the edge of the booth, if she wanted to dance.

Bob replied for her, "Move along, youngblood."

The kid looked over at Bob. "I wasn't talking to you, Pop."

Bob looked at the two girls blocking his way and said, "Excuse me." The girls slid out of the booth, and he followed.

The kid didn't move, stood his ground, a boxer with broad shoulders and clenched fists, ready to land a blow.

Bob stood and, in the same motion, pulled a knife from somewhere in his pinstripe, knee-length suit coat. He did it casually like a high roller readying a ten-dollar tip. Deedee saw it, and so did the kid.

Bob's solid gold rope chain with its coaster-sized pendant swung back and forth like a pendulum, time ticking.

The kid said, "You think you're going to cut me, old man?" Now other guys from the Kronk gym stepped beside and behind him.

Two of the doormen watched and then glanced toward Deedee to see what she'd do. A simple signal, a head nod, and they'd try to break it up. They'd be in over their heads—a knife, professional boxers, all tough street fighters.

The music was loud, people were still dancing, but many in the club had their eyes glued to the potential violence.

Deedee stepped between Iceberg Slim and the Kronk guys. She'd been on the streets herself, once a high-priced escort, then a junky and street hooker. She'd been cut, beaten, and raped. She knew instinctively that Bob would never cut her. The Kronk guys? They hit her, and half the club would descend and beat all four near death. She was not scared and did not have to say anything. The implications were obvious.

Bob kept the knife close to his thigh, and the boxers stared him down. It took minutes for the tension to settle. Deedee now stood with her back to Bob and faced the Kronk guys. She could see their shoulders slowly relax, their eyes roaming the room.

Finally, she smiled and said, "Let me buy you boys a drink."

The one who'd started the incident said, "Fuck it." Then, to the others, "Let this nice lady buy us a drink."

She knew Iceberg Slim was not someone to let the disrespect go unpunished, but he wouldn't do anything now inside the club. And what happened outside the club was like that tree that falls in the forest.

At 7 a.m., the music still pulsed loudly, and drinks were still being served. But the crowd had thinned, and Deedee felt done. She'd wait through the shift change and then do the deposit.

She sat at a small table close to the kitchen and drank coffee. And for whatever reason, her mind wandered toward things she rarely thought about, maybe it was her age coming on or the incident with Bob and the boxers. She thought about her life and wondered if it somehow made sense—or if it was just a string of stories with no moral, no revelation with an aha moment. She'd been on top of the world in her twenties with a husband she loved, a family, and a great job working for casinos as a hostess for high rollers. Was it booze, drugs, money, or the feeling of power? Her hostess job had turned into an escort gig with all that entailed. She'd gone out with celebrities. But then the drugs and booze took over, and she ended up on the street, her family estranged. Ironically, she was saved by an acquaintance who needed someone to manage the girls at the Chicken Ranch, a brothel just out of town in Pahrump. It saved her from certain death because, for the employees, booze and drugs were not allowed. Then Claire, her daughter, came back into her life along with Deedee's grandson, Frankie. Now Deedee was running Tramps, playing hostess again. Did her life make sense? Was there that revelation, a moral? She guessed the simple moral to her story was, *Don't do drugs and alcohol.* Or maybe the message was, *Family matters most.* That, or her life was just a long string of stories. And, oh, did she have stories to tell.

She had the next Sunday and Monday off. Ed, her bar manager, would take care of the club. After making the bank deposit, she'd go see Claire, her partner Red, and Frankie to make breakfast. She wouldn't be back at Tramps until Tuesday morning, when she'd do the next deposit and deal with the diamonds. She'd call Emmy to set it up.

◆ ◆ ◆

In the years spent managing the girls at the Chicken Ranch, she loved making breakfast. Mornings were the one time they rarely worked, and the girls could settle around the huge kitchen table, talk about their lives, and just relax. It was a time she didn't have to greet guests, do the lineup, take money, and worry about what could go wrong. She'd have everything laid out: cereal, juice, coffee, donuts, yogurt, muffins, bagels—a whole spread. She'd cook hot food to order, like eggs, bacon, sausage, home fries, and pancakes. She guessed it was a motherly thing. But she sometimes felt deep guilt and remorse that she hadn't done the same for her own family. She could now.

Deedee pulled into the dirt driveway of their old adobe house. Sunday morning at 8:30, and they'd still be asleep. Claire, because she worked late hours at the hospital, Frankie, because that's what thirteen-year-olds did, and Red, because he was kinda lazy. She let herself into the house through the back kitchen door and started cooking.

An hour later, they were all up and around her, eating and talking, though Frankie, with his autism, still said little beyond acknowledging her with "Lita," short for *abuelita*— granny in Spanish. That was her family now, and she'd do anything for them. And she thought they'd do anything for her. It was a new and strange concept—family. Her life now felt like more than just a string of stories.

Deedee had a life of her own outside Tramps and her family—a townhome which once belonged to her husband and now a boyfriend, Pete. Pete was a detective with Metro, and they'd first met after Frank had been shot and killed. She'd seen him at the funeral and knew there was some sort of relationship, some quid pro quo. A month later, he stopped by Tramps and introduced himself. He explained the situation in plain and straightforward language. Frank had paid him five grand a month in exchange for protection. The deal was, Pete's officers would not step inside the club to handle incidents that the doormen could handle on their own. They would come around to pick up and book anyone in a fight or otherwise unruly as long as they were already wrapped up in handcuffs. They would look the other way if a minor somehow entered the club with a fake ID. They also wouldn't enforce fire code restrictions on the number of people inside the club. He suggested to Deedee that she continue paying for the protection.

Deedee was not offended. She knew how things ran in Las Vegas. The mob or anyone else only did business at the pleasure of the cowboys who ultimately ran the town and ran Metro. Many people who didn't understand that rule had disappeared. And the facts were evident: fake IDs had become almost undetectable, fights had to be broken up and Metro called, and on weekend nights they packed fifteen hundred people in a nightclub with a maximum fire code capacity of five hundred. She paid, and every month around the first of the month, Pete would stop by to collect his envelope. One morning, he asked her out for dinner. Pete, it turned out, was divorced.

She could have written a book, the old hooker and the hard-boiled detective.

That Monday after breakfast, she and Pete got together for an afternoon on Lake Mead in his speedboat. After anchoring in a secluded bay, he proposed. Detective Pete Askoff got down on one knee and held up a little velvet box. He opened it to reveal a beautiful diamond ring. She slipped it on—too easily, it would need to be resized. Sadly, she remembered selling her first wedding ring from Frank to a pawnshop on Main Street. But that was so long ago, and she hadn't touched drugs or alcohol in nearly twenty years. She thought she loved Pete. He was nice to her, gentle. She could see him become part of her family. And she deserved this.

◆ ◆ ◆

Tuesday morning, she unlocked the front doors to Tramps, walked in, and turned on the lights. She then unlocked the office door.

A boy knelt at the opened safe. A fucking kid.

"You motherfucker." Then, "Stay right the fuck there." She dialed 911.

She looked at the kid sitting on the floor, like a child at a box of toys. He wore the black pants all service employees wore in Vegas, likely a waiter somewhere. His hair was short and curly, like it was permed, and on his upper lip was something resembling a mustache. She could see the bank deposit pouch stuffed into his waistband. Likely, he'd found the diamonds.

The operator answered, "What is your emergency?"

"My name is Dolores Welch from Tramps on Flamingo and Arville. I'd like to report a robbery in progress."

He held a gun, the one from inside the safe. "Hang up." The gun had been Frank's. He'd kept it there in the event of a robbery. A shotgun once stood between the side of the safe and the wall, but she'd gotten rid of that. She did not like guns, but they also didn't scare her; Frank had kept guns all over the house when they lived together. She wasn't scared of knives or guns or men.

The kid pulled back the gun's slide to chamber a round. Loaded. He said again, "Hang up."

The operator asked, "Is the perpetrator still on the premises?"

"Yes, he's right here in front of me." She glared at the boy, daring him to pull the trigger.

"Ma'am, you need to hang up and leave the premises immediately. Please do it now."

He pulled the trigger.

The force of the bullet sent her to the floor, her head slamming against the back wall. She couldn't move. She watched as the boy took the pouch with the diamonds from the safe and then scrambled to his feet. He dropped the gun and moved past her. But then he paused. She could not move or speak, as though her body was entombed in cement. He looked at her ring, the ring Pete had given her the day before. He slipped it easily off her twitching finger. She remembered the ring needed to be resized.

She knew she was dying. She couldn't move and could barely exchange air through her lungs. She felt no pain. She knew she had just seconds to live and think. What did she want her last thoughts to be? She had a life to be bitter about, but she didn't go there. Where she went was to her family. She tried to freeze in her mind the image of them all together, and what came to her was a photo taken at Frank's funeral right there at

Tramps. Someone took a photo of the three of them and gave it to her months later, and she kept it in a frame next to her bed. She remembered it was Pete who took the photo. He was there, too. She wanted to think that she'd had a decent life considering everything she'd been through.

But what she thought as she lay dying was that the good part was just beginning.

CHAPTER 10 – EMMY
That Same Tuesday

Tuesday morning, Emmy waited for Deedee to bring in the diamonds. It was almost a routine. He knew she received most of the stuff from a porter who swept the floors throughout the busy weekend nights. He knew Deedee took Sundays and Mondays off, so she always came by on Tuesdays after she'd gone to the bank. They'd do their business and then go next door to the German restaurant to get coffee and a slice of Black Forest cake, closing the store for an hour or so. Both had deeply checkered pasts, and that's what they mostly talked about, old war stories. They were coffee friends. So when she didn't show up, Emmy worried.

Fuck it, he thought, then closed the store and drove to Tramps.

The place was a crime scene—three Metro squad cars, an unmarked, and the Clark County Coroner van. The club was taped up in yellow. He parked down Arville and stood at the edge of the crime scene with a few gawkers. The unmarked looked like Pete's car. Then Pete walked out of the club. He walked stiffly and ignored the other uniformed cops outside.

Emmy called out his name.

Pete looked over and saw him. He motioned Emmy to cross the tape, then said to the cop nearby, "It's okay."

Pete's face looked pale and slack. His reddened eyes were bulging against their sockets, holding back tears.

Emmy asked, "What happened?"

"Someone robbed the place. Deedee must have caught them in the act. They shot her."

"She's dead?"

Pete nodded.

Emmy knew that Pete was either going to propose to her or had just done so. Emmy had sold him the ring. What'd happened was deeply personal. "I'm sorry."

And then Pete silently wept.

Emmy put his arm around the detective and moved him away from the cops and gawkers. He said again, "I'm so sorry."

Pete sobbed and Emmy held him.

It took the detective a few minutes to regain his composure. He said, "I've got a job to do," and then stepped away from Emmy's arm. Then he asked, "Why are you here?"

Maybe it was the cop talking, or maybe the friend. Pete knew that if a robbery took place in the city, the stolen stuff, especially jewelry, could easily end up at The Gold Rush. Pete himself had fenced stuff in the past. Maybe they had a relationship of sorts, but Pete kept him at arm's length, always reminding Emmy who was boss. So, he guessed it was the cop talking. "Deedee was supposed to drop something off. When she didn't, I came over."

"What something?"

"Had to do with that kid, Skinny, I asked you to track

down. He stole a package from me, uncut diamonds. Then, coincidentally, Deedee called on Monday to say she was holding onto uncut diamonds a porter had found on the dance floor—no doubt the same ones."

Now, whatever sorrow was left on the detective's face was replaced by pure anger. His eyes moved right and left beyond Emmy, looking for something that probably wasn't there. "He was staying at the Oasis, right?"

"Yeah, that's what you told me."

Then, with nothing else said, the detective turned and walked away.

Emmy guessed their relationship was back where it had begun, at arm's length.

◆ ◆ ◆

That afternoon, Swede called from Chicago. He asked about the diamonds—did Emmy have them? He tried to explain— the theft of the FedEx box, the kid Skinny, Tramps and the recovery of the diamonds, Deedee, a robbery, and her death. Even as he spoke the string of convoluted words, they sounded like some made-up story, the kind that in Chicago could get you killed. He ended it like any guilty asshole would, "Swear to God, Swede, I know it sounds far-fetched, but it's the God-honest truth." If someone put "God" into a sentence twice, Emmy himself would have killed him.

Swede said, "I'm coming out."

◆ ◆ ◆

The service for Deedee took place the following Sunday afternoon at Tramps. Emmy arrived alone and stood around like the others, talking and drinking while scanning the room, aware of the closed coffin resting on tables in the center of the dance floor. He'd never gone there to drink and dance—he guessed he was too old for that—and knew none of the employees or Deedee's family. He saw Pete with a younger woman who bore a resemblance to Deedee, next to a big guy with a graying red beard, and a kid who stood like he'd been frozen on the spot, a statue with eyes staring at the floor. He figured those were Deedee's people. Pete looked over once but didn't smile or acknowledge him. That was okay; Emmy was there to show his respects, and the detective might have felt slighted if he hadn't shown up at all.

The service started, and a DJ in the booth played some mood music that focused everyone's attention on the dance floor. Then, mourners made speeches while standing next to the coffin. One guy introduced himself as Ed, the bar manager, and told how Deedee had taken over for Frank, whom he loved. How Deedee was generous and kind but also demanding, and that brought some chuckles. The daughter, Claire, spoke about reconnecting with her mother and how Deedee had become a doting grandmother to Frankie. She looked at the boy standing beside her and tried to touch the top of his head. He would have none of it and stepped aside. She finished by saying that Deedee could now be reunited with Frank somewhere, in heaven or the universe. Pete stepped up last. He was stoic as he spoke, telling how they'd met over a dinner date at Hugo's Cellar and how she lit up the place with her beauty and personality. He finished by telling the details of how he'd just proposed to Deedee and that she'd accepted. Toward the end, his stoicism cracked, the edges of his mouth quivered, and he held up a hand to cover his face. Others in the crowd openly wept.

The DJ played another song, one he said was her favorite. It sounded familiar to Emmy, but he couldn't place it. But then the song brought back memories of his own deceased wife, Vivian. A few times, they'd gone out to the cocktail lounge at the Dunes, the Top O' The Strip. They had a piano player there who performed crooner oldies, and he and Vivian would often dance. Once, she kissed him right there on the dance floor. The song the DJ played reminded him of that. Still, he couldn't place the song.

It took him a second to snap out of it.

After the song, everyone bought more drinks at the bar and mingled.

Emmy noticed the kid then, the one who'd driven Tanya home on his minibike and kissed her on the street. The kid was talking to others, and Emmy waited until that conversation stopped before approaching.

The kid saw him coming and then looked around for someplace to escape. But he just stood still, frightened.

Emmy took the edge off. In a friendly voice, he said, "How you doin', kid? Didn't know you knew the deceased."

The kid looked down at his shoes. "I work here."

Emmy continued in his friendly tone. "Sorry about the other day. Maybe I went too far. Tanya can be a handful, but whatever she does, she means to. I know it wasn't your fault." The kid's shoulders seemed to relax. He added, "I don't think we've been introduced to each other. I'm Tanya's stepdad. Everyone calls me Emmy."

He put out his hand to shake. The kid looked up and then took it. He said, "I'm Cory."

"Glad to know you. So, what's your job at Tramps? I assume it's part-time, seeing you have high school."

"I'm a porter. I work weekends cleaning the bathrooms

and sweeping the floors."

There it was, his connection. Emmy knew that a porter had found most of the merchandise that passed through Deedee to the store. He made the connection for the kid. "I'm the guy who owns The Gold Rush on Sahara. I'm the guy Deedee sold lost stuff to. I assume you might have been the beneficiary of those proceeds."

The kid looked at him hard. "I guess so."

Emmy went for it. "She was supposed to have had some diamonds. I think those diamonds were in the safe when it was robbed. Are you the one who found them?"

Now, the kid looked scared again. "All I do is sweep up. Anything I find, I turn in."

"Hey, kid, I'm not accusing you of anything. Just want to know. I think they belong to a friend of mine."

"Like I said, whatever I find, I turn over to Deedee."

"So you did find those diamonds?"

"Yes."

"They look like twenty or so raw diamonds that'd never been cut?"

"Deedee said they were diamonds. Looked like little white pebbles to me."

"You got any idea who could have dropped them?"

The kid took a different stance then. "I'm no thief. If I knew who dropped them, I'd have given them back."

"Sure."

"Listen, Mister, on a Saturday night, there's like two hundred people packed on the dance floor all crammed together like turds in an outhouse. I find something on the dance floor; it could be any piece of shit."

Emmy had to laugh at that. The kid, Cory, was funny. "Sure, I get it."

The kid now looked a little put-off. "And listen, I won't have anything more to do with Tanya. Like, that's over."

Emmy thought about what Cory was saying. He felt bad for getting irritated like he had, threatening the kid in front of his stepdaughter. "If it's over, it's over. Not like I can get in the way of what she does in her life."

The kid gave him a look, like, *What, are you kidding?* What he said, though, was simply, "Yeah, I gotta go." And then he left.

Emmy stood alone and looked around. People were beginning to leave. Pete had left along with the family, the music had stopped, and someone had turned up the lights so that the stark interior was illuminated. And then it struck him, Tramps had nothing to do with sluts or prostitutes. The walls were decorated with rough-cut beams and old stuff from railroad yards: crossing signs, antique depot signs, and signal lanterns. A toy locomotive ran in a circle around the bar in the back. Tramps meant hobos. He wondered how this all began. For sure, it wasn't Deedee's idea. For her, Tramps would have meant hookers and sluts, and the place would've been littered with red velvet, brass rails, and dance poles. Had she put her mark on this place? Did it matter now? He figured once you were dead, you were dead.

And in the land of the living, the difference between life and death was finding those fucking diamonds. Swede was arriving tomorrow.

CHAPTER 11 – SKINNY
Thursday

Kitchen paid ten dollars for a stolen credit card, payable in heroin. Skinny had gone through what was left of the four hundred he'd received from Nuts at The Gold Rush. The last of it had gone to pay the bar tab at Tramps after Niven and his friends from Fridays had ditched him. Now, he was tweaking hard and just needed anything to top him off. He had three credit cards, all in the same name, Rhonda Gubbins.

He'd been at one of his spots, this one between the Barbary Coast and the Maxim on Flamingo. A woman with another lady friend came out from the Maxim and walked toward him as he stood against the wall of a dive bar called The Stage Door. No one else was around, and both ladies were older and boxy like they couldn't outrun a one-legged chicken. He watched them pass by. Neither noticed him standing there nor looked in his direction. Invisible. He moved, running up from behind, snatching the one lady's purse that she held by the strap. But along with her being boxy and heavy, she was also sturdy and wouldn't let go. Skinny was jerked back and onto the pavement like a dog at the end of its leash. The lady yanked her handbag away from Skinny, who was now scrambling to his feet. The other lady yelled, "Help, somebody, help!" He ran empty-handed to the back exit door of Barbary Coast, which he'd previously propped open. Then, by sheer luck, he ran past another woman playing the slots who'd set her purse next to the machine on the carpeted floor. As he ran past, Skinny scooped up the purse and kept going. The woman, Rhonda Gubbins, was so focused on dropping quarters into the machine that she never looked up or noticed. Seconds later, he was out the front door and on Las Vegas Boulevard. He slowed down then and walked casually, he hoped inconspicuously, a skinny street kid carrying a woman's purse. On the Strip, there were more stare-worthy oddities.

All she carried in her purse were credit cards, no cash money or casino chips.

The problem was, Kitchen wasn't paying thirty dollars for three credit cards, all with the same name.

Skinny said, "What difference does it make?"

Kitchen thought on that. "It doesn't seem right, you getting thirty dollars for one snatch."

"You're not paying for the snatch; you're paying for the cards, and there's three—Visa, Mastercard, and Amex. I'm guessing you can walk up to Homer or whatever his name is at the Cash 'n Go and get twenty dollars each. Am I right? And Homer doesn't know a Mrs. Gubbins from Marge Simpson. He gets a card and gives you the cash."

"I'm not saying who I sell the cards to. That's my business."

"And I don't give a fuck. You pay me ten dollars for each credit card. That's the deal. You never said anything about names."

Kitchen thought some more. "Okay, how about I give you one bag for the three cards?"

"Then you still owe me five bucks."

"Take it or leave it, Skinny. Frankly, I don't give a shit."

He was sweating, tweaking, and Kitchen knew it. If he didn't get his fix, he'd be back on the street trying to hustle a fix from one of the tunnel-dweller junkies that lived in the flood channels under the Strip. He might get a fix there, but he also might get stabbed and raped. "Fine, I'll take it."

Fifteen minutes later, he was back in his room with the needle a half inch under his skin, the drug entering his veins like little worms. He sometimes thought of the drug that way, little worms floating upstream to his brain and smothering it like caramel on a wormy green apple. A fucked-up thought, he knew.

The worms were just starting to swim when someone banged on the door. "This is Metro Police. Open up now!"

Right before the worms did their smothering thing, it came to him how stupid he'd been. At The Gold Rush, he'd instinctively signed his real name, Leopold Skinner, in very legible cursive. Those diamonds wouldn't have gone unnoticed—Nuts would've tracked down his signature with the FedEx man, then put two and two together. No doubt he reported the theft to the cops, who would have tracked him down to the Oasis. He did not answer the door.

"I know you're in there, Skinny. Don't make me go get the clerk. That will just make it harder on you."

The smack hit his system then, the worms and caramel, and he leaned back against the soft bed. He did not answer the cop or open the door. He didn't know what would happen, but for those few minutes, he savored the enveloping high.

He heard the cop say, "Just open it." He wasn't talking

to Skinny.

Then the clerk—he could tell it was Sweet by her rough, cigarette-mangled voice. "Pete, you're supposed to have a search warrant."

Then back to Sweet, "You don't open it, I'll bust it open. Don't expect the city to pay for the fix."

"Okay, Okay."

Skinny could hear keys fumbling. It wasn't until he heard the scratch of the passkey against the lock that he jumped to his feet.

He had no place to hide. One room, one chair, a bed, a bathroom. He thought about the window in the bathroom, whether he could open it or squeeze through. That idea was so incomprehensible, like the thought of how he'd get his next fix.

He stood and pulled the white top sheet from the bed. He tossed the sheet over his head and then sank to the floor. He rolled his thin body beneath the bed.

The door opened. He could hear the cop, Pete, step in. Then, "Skinny?"

He stayed silent and did not move a muscle.

The cop walked through the room, his shoe soles making a squishy sound against the old carpet. He entered the bathroom, the soles now like crickets on the cold tiles. He said again, "Skinny?"

The cop moved back into the room, and Skinny heard the bed mattress being flipped just above him. He was looking for something. The diamonds. Skinny heard him go through each of the two pillows, pounding them to feel for a package. The cop stepped back into the bathroom, the soles of his shoes again like crickets. The squeaking door of the medicine cabinet opened and closed. Even if he had the diamonds, there'd be no place in the small room that Skinny could think to hide them.

He heard the light footsteps of Sweet pass over the threshold, heard her now smoking, the movement of air into her lungs, holding it, then the exhale. He could smell the smoke.

She said, "He's not here."

The cop stepped out of the bathroom, and for a brief moment, Skinny thought he could feel the cop looking under the bed, staring at his head and body covered in the white sheet. He was ready to be discovered, tossed around, and handcuffed.

He held his breath.

Then he heard the door to the small motel room close.

He lay under the bed for what seemed an eternity, waiting for the cop and Sweet to realize their mistake. Nothing happened; no one returned. Finally, he moved, squirming out, standing, and tossing the bed sheet to the floor.

What did it all mean? The cop must have looked under the bed—like under the bed was where people hid stuff. But the cop didn't see him. Was he invisible? The woman on the street today hadn't seen him until he ran past and tried to snatch her purse—and she'd walked right by within ten feet. But Kitchen had seen him; that was a fact, and he had the smack to prove it.

The cop *for sure* looked.

He always thought people just didn't see him, but now Skinny was convinced that some people *couldn't* see him. Was he actually able to become invisible? Was it just his adversaries? Was there a way to turn his invisibility on and off like a light bulb? He didn't know and doubted everything he thought.

That he was high didn't help.

◆ ◆ ◆

Skinny packed up what he had—his fix kit, a toothbrush, a bar of motel soap, two extra T-shirts, a pair of long jeans, a long-sleeved flannel shirt, and an extra pair of underwear—which all fit into his blue draw-string laundry bag with the One-Hour Martinizing logo. He couldn't stay at the Oasis. The cops would be back looking for him, and he couldn't just rely on his invisibility. He used the clean and private bathroom one last time before leaving. He thought Niven might let him crash at his place since he was the one who probably had the fucking diamonds.

He walked the five blocks to Niven's apartment. He saw the Jetta parked in the lot and climbed the outside stairs to the second floor. He knocked.

No one answered, and he knocked again. "Niven, come on, open the door. I know you're in there." He knocked one more time. "Niven?"

The door opened, a chain across the gap. "What do you want?"

"Come on, man, open the door."

"No, you can't be around here." Niven whispered like someone could hear, but the apartment complex appeared deserted.

"Why, man? What's going on?"

"None of your beeswax. Just get the fuck out of here and don't come back."

"You got my diamonds? Is that it? Fuck, man, I don't care anymore. Those diamonds are hot, and the cops have been around to the Oasis already. I got to lie low for a while."

"The cops? You talk to them?"

"No, I was like ..." He didn't know how to put it without sounding stupid. "... Invisible. They didn't see me." When it came out, the invisible part sounded like a figure of speech, like saying, "The smack cost me an arm and a leg," when a bag just cost twenty-five in paper dollars.

"I don't have those diamonds, and if you get caught on the street, I don't want you saying I do. Because I don't."

"Cool, but why can't I just crash here for a while?"

"Because you can't. Now Skinny," and his voice got louder, "get the fuck out of here and don't come back."

"Fine, but you stiffed me on that bar tab, and I got next to nothing left of the pearl score."

He heard some rustling inside; he guessed Niven was looking through his pockets. A few crumpled dollars then squeezed out the gap in the door and landed on the concrete walkway outside. Skinny picked up the bills before they blew away. The door then shut, and the lock bolt slammed home.

He couldn't be on the street, and even if he had the money, he couldn't get a motel room somewhere else. They'd find him. The only place to go was into the flood channels—the tunnels—and hole up there until things cooled.

Skinny walked west on Sahara and then up the Interstate overpass. On the other side was an embankment that led to a fenced-off area where the freight trains moved through the city. The fence had been cut ages ago, and just past it was the tunnel entrance he'd used before. The entrance itself was a series of five square concrete tunnels about chest-high that passed below the Interstate. He knew the tunnels converged on the other side into a larger tunnel big enough to drive cars through, which eventually joined with miles of other tunnels, some right under the Strip. A whole ghost city was down in those tunnels. He'd been through a few times to get a fix when Kitchen wasn't around or wouldn't sell him drugs. He'd never stayed long or overnight. The tunnels were creepy.

Skinny crouched into one of the entrances and crab walked to where they converged. He didn't have a flashlight and went in only to where he could still see his hands and the graffiti-covered concrete walls. He sat down.

An hour later, he pulled his fix kit from the laundry bag along with the little bag of smack. He was just cooking, focused on his work, when he looked up to see a man hovering above. The guy looked strong, muscled, with arms covered in tats. His reddish hair was cut unevenly short, but his long, gray-streaked beard hung to the top of his black T-shirt. He carried a military-looking backpack, a gallon jug of water, and a chunk of wood shaped like an axe handle—it probably *was* an axe handle. One eye looked at Skinny while the other focused in another direction—like he could see two things simultaneously, like a horse or a fish.

The man said, "You got enough for me?"

Skinny didn't think it was a question. He nodded, and the man swung off his backpack and settled down beside him. Skinny had already tied off his arm and now stabbed the needle into the flesh just above his wrist. He untied his arm and felt that familiar rush. He passed the kit and bag over to the man who helped himself.

The man asked, "What do you go by?"

"Skinny."

The man nodded but said no more. Just as the smack hit Skinny's nervous system, before he wouldn't care, he asked, "What about you?"

"They call me Rat King."

Rat King. He didn't know what that meant or whether to call him Rat or King or the full Rat King. Or was it *The* Rat King? He said nothing back to the man.

When Rat King was done with the needle, he reached inside a pocket to retrieve a Zippo lighter. He sterilized the used needle over the flame. He said, "Precaution," then asked, "You got any money?"

It was just the two of them in the tunnels, deep enough inside so that any noise or scream would be muffled and silenced. Skinny had never been much of a fighter, more into running—*flight*. And he didn't think that what the King of Rats was asking was really a question.

CHAPTER 12 – CORY
Friday

Tanya yanked Cory aside as he made his way to the school cafeteria. She'd taken to dressing preppy in the last few days and now seemed to be one of the popular girls. He didn't think she still had any interest in him with all the boys now hitting on her. She backed him up against a locker and got close to his ear with her mouth.

She whispered, "Let's get out of here. Go to the lake."

He couldn't argue with that. No tests or finals were scheduled that Friday afternoon, and few would notice their absence. If a teacher did notice and decided to do something about it—well, fuck it. He hated high school and just wanted it to be done. In six weeks, he would be, and then he'd pursue his newfound career as a stand-up comedian. He didn't need good grades to be funny.

He responded, "Okay."

They drove out to Lake Mead on his dirtbike. It could do fifty miles per hour, fast enough to cover the minimum speed limit on Boulder Highway. Cars, pick-ups, trucks, and other motorcycles—pretty much anything with an engine—whizzed past. Pissed-off drivers flipped a middle finger, and one semi-truck passing too close blasted a concussion of air that sent the dirtbike into a wobble. Tanya was on the back wearing his helmet, her Nikon camera strapped around her neck and shoulder. She held tight, her hands clasped around his waist. It made his peeder hum.

He knew a turn-off to a dirt road about four miles north of the marina that led to a hidden beach. He parked above it, and they walked down a gravel path to the lake's edge. A few others knew about the place, but there wasn't a fire pit or scattered beer cans to spoil the charm. The beach was deserted and as private as a locked toilet stall.

Tanya said, "Cool," then immediately began removing her clothes.

Cory was shocked, stunned, but followed her lead. She ran splashing through the water before Cory was half undressed. What he noticed and tried not to stare at was her breasts, which, to any kid his age, were just about perfect. He finished undressing and splashed in after.

In water up to their shoulders, she kissed him deep and hard. His stiff dick pushed against her stomach, and she grabbed it like a door handle. Tanya then wrapped her legs around his chest and used a hand to guide him in. She pulled her mouth briefly away from his and said, "Don't cum in me." Cory withdrew at the last moment, only seconds into the fuck, and felt his sperm pulsing out and merging with the cool water.

The release was emotional, and it took him some time to get his head together. He thought about saying, "That was great," or "Gee, I really like you." Both of which sounded phony and contrived. In the end, he said nothing.

Tanya swam back toward the shore, and he followed.

They then sat on the beach naked and dried under the hot May sun.

She asked him, "So what's your deal?"

"What do you mean?"

"Like, do you have any brothers or sisters? I wish I had a sister."

"No, it's just me and my mom, that is, until her new husband moved in, and I, like, moved out. He's a real asshole. I have my own apartment now, just off the Strip." He thought about what had happened with his mom and her husband, his stepdad. He'd never told anyone, but Tanya was there, and they had the whole afternoon. And he *wanted* to tell someone. "Mom and I were cool before he showed up. She worked as a keno girl at the Showboat, and we had this nice two-bedroom townhome. They let you have dogs there, and I had this small lab named Sulu after that guy in *Star Trek*."

She stopped him. "That's a cute name. If I had a dog, I'd name her Ginger, like after the Hollywood starlet in *Gilligan's Island*. The way she dresses up and shows herself—you know there's something behind the makeup, something mysterious."

"I always liked Mary Ann."

"Why is it that all you boys like Mary Ann? There are no layers to Mary Ann. Like that song, 'Whatcha see is whatcha get …'"

"Some people like that." He thought for a second, then added, "the simplicity."

"Some people like vanilla ice cream. I like cotton candy with streaks of blue, pink, and purple. But sorry, go on with what you were saying."

"Okay, so this new husband of hers moves in. They'd gotten a quickie marriage at the Little White Chapel. He's a security guard at the Showboat and is all authoritarian and shit.

You know, he thinks he's a real cop or something. He doesn't like Sulu and doesn't like me. Says to my mom that it's not good that I watch so much TV, so he sends me to my room to study every night. I don't need to study; I can almost always finish my homework in class while ignoring teachers like Tierney."

She snorted, "Yeah."

"I know he just wants me out of the way—you know, out of sight, out of mind. He tells me to take the dog along wherever I go, but I can't take Sulu to school, and I know the asshole hates the dog. I come home one day, and Sulu's under the kitchen table. He looks scared and won't come out to greet me like he usually does. I try to give him a treat, a milk bone, but he won't take it. I know that asshole, his name is Greg, was beating the dog. I know because Sulu wouldn't let me hold him, and he cried out when I touched his side. I think a rib was broken.

"I yelled at Greg when I saw him, telling the creep to stay away from my dog. My mom was there, and he just lied and denied everything. My mom stood up for him, saying Greg wouldn't do anything to hurt Sulu. Then, one day, I actually saw him through the kitchen window. He hit Sulu twice with something, right in the ribs. I thought, fuck that.

"I started to sabotage him. I put sugar in his gas tank one night. Then, a few days later, I planted someone else's panties in their bedroom for my mom to find. Of course, he knew it was me, though I denied it just like he'd denied beating Sulu.

"Then, a week later, I come home and Sulu is gone. I ask my mom, and she says she doesn't know. I look at Greg, who says maybe the dog just ran away. Sulu would never run away; he wouldn't even leave the yard."

"So, what happened?" Tanya now had her camera out

and was snapping photos.

He sat there naked, lost in his own story, and continued. "I don't know where I found it, I don't remember picking it up, but only minutes after Greg lied to me, I had this old table leg in my hand—it could have been what Greg used to hurt my dog. I swung it up into his head, catching him square above the ear. He went down like he'd been shot. Blood was spattered all over, and my mom was screaming her head off, 'Get out, get out.' So I did. And I've never been back."

Tanya put down her camera. "Did you kill him?"

He felt tears now streaming down his face. "I've never been back. I don't think so. No one's been around to arrest me, and my mom knows where I work, where I go to school."

She then put her hand on his thigh and gave him that pity look—he guessed the story was kind of pitiful. Her hand stayed where it was, and whatever sympathy he felt from her was overtaken by that familiar humming.

His peeder had a seventeen-year-old mind of its own and now rose in his lap. She grabbed it like before, like a doorknob, and then began to twist and turn to open the door. Cory closed his eyes and waited, transported. Then he could swear he heard the click of that camera. One-handed, he guessed. He kept his eyes closed until after he finished, his semen seeping into the sand and dissolving under the hot sun. He heard another click.

Cory opened his eyes, taking a minute to regain some composure. Then he asked, "What about your stepdad? How does that work?"

"He married my mom five years ago. He came here from Chicago. He doesn't talk about it, but I think he was a mafia guy. Might still be a mafia guy, but he doesn't talk about it. Just runs a jewelry store on Sahara called The Gold Rush. My mom died two years after they married. Breast cancer."

"I'm sorry. That must suck."

"It's been a few years now. I miss her, but you know, shit happens. Now I'm stuck with my stepdad."

"You get along with him?"

"I guess. It's not as bad as he let on that other day. He said later he was sorry, that he'd been all jacked up after some road rage thing. The fact is, he's a million times better than my real dad. Total drunk and a liar. I haven't seen him since I was ten."

"I saw your stepdad at this funeral. He introduced himself. Emmy, right?"

"Emilio Nuzzarello, but he goes by Emmy. Apparently, back in Chicago, he was called Nuts. He didn't do anything, right?"

"He was cool, and I guess he apologized in his own way. But then it got weird. I'd found this little velvet baggy while cleaning up on the dance floor a week ago. Inside were diamonds, milky-looking, uncut diamonds. They were stolen when my boss, Deedee, got shot. Your stepdad knew about the diamonds, and he knows that it was me who found them. I didn't steal those diamonds. Like I told him, I found them on the dance floor and turned them over to Deedee."

"I wouldn't worry about it. He's not as scary as he looks."

Then he remembered something, and he asked Tanya, "Did you take photos of my dick?"

She smiled and gave him a slow-motion, theatrical wink. "Maybe."

CHAPTER 13 – THE SWEDE
That Same Friday

Karol flew coach on a direct United flight to Las Vegas. The tickets were purchased last minute, were criminally expensive, and the only seat available was sandwiched between the window and aisle seats, both occupied by large men. The man on the aisle was dressed in some vacation outfit—shorts and a Hawaiian shirt—and seemingly ready for a poolside lounger. The other man wore a suit like his and, for the long five-hour flight, stared out the window and never left his seat to use the toilet, which was perfectly fine with Karol. It was the vacation guy who was annoying. First, he attempted to badger him with conversation—best Vegas restaurants, sports betting, and favorite table games. Karol had no thoughts on any of those subjects—he was not a gambler, and eating for him was more about appeasing appetites, like jerking off. He answered curtly, then pulled a magazine called *Hemispheres* from the seat back pocket and flipped through photos of people and places that had no relevance to his life. The man got the message and started in on a paperback novel. Then, holding his book, the vacation man's elbow not only took up the shared armrest but also poked over and touched him. Karol did not like being touched by anyone. He gently pushed back at the elbow with his forearm. The vacation man withdrew it but still controlled the shared armrest. Though Karol did not fly often, he figured the center seat person should get the shared armrests, considering both window and aisle seats had their own. Fifteen minutes later, the man's elbow was back into his territory, again nearly touching him. Karol desired to break one of the man's fingers, one quick yank in an unnatural direction. Short of that, *threaten* to break a finger. He knew, though, that if the man complained, Karol would get in some kind of trouble and still wouldn't be able to follow through with the finger breaking. Instead, he ordered hot coffee from the stewardess. A minute later, she was back, but Karol did not pull down his tray. Instead, he held the coffee in his left hand and waited for the eventual turbulence. When it hit, the coffee spilled, and the man let out a high-pitched shriek. Karol apologized a few times—no big deal—and the stewardess brought a towel to clean up the mess. After that, the vacation man gave up the armrest and created another two inches of buffer space by nearly blocking the aisle. Karol made a mental note to not be so cheap next time and fly first class.

He rented a Ford Taurus at the airport because it wasn't a car that screamed *Big Shot, Fat Cat,* or *Gangster.* In fact, the Taurus didn't scream anything other than *The Top Selling Car in America,* which meant they were as inconspicuous and ubiquitous in Vegas as lit-up slot machines.

He had a rented room at The Mirage but was not eager to get to the hotel. He wasn't a Vegas guy—he didn't gamble, get hookers, and did not especially like sitting by a pool. He wondered what it was, sitting by a pool. He thought he'd be bored to death lying in a lounger, and he had no interest in allowing his skin to turn dark. Furthermore, he didn't know how to swim.

Karol first drove to The Gold Rush to make his presence known.

He'd been to Vegas before, back when Aiuppa was skimming money at the Stardust, and his job then was to run the suitcase of cash back to Chicago. Aiuppa flew him first class, and he inhabited a whole suite at the Stardust that he rarely left. He liked to order room service and watch TV. Sometimes, he took in a show, sitting by himself in a comped booth that could accommodate four people. He enjoyed the shows, the glitz and glamour, and the showgirls, like walking, talking porcelain dolls. That was years ago. Aiuppa, Joey O, was now doing twenty-eight years for the skim.

He drove past all the casinos the Outfit had run: The Tropicana, the Desert Inn, the Stardust, and the Riviera. He'd seen Frank Marino at the Riviera, "An Evening at La Cage." The guy could do a pretty good Joan Rivers.

He took a right on Sahara and another right into the parking lot of The Gold Rush. He remembered Tony Spilotro used to run the place, a real asshole now dead and buried along with his asshole brother in a shallow grave under an Indiana cornfield.

Karol parked around back of the jewelry store. He walked into the place and peered through the cases of mostly chains and jewelry while Nuts finished up with some guy buying a pinky ring. That's something he remembered about Las Vegas—every guy wanted to be a bigshot, and they wore rings, gold chains, and bracelets. In Chicago, you'd get your ass kicked wearing bracelets.

Nuts said to him, "Sir, I'll be right with you."

When the guy with the pinky ring left, Nuts locked the front door, and they moved into the back office.

Karol asked, "Nuts, how you doin'?"

"Hey, no one knows me by Nuts around here. I go by Emmy now. No big deal, just sayin'."

Emmy. Everyone in Vegas had to be a big shot. "Okay, Emmy, how you doin'?"

"Good, Karol." Nuts, or Emmy, called him Karol. They'd known each other since they were kids, back when Nuts was Nuts and The Swede was just Karol.

"So, tell me about the diamonds again."

Emmy sat down in his desk chair while Karol stood. The desk was clean of any papers or bric-a-brac, like pen stands and paperweights. He liked that Nuts kept it tidy. "As I said on the phone, this street kid who goes by Skinny signed for the package while I was in the back getting money I owed him. Didn't know it was missing until you called, and then I checked the signature at the FedEx office. Then this Skinny must have dropped the pouch of diamonds at a nightclub called Tramps because a woman who runs the club, whose name is Deedee, called me to say that she wanted to sell the diamonds. She said they were uncut, so I figured they were the diamonds you sent me."

"So this Deedee has my diamonds?"

"No, Deedee was shot dead in a robbery. The diamonds are missing."

"So, this Skinny kid did the robbery to get back the diamonds he dropped?"

"Has to be, though he doesn't seem like someone who could open a safe. He's more of a street thief, snatch and dash stuff like we did when we were kids, and he's into dope."

"So, you know the whereabouts of this Skinny?"

"This detective friend of mine has been searching, but no luck. The last I knew, he was staying at this flop called the Oasis Motel."

"So, a cop is involved?"

"I do jobs for him. He was engaged to Deedee, so he has a personal interest."

"Okay, who's Deedee again?"

"The woman who ran Tramps nightclub, where the diamonds were stolen." Nuts looked exasperated, like someone had just asked him to explain the laws of physics.

Karol tried to think through the story and get it down like something he could tell himself, but the line-by-line wasn't working. He pulled out a leather-bound notebook with an attached pen from his inside coat pocket. Then he asked Nuts to go through the events again while he wrote them down, drawing little arrows for each turn in the storyline. Both times through, Nuts seemed to be consistent—and this was not a story he would even make up. They'd known each other for years, and not a lie between them. Maybe details were left out, but never a bald-faced lie.

When Nuts was through with the second go-round, Karol said, "Okay, we start with the Skinny kid. We go back to this Oasis Motel. Ask around."

◆ ◆ ◆

Emmy drove his Cadillac down Sahara with Swede in the passenger's seat. The man was the same except for his hair, which he'd dyed bleached blond. He had the same cold stare and stiff posture, like a guy strapped to an electric chair, waiting for the switch to be pulled. But he knew Swede better than that; the man had never been nervous or scared in his life. It was more like Swede's mind was deep in thought, thinking about the next move and the move after that. He did not say a word during the ride, and Emmy was not going to ask about his hair color or provide any chitchat—the man did not do chitchat. He pulled the Cadillac into the courtyard and parked where they could surveil every motel room door.

Emmy said, "You want me to go in and ask the clerk where the kid is staying?"

"No, let's not spook anyone. Just sit here and see what happens."

They waited in the idling car with the AC on and watched. A middle-aged man walked out of number eight, got into an old four-door Impala, and drove off. A few minutes later, a hooker wearing four-inch heels and a short skirt tugged over her ample ass walked out of the same room. They watched other residents come and go—hookers, users, losers. Each time, Karol marked the movement down in his notebook, including room numbers and descriptions. None resembled Skinny. They watched a cleaning lady go through a few rooms, changing bed sheets and mopping out bathrooms. He marked down which doors she knocked on and which ones she just entered with a passkey. Cars came and went, with a few guys knocking once on the window of number five and then doing quick business.

Swede asked, "Did you say this kid Skinny was a junky?"

"Track marks down his arms."

"Let's go visit number five. See what that guy knows."

Like others they'd watched, Emmy knocked once on the window while Karol stood at the door. The guy inside peeked out, and Emmy let himself be seen. Seconds later, the door opened a few inches with the swing bar latched. He said, "What do you fellas want?"

Karol said, "Just want to talk."

"So talk."

"Inside."

Swede wore a dark suit and tie, though it was ninety degrees outside. Emmy wore his blue suit with an open-collared shirt. He knew they looked like cops or maybe gangsters, but definitely not hopheads looking to get a fix.

The guy inside said, "Let me see some ID." Cops.

Karol was tall and built; not an ounce of fat or muscle wasted. With one quick blast of his shoulder, he busted through the door, the swing bar along with screws popping from the frame. The guy behind fell to the floor. Emmy and Swede walked in and shut what was left of the door behind them. Swede helped the guy up and then moved him toward the one chair in the room.

Emmy noticed the wallpaper, a collage of palms, tropical birds, snakes, and monkeys. He guessed it was supposed to be a fantasy room, the Garden of Eden, though that didn't make sense.

Swede asked, "Kid, you got a name?"

"Stewart. Stewart Kitchen." The kid touched his forehead and then looked at his hand to see if there was any blood. His head was fine.

"Stew Kitchen?" Emmy asked.

"Stewart, it's Stewart. That or just Kitchen." The kid was adamant. "So, what are you, like cops? Don't you know who I work for?"

Karol asked, "So, who do you work for?"

"Ricky Nicolo."

Karol looked at Emmy. He had no idea who the drug kingpins in Vegas were; he couldn't even tell you who the current mayor was. The name Nicolo did sound vaguely familiar, though, a name from another neighborhood back home. But he didn't think it was a name he was *supposed* to remember. He shrugged.

Karol stepped toward the kid, who sat slumped in the chair. He gently reached down, took his hand, and lifted it. The kid, Kitchen, let him. Then, in one quick motion, he took the kid's pinky and snapped it back until it touched his wrist. Emmy heard the subtle cracking noise of tiny bones breaking.

The kid let out a scream that Karol muffled with his hand. He said, "Relax. Now answer questions."

Karol's hand moved away, and the kid looked at his broken pinky. It was still bent and reminded Emmy of a fancy lady drinking tea, maybe something he'd seen in a late-night movie.

Kitchen looked at the misaligned pinky. In a shaky voice, he asked, "What?"

"You know this junky kid with the street name Skinny?"

"Yeah."

"Where's he staying?"

"He was in number twelve, but your guys have already been there and scared him off."

"Our guys?"

"Aren't you cops?"

"No. So he was there, then cops came, but they didn't find him?"

"Yes."

"Yes, they found him?"

The kid looked up, too scared to say anything flippant. "No—no, they didn't find him."

Swede pulled out his notebook and turned to the pages where he'd written down the room numbers. Number twelve was there, one of the rooms cleaned and opened with a passkey. Swede said, "He's gone."

The kid looked at his hand again and gently laid it on the chair's padded armrest. He whined, "Look what you've done to my finger."

Swede stepped over, now looking. In two quick movements, he pinned the hand down to the armrest and then pulled the pinky straight. The kid screamed again, just a short burst, a squeal.

Swede asked, "Does this Skinny have any friends or family he might go to?"

"His family's back in LA somewhere. He used to hang out a lot with this guy named Niven."

Swede wrote it down. "Is that a first name?"

"I don't know. It's just Niven."

"Where does this Niven live?"

"I don't know."

Swede made another motion toward the kid, who leaned back in his chair, squirming. "Really, I don't know. He drives a VW Jetta, silver with these custom rims."

"Does he buy from you?"

"Sometimes. Maybe once or twice a week. Always coke now. Never junk."

"You call us when he comes back. You find out where he lives."

"Yes. Sure. Where?"

Emmy lifted out his wallet and gave the kid a business card. He had a pen and wrote down his home number on the back. "Call me here at The Gold Rush first. Leave a message if I don't answer but then call me at this number on the back. Don't talk to anyone but me on that number."

The kid took the card with his good hand.

"Where do you think this Skinny is staying now?" Swede

asked.

"Could be with Niven, I don't know. Though probably on the streets. Or below the streets."

"Below the streets?"

"The flood channels, like sewers. It's where a lot of the bums and junkies live. Never been down there myself, but I've heard there are miles and miles of tunnels."

Just as they were leaving, Emmy got it. Not the Garden of Eden, the Jungle Room. He said it as a question to Kitchen, "The Jungle Room?"

Emmy could see the kid's pinky now swollen to the size of a *Robusto* cigar. It didn't seem to bother him when he responded, "Oo, Oo, Oo," and scratched under his armpits like a monkey. Rough business, selling drugs.

♦ ♦ ♦

Karol checked into the Mirage Hotel and Casino that night. It was the newest gambling joint on the Strip, with an active volcano out front that erupted every hour on the hour like Old Faithful. He didn't know anyone in Vegas outside Nuts; every Outfit guy he'd known was either in prison or dead. He stood in the roped registration line with all the other tourists, waiting for a room key.

His room was nothing special—two queens, a desk, and a minibar. He did not drink alcohol. The bathroom had a separate shower and tub, and before he ordered room service, he took a long bath to wash off the grime and dust the town seemed to give off. His dinner was a New York steak, mashed potatoes, and a mixture of vegetables sauteed in butter and garlic. After the porter left, he switched on the television. The TV was pre-programmed to the Mirage in-house station and advertised the act currently playing, Siegfried and Roy, flamboyant magicians with their white tigers. He'd seen them at The Frontier hotel years before and remembered they were top-notch. If the thing with the diamonds lasted more than a few days, he'd take in the show.

The next morning, Nuts called and said his detective friend had a couple of guys who would check for Skinny on the streets and in the flood channels. He also said that his friend had looked through the county computer system for anyone named Niven, first name or last. So far, nothing had come up. Nothing to do but wait.

Karol was a patient man, he thought. Up to a point.

Karol decided to take in the Liberace Museum. He received directions from the valet when his Ford Taurus was brought around: south on Las Vegas Boulevard, left on Tropicana, and then about a mile down on the right. When he finally arrived, Karol was surprised to see that the museum was in a cheap strip mall filled with stupid shops like a dry cleaner, dive bar, and nail salon. But there it stood, the sign lit in gold letters, LIBERACE MUSEUM. On that Monday, the parking lot was mostly empty.

A woman took his three-dollar and fifty-cent admission. She wore a long, flowing red dress with a collar that puffed up around her chin and cheeks, no doubt covering the loose chicken skin that hung from her neck. Her hair was in a fifties updo-style and dyed brown. Her nametag said, "Doris Liberace." Karol was dumbstruck to be in the presence of a relation.

His mother had been a big fan and collected any

clippings or memorabilia she could get her hands on, which, in the fifties, was a lot. It seemed Liberace's mug was on the cover of every magazine, and his whereabouts and the extravagant things he bought were chronicled in the daily newspapers. His mother had seen a young Liberace when he first debuted with the Chicago Symphony Orchestra at the old Pabst Theater in Milwaukee, back when she lived there in the forties. Karol had gone with her to see him twenty years later at the Chicago Stadium on Madison Street. He was only ten years old then and was mesmerized by the piano covered in little shards of mirror, the elaborate candelabra, and the outfits of sequins and fur that changed four times throughout the show.

Later that year, his mother paid a neighbor lady to give him piano lessons. He loved learning, but the lessons turned sour when the lady's husband got him alone in the bathroom. The molestations went on for a few months before Karol had had enough. His mother was upset when he quit, and to this day, Karol felt he should have figured out a way to stay with it. The teacher had said he showed promise. And he could have gone back right after the husband hung himself a year later, right there in that very same bathroom. But by then, Karol had moved on to other things.

What he remembered about Liberace was that he never married, and his one sibling was his close brother George. He said to the woman, "You must be George's wife."

"I am. Are you a fan?"

"My mother was."

"Well, enjoy the collection. If you have any questions, I'm right here."

As he walked in, the wall on his right was lined with mannequins dressed in many of the stage outfits worn: a bright red cape fringed in white fur, a long-tailed jewel-studded coat like something from the Renaissance, and a cape covered in sequins that might have been the one he'd seen when he was ten. Another cape on a blank-faced mannequin stood completely enveloped in black raven feathers like something out of a horror movie. Glass cases in front of the mannequins held his shoes, belts, and other accessories. Lighting the whole room were chandeliers dripping with crystals. Karol walked through an arched entrance into another showroom, this one showcasing a Steinway grand piano overlaid in the shards of mirror—for sure, the one he'd seen in Chicago.

Then, in another room, stood floor-to-ceiling glass cases filled with porcelain figurines. All were Hummels, but Karol could tell many were extremely collectible and valuable. Seven little boys called "Adventure Bound" could go for a couple grand, and "Apple Tree Boy and Apple Tree Girl" was worth over five. "Merry Wanderer" was worth two to three grand, and there were dozens more.

He walked back to the front counter. The museum was still empty of visitors, and Doris sat on a high stool reading a *People* magazine. She looked up when he approached. "What can I do for you?"

Karol stood silent for a moment, unsure what to say. Behind her, on the wall, was a photograph of Liberace and his brother George with Doris. The resemblance was astonishing. He asked, "Were they twins?"

Doris looked at the photo. "No, but fans could confuse them. Though an interesting fact, Liberace did have a twin, but he died at birth."

That was it for his pleasantries, and he segued into a more pressing interest. "I was looking at the Hummel figurines. What's the story there?"

"Those were his mother's. Frances died ten years ago.

She loved the little porcelain characters, and Liberace—she called him Walter—would bring one or two back whenever he toured in Europe.

"May I ask, are they for sale?"

Doris put the magazine down on the counter. "Excuse me?"

"Are any for sale? Would you ever sell the Hummels?"

She now had that look as though she'd just found a fly in her soup. Some prude. "Nothing in this museum is for sale. We've kept the whole collection intact from the moment Liberace himself donated everything for the sake of the fans who loved him. People come from all over the world to see the collection and pay homage. Those figurines were his mother's prized possession, all given to her by her beloved son."

Karol did not need the lecture. "So I'm guessing the answer is no?"

The woman took her time, and he could feel another lecture coming. He thought he might have to strangle Doris. To his relief, she simply said, "Definitely no."

Karol thanked her and went back into the museum. He toured everything again, going into the back garage where Liberace's collection of Rolls-Royces, Bentleys, and others was displayed, some bejeweled like his costumes and pianos. He walked slowly back to the entrance, this time with his notebook out. He sketched the museum's layout and noted any motion detectors or cameras. The only security he could find was on the front and back doors and the windows facing the street.

He did not like how Doris had spoken to him.

CHAPTER 14 – CORY
Saturday

Cory stood in the middle of his one-room apartment and practiced another bit in his routine. He was going with the stories of his Social Studies class and work at Tramps. He improvised one about the diamonds he found.

"So I have this job working at Tramps, a nightclub in Vegas. My title is porter, which most people think of as one of those guys at a hotel in a monkey suit who smiles a lot, totes your luggage, and then stands around waiting for a tip. At Tramps, it's cleaning up, which is really the lowest job they have. And a lot of the job is cleaning up bathrooms, which, seriously, is gross. Women are by far the worst. You can't imagine the things I've pulled out of toilets: of course, sanitary napkins—big-ass pads like a whole roll of Bounty, you know, The Quicker Picker Upper—but also socks, panties, and bras. One assumes quickie, dirty toilet-stall sex. But why wouldn't you take the time to put that shit back on? Now, if I can't unclog a toilet, I have to close it down. Then you can't just lock it. I've done that, and those women will go right under the door and unlatch it. Then they'll shit on top of the clog, shit on top of other people's shit until it's literally spilling over. Disgusting. Seriously. The guys are a piece of cake in comparison. They just like to piss all over the floor.

"I did see a guy do something really disgusting the other day. I was standing next to the bar, drinking a Coke, all chill, and watching the customers. One guy on a barstool was dressed really nice, like in a suit and tie, with his hair combed perfectly across his scalp. You know, like that guy Gordon Gekko in the movie *Wall Street*. He was alone and not really talking to anyone. Then I notice his hand rise slowly from beneath the bar top and move to his chin. He nonchalantly scratched his chin, then ever so casually moved in for the nose pick. He must have known a nugget resided there because it didn't take long for him to snag it out. But then here's the really disgusting part—he ate it. No shit, ate it like a bread crumb that might've landed on his silk tie. And you wonder if the guy keeps a jar of boogers in the fridge, you know, to season a salad or for a midnight snack.

"Another part of my job is to carry around one of those little brooms and dust pans with the long handle, like something an old lady would use to pick up dog poop in the yard. This is actually the best part of my job because of the things people drop and lose. Of course, it's mostly coins and dollar bills that embellish my wages. But I also find little vials of cocaine, which I can turn around and sell to the bartenders. A week ago, I found not only an open condom wrapper but the used condom itself. Is it possible to fornicate in tight and crowded spaces? On the dance floor? I've seen it done. Seriously. Then, just the other day, I found a little velvet pouch. It was right after the DJ had played that *Animal House* song, "Shout," where everyone is jumping up and then squirming on the floor. That song is a bonus for me, you know, with everything flying from pockets. So I take the pouch into the back and look inside. Diamonds. Seriously. A sack full of uncut diamonds. I'm rich, right?"

He stopped there, not knowing where the story would go. He'd had the diamonds and then given them to Deedee, who was now dead. The diamonds were likely in the safe when they were robbed. He didn't know for certain, but he also couldn't start asking around. Regardless, the end of his diamond story was anything but funny. The other stuff about the bathrooms and the guy picking his nose was solid gold.

Then he wondered about his new catch phrase, "Seriously." He wondered if he wasn't overplaying it.

◆ ◆ ◆

On Monday, he was back at school. It wasn't until Social Studies class in the afternoon that he saw Tanya. The preppy outfit was gone, and now she was wearing white tennis shoes, a pleated skirt that fell mid-thigh, and a T-shirt that said GO WARRIORS! He was certain Tanya was dressed up to be a cheerleader, and as far as he knew, she was not part of the squad. That, and the Chaparral High School mascot was a cowboy. She did not look over at him or acknowledge his presence in any way. That hurt.

She sat in front of him in class, and halfway through, he wadded up a piece of notebook paper in his mouth and then made a shooter out of his BIC pen. When the teacher wasn't looking, he shot the wad and hit Tanya in the back of the neck. She reached behind and wiped the spitball off. She did not turn around.

After the bell rang, Tanya beelined toward the door and

walked briskly down the hallway, her ubiquitous camera swinging back and forth from her neck.

Cory ran to catch up. He got beside her and said, "Tanya?"

She did not look at him or respond.

"Tanya, what's going on?"

She stopped, still ignoring him, and smiled at another guy walking toward her. His name was Biff or something, and he was captain of the varsity baseball team. He stopped and said, "Hey, Tanya, see you after school?"

Cory had also stopped and stood next to her while she and the jock conversed. She said, "Sure."

The jock kept going, and Tanya started walking again. Cory tried to keep up.

He asked, "What's going on? What are you doing?"

She kept walking. "I don't know what you're talking about."

Was he in Bizarro Land? Didn't they just have sex three days ago on the beach at Lake Mead? Did he imagine all of it? He wanted to explain to her what they'd done.

He started to say, "What about last Friday ..." Then he felt like a fool and stopped.

Tanya walked away.

She'd officially ghosted him.

He was hurt. But as Cory walked toward his last class of the day, trying to move past the exchange, he wondered how this could be turned into a funny story, a bit about the girl who ghosted him at school. He tried to put the bit together in his head—spitballs, costumes, jocks, sex, ghosted. Then what?

Then nothing. Beneath all the funny storytelling, he was still hurt. Devastated, in fact.

CHAPTER 15 – SKINNY
Sunday

That afternoon, he and Rat King did what was left of the twenty-five-dollar bag. Afterward, they sat side by side, spacing out, with Skinny drooling like the village idiot but contemplating his situation, nonetheless. Shit was stacked up—invisibleness (what did that mean?), cops out to get him, diamonds he didn't have, three more days of a clean room at the Oasis he couldn't use, and the flood channel tunnels underneath the streets of Vegas, crawling with an element of the city he'd avoided like rancid puke on the sidewalk. Skinny knew he was on the lower rung of the humanity ladder, but he guessed, like everyone else, there were a few rungs below. The thing about smack, though, was that all that shit felt meaningless and out-of-body, some other dude's problem. All he had to do was sit there and be invisible.

The man next to him, with his all-seeing wandering eye, said nothing for that restful hour. Nothing until the hour was up. He then stood, looking around as though for the first time he saw the surrounding concrete and graffiti. He said to

Skinny, "Let's go." From his backpack, Rat King took out a flashlight the size of a large dildo and switched it on.

Rat King spoke as he walked, his voice gravelly and southern, like one of those hillbillies in *Deliverance*. "This here is called the Underground. We got like a hundred people all up and down the tunnels that stretch from one side of the valley to the other. Most of us live right under the Strip. We keep it together, if you know what I mean. We share and share alike. No killin' or stealin' like the Bible says. We keep it clean; do your shitting business in a bucket, which gets dumped in the dumping place. We do not appreciate unwanted fleshy advances, if you know what I mean. You break the rules, you get broken."

It all seemed reasonable to Skinny—sounded safe, in fact.

The man paused for a second, then added, "That's the law down here, and I'm like the sheriff."

"The King?"

"Yes, boy. The Rat King. You can call me King. Name's Ignatius King, but no one ever called me Ignatius or Iggy but my folks. Always King."

Skinny told his story then, how the cops were looking for him because he'd stolen these diamonds, that he didn't have the diamonds, and thought maybe his friend Niven had ripped him off. He needed to stay out of sight for a while.

With his dildo flashlight, King led the way into the channels, now ten feet high and just as wide. The floor was slick with water, some constrained in puddles they could walk around, other times wall to wall, and Skinny stepped through, his sockless feet and slip-on Vans getting soaked. It smelled of dank mildew and urine—the shitting rule obviously not covering piss. King's flashlight lit up the walls from time to time, and Skinny could see hundreds or thousands of cockroaches scurrying to avoid the light. He was not unaccustomed to roaches and, in fact, sometimes thought of them as clean, like nature's little Hoover vacuums. The flashlight also revealed peeling graffiti. One tag spelled out UDRGRD, which he took to mean UNDERGROUND. He guessed he was part of some gang now. He'd never been in a gang before, and it seemed kind of cool, like he belonged.

About two city blocks in, Skinny started to see the bums who lived there. Some had lit candles, and he could see their accumulation of stuff—sleeping bags, blankets, clothes, little Sterno cook stoves, grocery carts, and straight-up garbage. A woman his age talked to herself. Her hair was tangled in dreads. She was missing front teeth and had sores on her face, which could either mean crystal meth, AIDS, or both. Skinny had never been much into meth, but AIDS and all those shared needles scared him.

At times, they passed beneath overhead tunnels leading to surface manhole covers that let in small bits of light from the luminous city. The light reflected off bent rebar ladder rungs that Skinny guessed allowed city workers to clear clogs, or whatever the fuck they did.

They were so far in that Skinny hadn't a clue where they were. Ahead, more lights flickered, and as they came closer, more people milled about, and more elaborate shelters lined the walls. One, the size of a minivan, was entirely sheathed in cut-up beer and soda cans. The shelters were lit with candles and lanterns, some the old kind with wicks, and some the newer kind that burned gas. Rat King acknowledged the bums as they passed with a nod, and some returned the nod, saying, "King."

Further on, they walked into a central tunnel hub,

channels going off in five different directions. The whole area was now lit by a spillway that slanted up to the surface, letting in sunlight through a grated entrance. He could see the tunnel roof, over twenty feet above, and the hub itself was the size of his high school gymnasium. Other, smaller shacks were scattered around, and from Skinny's brief experience in the school system, it looked like a third-world slum he'd seen in a *National Geographic* magazine.

Rat King's shack, the size of a single-car garage, leaned against one wall. Skinny guessed that for a place underground and in the sewers, it was made for a king. The walls were solid pieces of plywood stacked on a pad of wood pallets. The entrance had an actual hinged door with a padlock. Rat King pulled out a set of keys tethered by a three-foot chain to his leather belt and opened the lock. It was the only shelter he'd seen that had a lock, and Skinny wondered how compliant everyone was with no stealin'. Inside lay a single mattress on the floor, two mismatched kitchen chairs, and a trunk with another padlock. The shelter had no roof, and Skinny guessed none was needed for a structure built in a tunnel.

Rat King said, "You can stay here until you get situated. I got an extra blanket, but you might want to find some cardboard to lie on."

Skinny found cardboard stacked against one wall of the tunnel hub and collected what he could carry. He did not talk to the other inhabitants, and they didn't talk to him.

Once back in the shelter, Rat King laid out some more rules. "Tomorrow, you'll need to contribute. I know you don't want to be seen on the topside, but we'll get y'all a disguise so you can panhandle. Good place to start until you find a worthy trade."

"A trade?"

"We got musicians, kiddy characters like robots and fuzzy animals who'll pose for tourist photos, street corner squeegee boys, wheelchair cripples, and the like. Most start off panhandling with a cardboard sign and a plastic cup. You got to start somewheres."

"I've been purse snatching and stuff."

Rat King clicked on his flashlight and shined it in Skinny's face. "Remember, no stealin'. That means no stealin' from the Underground and no stealin' from people up top. We don't need the hassle. There's an understanding with Metro. We don't steal from tourists, and they don't fuck with the tunnels."

◆ ◆ ◆

In the morning, King took him to where clothes were piled on four pallets, keeping them dry above the water that pooled and seeped everywhere. He talked to someone Skinny couldn't see. "Marie, can you get this kid some begging clothes?"

Marie was beneath the edge of the pile and crawled out like a rodent from its hole. To Skinny, she looked like a witch. She made a squeaky sound—nothing that could be construed as English—and then began going through the pile. The clothes he was given stunk like piss and vomit and were way too large for his slight frame. Regardless, he pulled them on over his shorts and long-sleeved t-shirt. She handed him an olive green wool cap. When he was done, the woman looked him up and down, then said something that sounded like "globule." It could have been "Congrats," or short for "Good looking." He wasn't sure.

King instructed, "Sit on the sidewalk in front of the Flamingo," and then gave him a cardboard sign, NEED

BOOZE OR WEED, PLEASE HELP, along with a red beer cup and flashlight. He added, "Funny works better than pathetic." Rat King pointed him down a dark tunnel. "You'll see daylight in a few hundred yards. That's Paradise." As an afterthought, he added, "Paradise Road."

Skinny collected over forty dollars along with Styrofoam cartons filled with leftovers: beef filet, sweet and sour Chinese, half a pizza pie, noodles covered with cream and shrimp, and a complete slice of cheesecake. In the disguise, he was both invisible and conspicuous. Cops walked by without seeming to notice him. The tourists who dropped coins or bills into his cup laughed at the sign but did not look at *him*. But, of course, they saw him. Skinny figure that giving was a penance of sorts, the alleviation of guilt, and they needed to recognize his utter destitution to get the payoff. Skinny sat there most of the day, sweating in the heavy garments and then twitchy and irritable without his fix.

Back underground, Rat King was waiting for him and others. Two men stood at his door, and one handed over a wad of cash. Skinny had seen the guy before, on the streets. Skinny remembered that he wore perfectly good clothes that had been deliberately torn and fastened together with bits of string. His gimmick was to approach tourists and explain, "If you got a dime, I've got ninety cents, and a dime will get me a dollar." The rigmarole apparently worked.

Skinny waited around until they left and then approached Rat King. He held out what he had in the cup, forty dollars and maybe another ten in change. Rat King took the bills and left him with the coins.

Skinny said, "I need a fix."

King looked at him and then gave back twenty. "Down the south channel is Blinky. Twenty-five will get you a bag."

Skinny didn't understand how anyone knew the points of the compass down in the tunnels. He looked up, expecting more instructions. King just pointed, "There."

Later, they cooked up together.

After his initial high leveled off, Skinny wanted to talk. He asked Rat King how he found Vegas and the Underground.

"I was escaping—like everyone else, like you. Grew up in a small mining town in West Virginia and did a tour in Vietnam. Never went back. You ever seen the movie *First Blood*?"

"Stallone kicks ass on some hick town cop. You kick some ass?"

"No, I was just that guy wandering from town to town. Sometimes, I got into it with local cops, but nothing came of it, no Bowie knife or machine gun. I just moved on. Then, I wandered into Vegas. I walked around for a few days, sleeping in alleyways or out in some open desert lot and eating from trash cans. Then, I discovered the tunnels. I understood the folks down here, and they seemed to understand me. Like this is where I was meant to be.

"The people here were all broken—I was broken—but now I was there to help. Though help isn't the word. I was one of them, and I was there to belong. One guy asked me my name, and I said, 'King.' He looked at me like he'd just discovered the second coming of Jesus Christ. He said, 'The Rat King is here.' Don't know where all that rat business came from, but the fact was, we were underground like rats. After that, I was put in charge. They wanted some kind of order, maybe like a hive needs its queen."

Kings and queens and Jesus Christ. Skinny listened to the story as best he could, spacing out and catching every other word. What struck him, though, was the comment about the second coming. He'd never spent much time around religion but knew enough. He knew about Jesus and thought the guy must have been a relief to people on the bottom rungs. Why wouldn't there be a second coming? It seemed as obvious as other forms of life kicking around in the universe somewhere. If there could be a Martian space man, there could be a second Jesus. And why wouldn't he be called The Rat King?

King paused, then asked, "You want a measure of order in your life?"

Order to him had always meant parents or cops. He didn't think he wanted that kind of order, but he did want something in his life—a transformation.

He said, "I want something."

King nodded like that made sense. "I think we all, sooner or later, want something and some meaning. The underground, the *real* underground, is full of worms and grubs and chrysalises. Like worms, some of us will never make it to the surface. Like grubs, some of us will become beetles and be lured to dung and death. And like a chrysalis, some of us will turn into a butterfly and be free to spread beauty and cross-pollinate the world." King's hands performed a fluttering motion, wings taking flight.

Skinny looked up. "What's cross-pollinate?"

"Be like a preacher, bring people together, spread love."

"What about you? What do you think you'll be?"

"I know what I am. A worm. I'll never see the light of day. I'll stay here and take care of the Underground."

Skinny was barely paying attention to King's reply. He was thinking of himself. He did not want to be a worm and be underground forever. He didn't think he'd ever be attracted to dung or death, though he knew some people were and had no choice in the matter. Skinny wanted to be a butterfly. It sounded so cool. He said it. "I want to be a butterfly."

Rat King laid his hand on Skinny's head and gently scratched his scalp. "So be it."

◆◆◆

The Metro cops descended on the evening of the next day. Just two of them walking side by side with flashlights as big as lunch boxes. They wore uniforms, and the beams of light were so bright they illuminated their chrome badges. They spotlighted the faces of those sitting or lying against the tunnel walls, looking for someone. All this was relayed to Rat King before the Metro cops drew near. Skinny knew it was him they were looking for.

He saw their knee-high rubber boots, hospital masks, and thick rubber gloves like those worn by the cleaning ladies at the Oasis. They stopped in front of Rat King's shack, first shining their flashlights at his bearded face and then at Skinny. He wanted to run, but, sensing this, Rat King touched his shoulder.

One cop asked, "Are you Leopold Skinner, Skinny?" The cop's face was hidden behind the bright light and surgical mask. His loud voice penetrated the mask's thin fabric.

Skinny squinted. His mouth contorted into a grimace, and he raised one hand to shield his eyes.

It was King who responded. "Officers, y'all know better than to come foraging in the Underground. Who sent you?"

The other cop answered, "Detective Askoff." His voice seemed calm and confident. Instinctively, Skinny thought he was the one in charge.

"He knows better."

The calm voice. "He's pissed."

"It's a breach of trust."

The cop shined his light on King and then back on Skinny. "He doesn't give a fuck about the Underground. He wants the kid, Skinny."

"Gentlemen, look around. Y'all are deep beneath the Vegas Strip and close to a mile away from a taste of sunlight. Your radios are useless down here—you might as well be on the moon. And around you are more moonmen than you can handle."

The cops swiveled their flashlights through the tunnel. Beside them and in back crept thirty or more of the Underground people. Skinny had not heard them approach, silent and invisible. The invisible underground people, moonmen, undergrounders. Skinny was now one of them.

He heard the squeak of leather and the snap of a holster strap.

King said, "Your loved ones, if you have any, will never find your bodies. They will live the rest of their lives thinking about where you'd gone to. Or maybe they won't. It's a riddle."

The flashlight turned on King. He stood to his full height and spread his legs. He didn't blink or squint under the harsh lights, and Skinny could see that his lazy eyes were now focused on the two cops. He added, "Tell Askoff that you did not find this Skinny. Or tell him whatever you want. But if Askoff decides to break the understanding we have, he may or may not live to regret it.

The cop with the calm voice said, "Jack, let's go." The flashlights swung in the direction they'd come, and minutes later, their lights faded until they were just a candlelight glow in the distance.

King then told Skinny, "Why don't you get us another bag of the good stuff?"

He slipped a few bills into Skinny's still-shaking hand.

CHAPTER 16 – THE SWEDE
A Week Later, Saturday

Karol had money no one knew about. Some was wrapped up in the figurines, but most was spread around in banks across the country, big banks like Chase Manhattan, Citicorp, and Bank of America. He could have afforded a suite at The Mirage, but he didn't need more than a bed and television, and why throw his money away on things that didn't enhance his emotional well-being? But he thought seeing the Siegfried & Roy show would be an enhancement, and sitting as close as possible. He bought a block of four seats—an entire booth. He wouldn't repeat the plane incident where he fought for the armrest.

Siegfried and Roy exuded showmanship that rivaled Liberace. One had a German accent—Karol assumed Siegfried—while the other, Roy, sounded bland, like from California. Both talked to the audience as though friends at a fancy party, little stories about their past, where they grew up, and where they met. Then the magic itself—unbelievable, mind-blowing, larger than life. In one trick, they made a six-ton elephant disappear. Like Liberace, the two magicians changed in and out of matching costumes throughout the show. Alongside the white tigers, both wore white suits with tiger stripes. Then, it was dark suits covered in sequins, one with a shawl lapel and the other with a high collar like something Elvis would have worn.

Back in his room, the message light on the phone blinked red. He called in. The message was from Nuts. The Vegas police had found the Skinny kid down in the flood channels. They could not get to the kid without a full-fledged SWAT team invasion. The detective Nuts knew, Pete, now offered a five-thousand-dollar bounty on the kid. Karol didn't care about the reward—the diamonds were worth ten times that.

He called Nuts the next morning. "What do you mean, a SWAT team invasion?"

"From what Pete tells me, there are lots of bums down in the flood channels, and they're organized somehow."

"Really, organized bums?"

"That's what he said."

"Can you get us some scatter guns?"

"That's not something I want to do."

"Listen, Nuts, you owe me, and you fucked up this diamond deal. Get us some guns. I'll be at your place at noon. Find out how to get down there."

He knew Nuts was trying to make a clean break from The Life, become this Emmy character, but that was all bullshit. You didn't leave The Life; The Life left you.

Karol sat beside Nuts in the Cadillac as they drove down the frontage road that followed Interstate 15 and the railroad tracks. They stopped and parked on what looked like a dry creek bed. Not far away was an entrance to the flood channels, like a sewer runoff. He couldn't imagine the city ever getting an inch of rain, let alone flooding.

They walked in with their shotguns, both pump-action, both Winchesters with long stocks and barrels for killing birds. Karol would have liked something close-action in the tunnels, something sawed off with a pistol grip, but these would do. Nuts had also brought along battery-powered headlamps. Once inside the tunnel, Karol pulled his down around his forehead and switched it on. The first thing illuminated was a bum with a tattered cardboard sign that read, BEWARE. Karol walked past like he didn't exist. The next thing he lit up was the graffiti, UDRGRD.

Two blocks in, they passed more bums, most sitting in the dark but others with candles or lanterns. Wisps of light occasionally came through the overhead manhole covers. He led and Nuts followed. They passed a few makeshift shelters made from plastic sheeting, bits of wood, tar paper, scraps of beer cans, and filthy bed covers. It then occurred to Karol that he didn't know what the kid looked like.

He asked Nuts, "You sure you'll recognize this Skinny when you see him?"

"I haven't seen him."

"But you'll recognize the kid?"

"They all start to look alike. But yes."

They kept going. About two more blocks in, they reached a crossroads illuminated by an overhead sewer runoff. Tunnels went off in different directions, but the crossroads itself was like a small theater, like a bomb shelter beneath the city that could protect a few thousand souls from a nuclear explosion. Against one wall was a plywood shack lit up from inside by a lantern that shined brighter than the others. The light reflected off the ceiling and exposed the concrete with the imprint of the forms used to make it. Then the door opened, and a big man with a graying ginger beard walked out. A skinny kid followed.

From behind, Nuts said, "That's him."

Karol held the shotgun under his arm, the barrel now pointing up toward the big man. All around him, he could hear the shuffling of feet. He said, "Give us the kid."

The big man said, "We're all family here. The Underground family. A momma don't just give up her kin."

Strangely, the man's eyes acted independently. One appeared to focus on Emmy while the other stared Karol down. "Don't fuck with me. The kid, Skinny, hand him over." He pointed his shotgun at the boy beside the big man.

"Why?"

"None of your business. Just give us the kid and we'll be gone. One bum gone missing won't interfere with your little…" He recalled the word the big man used, "Family."

"I don't think so."

"Hand him over, or we'll take him." Karol pumped a round into the chamber of the shotgun. He did not hear Nuts do the same.

"Six rounds."

"What?"

"Six rounds is all you've got, then you'll need to reload. Takes time to reload. Some of us get cut down, but eventually, you'll be overcome by our implements—bats, knives, pliers, good old-fashioned clubs, and what have you."

"We want the diamonds he stole."

"Good, now we're getting somewhere." The big man

turned to Skinny. "Do you have the man's diamonds?"

The kid shifted his weight to one foot and looked Karol straight on. "No."

The big man raised his arms. "There you are. You have your answer. Now you can leave."

"Where are they?"

The man turned to Skinny and whispered something. The kid said something back. The man said, "It will cost you."

"How much?"

"One thousand."

Karol took his time. He did not want to be knifed or beaten to death by vagrants down in these creepy tunnels. He had more shells in his pocket, but *it did* take time to reload. In another pocket, he had over two thousand. He held the gun in the crook of his elbow and pulled out the folded bills. He peeled off ten hundreds and dropped them on the floor. "Okay."

The big man looked toward Skinny. "Please enlighten the gentlemen."

Skinny cleared his throat, like gunk that'd built up from nonuse. "I don't have them. I was at Tramps on the dance floor, and then they were gone."

From behind, Nuts spoke up. "The porter there found the diamonds and gave them to the manager. She had the diamonds in the safe, but someone robbed the safe. Killed her."

"It wasn't me."

"Then who?" Karol asked.

"I don't know."

"Who knew about the diamonds?"

Skinny paused then, unable or unwilling to answer. Karol could tell by the hesitancy that he was unwilling.

The big man said, "Skinny, my boy, if the person who knew is not underground, you are bound by my agreement with this gentleman. If he *is* underground, he'll be protected."

"Niven."

That name again, Niven. The drug dealer had given the same name. Karol asked the question he'd asked the dealer, "Is that his first or last name?"

"I don't know. Just Niven."

"Where does this Niven live?"

"The man touched the boy's shoulder. "Out with it."

"I don't know the address. An apartment just off Sahara on Tam Street. Naked City. Number 204."

Nuts spoke up, "I can find it."

The big man said, "Okay, your task is done. You can now officially fuck off."

Karol badly wanted to pull the trigger. One blast and the kid would be dead, five thousand for the bounty, four thousand minus the thousand he'd just dropped on the floor. His finger was on the trigger, and he sensed the pressure needed to make the gun jump. Six shells, a pump between each shot. But then the thought of those grubby hands on his clothes and body. Touching his hair. The image was repulsive. He lowered his barrel and stepped back.

Emmy, behind him, said, "Let's go."

Karol turned and left.

Minutes later, he looked behind. No one had followed. He kept walking. Then the graffiti, UNRGRD. They owned this place.

In the distance, he could see light. He kept walking, now toward the bum who'd held up the sign, BEWARE. He didn't have a sign now, but he looked at Karol with a funny smile, a smirk. Arrogant bastards for a bunch of homeless bums. He raised the barrel of his shotgun and swung it toward the man. The smirk was now a full-on gap-toothed smile.

Karol pulled the trigger.

The man's smile and face disappeared.

Nuts turned at the sound. His headlamp highlighted what was left—a pile of filthy clothes, a splatter of blood against the wall. Hair and pieces of brain. "What the fuck?"

Karol said nothing at first; what he'd done was all instinct, like chewing meat. He came up with a response, "Leaving a message."

"That you're insane?" And as he said it, Emmy realized it was true.

CHAPTER 17 – NIVEN
That Same Saturday

Saturday nights were a license to steal at TGI Fridays, and though Niven had plans to finally get into the safe, he wouldn't pass on an easy opportunity to make an extra fifty bucks. He worked through the dinner rush without pocketing a single dime; it was only later that he could run the scam.

In the meantime, he focused on the newest corporate contest simply called "Loaded." It was all about loading an item with cheese and bacon bits. The regular potato skins on the menu always came loaded with cheese and bacon, but a customer could order French fries loaded, a baked potato, or even soups like clam chowder and beer cheese. The winner would only get a silly logo'd pin with the word, WOW, but the big losers could lose shifts. So, he had to make an effort. At one point, he asked a lady who'd ordered a sirloin steak if she wanted the steak loaded, covered in cheese and bacon bits. She was totally delighted. He sold a few steaks that way, which impressed the asshole manager, Carl. Niven was on his way to winning that WOW pin.

After the dinner rush, the restaurant became more of a bar, a party atmosphere with mostly cocktails served. It was then that the servers were allowed to pay at the bar for the ordered cocktails and then charge the customers at the table. Called "cash and carry," it avoided the extra steps to ring up and close guest checks. The scam part was to upsell the customers on a premium alcohol like Tanqueray but at the bar, order and pay for a plain rail gin. The difference was anywhere from fifty cents to a dollar. By the end of the evening, with regular tips and the cash and carry extras, he had almost two hundred in his pocket.

Once last call was given and his shift ended, it was time to get into the safe.

Niven clocked out and then went into the employee bathroom to change out of his Friday's striped polo shirt. From there he snuck into the back dry-storage room and hid behind a stack of fryolator oil. He heard Carl count down the bartender tills and then finish whatever paperwork managers did before going home. He heard Carl lock the back door to the dumpsters, and then he could see from under the storage room door all the lights being switched off. Niven figured he had five hours to bust into the back office and crack the safe.

He'd seen Carl and others open the office door with the push-button code. Niven punched in Y0451C and turned the handle. It opened. Inside, he switched on the interior light.

He'd come prepared with graph paper already marked up to one hundred. He quickly learned that the Gardall safe had only three disks—three number combinations to figure out. It took him the next hour to graph the clusters of possible numbers and then another hour to pinpoint numbers on each cluster. He had it down to what he thought were six possibilities. An hour later, the heavy steel door swung open.

Inside was the bank deposit bag for that Saturday night, the second busiest of the week. Niven took the bag and then left.

He crashed the emergency exit bar on the back door, and immediately, the alarm rang out. Niven ran to his Jetta and drove away.

The sun was just coming up from behind Sunrise Mountain. He was tired but exhilarated. He'd cracked two safes in the last week and possessed more cash and stuff— diamonds—than he'd ever had. The cash from Tramps amounted to over fifteen thousand dollars. He wasn't sure what the uncut diamonds were worth—potentially tens of thousands—and he'd have to fence those in LA or elsewhere. The wedding ring he could sell locally, and it had to be worth five grand or more. He felt bad about the woman—it wasn't his thing to kill people—but he'd given her fair notice.

Niven drove west on back streets until he merged with the stream of cars going north on Las Vegas Boulevard. He was almost to Sahara, close to home, when he saw the Metro cruiser in his rearview mirror. Then, the light bar on top began flashing. Niven kept driving, hoping, and really praying that they were meant for someone else.

Then, over the loudspeaker, "You in the Jetta, pull over."

He pulled over. Everything he'd stolen was in the car. He never left valuables in the apartment—the supervisor and God knows who else had keys—so the haul from Tramps was in the locked trunk and the deposit envelope from Fridays right beside him. He stuffed the envelope beneath the seat. He was fucked if they searched the car.

Niven rolled down his window when the officer stepped up. "License and registration." Not even a "please."

"Yes sir." He pulled out his wallet to retrieve his Maryland driver's license, then found the Nevada registration in the glove box.

The cop took both. "I suppose you didn't see that traffic light back there. You went through the red."

Niven remembered. "I thought I entered while it was still yellow." He made his excuse, which he believed. But under all that, Niven was relieved—a ticket and then he'd be on his way.

"It was red."

"I'm sorry, officer."

"I'll be right back."

Niven saw the man return to his cruiser, then radio in the license and registration. Minutes passed, and then the officer stepped out onto the street.

Niven had not seen him write a citation. And for a moment, he thought he'd had the luckiest day of his life.

The officer walked back up to his window. "Get out of the vehicle and put your hands on the hood of the car." When Niven paused, he added in a loud, commanding voice, "Now!"

He did as the officer asked. The man then frisked him from head to toe, running his hands up the inside of his legs. Before he turned his pockets inside out, he asked, "Are you carrying any needles or blades?"

"No, sir." Then, "Officer, what have I done?"

The cop pulled Niven's arms down to his back and then handcuffed his wrists. "Your registration does not match the color of your vehicle. I'm guessing the VIN doesn't match either."

Niven stayed silent as the man checked the Jetta's VIN, which could be read through the bottom left of the windshield.

The officer said, "I guessed right."

Clever. He thought he'd been so clever when buying the Nevada registration from the chop shop guy. His was silver, while the other was metallic blue. All because his dad, back in Maryland, wouldn't sign over the original registration. It should have worked. Now he was fucked. They'd tow the car, find out who it really belonged to, then call his dad. He didn't know what his dad would do. In the meantime, the cops would assume the car was stolen.

The realization came as the officer led him to the squad car and guided his head into the back seat: *I'm going to jail.*

◆ ◆ ◆

The Metro cop did not search the Jetta before the cruiser drove away. Niven still had hope that he'd get his loot back. He was driven downtown to one of the government buildings that housed police and jail cells. He was fingerprinted and his mug shot taken. Then, he was led to the communal holding cell where he'd spend the next seventy-two hours.

The cell was the size of his apartment with a wall of windows that looked out to the hallway where guards and other people occasionally walked past and stared in like gawkers at the zoo. He guessed, in a way, they *were* exotic animals. Lining the room on three sides were benches facing the empty center and the one-floor drain. Against the back wall was a bathroom privacy divider, though it was anything but private. A wash basin and drinking fountain were attached to the front and behind stood a single stainless steel toilet. Most in the cell could see into the bathroom. If the guy had to take a piss, you could see his back or dick, and the stream, which made an echoey sound against the stainless steel. The place had a boredom to it with everyone waiting to either be bailed out, cut loose, or processed into the regular jail with, Nevin guessed, beds and bars.

He was there an hour before someone had to crap. Niven sat to one side and watched as the man unzipped his pants, pulled them down to his knees, and squatted. The man sat looking at the floor. He let out a pre-fart, and someone said, "Nice," and others laughed. Then the sound of the turd hitting the water, a plop. Another guy said, "Good one," and Niven, out of sheer boredom, waited to see how much single-ply toilet paper the guy would use. The man took a handful and wiped once. Niven thought it wasn't enough, that he'd have skids later on—that he probably wore underwear full of skids. The thought of having to defecate in front of a crowd loomed in the back of Niven's mind. He didn't have the urge right then, but he was used to a daily shit, and he figured he'd be there until Monday or Tuesday when he'd be hauled in front of a judge. It was now just Sunday morning.

One phone hung on the wall. A sign above said to limit calls to three minutes, but that was routinely ignored, and some guys went on and on about how they'd been framed or mistaken or just plain stupid to get caught. One guy in loose-fitting shorts appeared to be pulling his junk as he whispered into the receiver. Another guy sat near the phone and seemed to be in charge, nodding to whoever was next in line. That guy wore black jeans and a plain white T-shirt. He was white, but like some black dude, had his hair all cornrowed around his head, the ends nipped with little red rubber bands. His teeth were outlined in gold, and his body was muscled and tattooed with fading blue ink. The tattoos looked like infant scribbling, but the images were all grown up: guns, knives, drops of blood, a heart with a name crossed out.

Niven said, "Let me know when I can use the phone."

He was ignored.

He waited the rest of that morning, past when a cop had come in with bag lunches of bologna and cheese sandwiches, cartons of milk, and green bananas. The clock was coming up on 2:00, and he was never given the opportunity to make a call. In the meantime, others had made two or three calls—he guessed friends of the cornrow-hair guy. Niven didn't push it but needed to call in to work. If he were a no-show, he'd be fired.

Then, for several minutes, the phone was unused. He walked forward and stood for some kind of approval. Cornrow looked at him and then nodded. Niven dialed the memorized number at TGI Fridays. Carl picked up with the customary greeting, "It's always Friday at TGI Fridays. How can I help you?"

Niven explained the situation. He told the truth, that he'd been pulled over after work and that his registration had been falsified. He explained that his dad held the title and wouldn't sign it over. The explanation was long, tedious, and Cornrow gave him a look like, *Hurry it up before I beat your ass.* Niven told the truth because the restaurant had just been robbed, and the incarceration was his convenient alibi. That he'd been pulled over *after* the robbery was a convenient omission.

Carl just said, "You stupid motherfucker," then hung up the phone.

People came and went in the night. The newbies were mostly drunk and looking banged up. Tough guys, and some didn't like Cornrow's rules, but the last thing most wanted was another brawl. But not all.

One kid stepped up to Cornrow. His hair was so blond it was nearly white. He said, "Fuck man, I need to use the phone, like now."

Cornrow said, "Sit your ass down, Blondie."

The kid looked right at him. "Fuck you."

"No, fuck you."

The blond-haired kid, Blondie, stood unmoving. He wasn't big, but his muscly shoulders and arms filled out his short-sleeved shirt. He was clean-shaven, and his hair neatly combed and parted. Despite the cut over his left eye, he looked like a college boy. Blondie stood waiting for Cornrow to make the first move.

He did, jumping up quickly and landing a fist on Blondie's jaw. "Motherfucker, you back the fuck off."

Blondie stepped back, anger burning in his face, concentration like a mean dog. His shoulders stiffened, and he stepped forward.

Someone said, "Aw shit." The excitement in the room amplified, the boredom not broken since the last guy had taken a shit.

Blondie charged and took Cornrow to the floor. Cornrow landed punches to the kid's head, and to Niven, it looked like Blondie was biting at a nipple. He was, and his teeth came up with a small chunk of bloody flesh and bits of cotton T-shirt that he spat onto the floor. Cornrow screamed out but continued throwing punches at the kid's head.

Near the locked door was a red panic button to call the guards. No one stood to press it.

Blondie was tougher than he looked and probably all jacked up on booze and coke. He used his fists now, and both traded blows as they rolled around the blood-smeared concrete floor.

Then Niven saw two uniformed guards standing at the window and staring in. They did nothing immediately, and now the fight was slowing down, both exhausted and bloody. Finally, Blondie had Cornrow in a choke hold, the guy inert and not breathing. The two guards then moved, opening the door and stepping through. One said, "Quit it now." Both had black thirty-inch batons held out to their sides and ready to swing. The kid let go. Cornrow, still unconscious, started to breathe.

The other guard added, "See you two fighting again, it's solitary and constraints.

Niven thought he wouldn't mind the solitary.

After the guards left, Blondie walked over to the phone and made his call. His face was swollen, with the left eye, which had been cut when he arrived, now completely shut. His shirt was torn and bloody. Into the receiver, he said, "Dad, I'm in jail." A pause, then, "Drunk and disorderly." A pause, then, "Yeah, again." Another pause, "Okay."

Cornrow sat up and looked at his torn shirt and missing nipple. He did not request any medical help, and it continued to seep blood the rest of the evening. After the fight, he lost all interest in the phone, and some other guy who looked equally menacing took over the job.

A guard came in Monday morning with more bologna and cheese sandwiches, milk, and unripe bananas. Niven ate the sandwich, even the banana, and drank the milk. Afterward, he had to shit but just clenched his butt cheeks tight. The urge dissipated.

Late Monday morning, he was visited for all of five minutes by a court-appointed attorney dressed in an ill-fitting suit who talked fast and nonstop. The gist was that he'd be arraigned in court that afternoon. His father had been called and confirmed that the Jetta had not been stolen. Regardless, he'd been charged with displaying a fictitious plate—a Class 2 misdemeanor—that could result in a fine and up to four months in jail. He would ask the judge to release Niven on his own recognizance. He had no priors in the State of Nevada, so the attorney thought the judge would release him without bail.

The lawyer asked if Niven had any questions.

He had just one. "Will they let me get my stuff out of the car?"

The lawyer didn't ask what stuff he was referring to. He said, "The impound lot cannot withhold your personal property or make you pay for getting it out of the car."

And after seeing one fight nearly to the death and eating three baloney and cheese sandwiches, Niven was in front of the judge for maybe two minutes before being allowed to leave without bail. But it wasn't until early Tuesday morning that he was actually processed out of jail and back onto the street. By then, he'd eaten another three bologna and cheese sandwiches, bananas, and milk, and now Niven wondered if he was permanently stopped up.

But once on the street, the urge hit him, and he looked for the closest casino to take a long and well-deserved shit.

Ewing Bros. Towing was an easy mile-and-a-half walk north from downtown. The lot was a huge flat concrete expanse surrounded by razor-wire-topped chain-link fencing. Out front was an old two-story cinder block building with one window covered by bars and wire mesh. The Ewing Bros. people were bulldogs, and everyone in Las Vegas hated them as much as federal taxes. Niven guessed everyone everywhere hated the company that impounded their vehicles.

He had paperwork, but the names were complicated. The false registration was in his name, Walter Niven Kolchek Jr., but the real registration was in his father's name, and this confused the stout lady who looked it all over. "It says here that the owner is Walter Niven Kolchek, but your license says Walter Niven Kolchek Junior. So, you must be Junior?" She emphasized the word Junior, having some fun at his expense.

He ignored her mocking tone. "Yes, I'm Walter Junior."

"Well, I can't let you have the car without having your dad, Walter Senior, present." She looked up, sure of herself, smacking on some piece of bubble gum. He could smell it.

"I don't want the car. I just want what's in it."

"What's in it belongs to the vehicle's owner, and according to this paperwork, the vehicle belongs to Walter Niven Kolchek Senior."

"He's my father."

"I get that." She looked down at the license in her hand, adding, "Walter."

"I actually go by Niven." He wasn't sure why he said that, but now the confusion was full on.

"So, are you Walter or Niven? And what kind of name is Niven anyway?"

Niven stood back and looked toward the ceiling. The place was empty and surprisingly quiet. He had the almost two hundred dollars from waiting on tables three nights ago and pulled out the folded bills. He counted out five twenties and returned to the bulletproof plexiglass window. He slid the bills through the small opening. He said, "I just need what I left in the car. It's my medicine."

She slid the bills down under the counter. "Medicine for

what?"

The nerve of this lady. The questions. He thought quickly, "Asthma," and breathed in and out, making a straining noise in the back of his throat.

"Well, since it's medicinal and all…" She stopped there, then yelled out, "Cleveland!"

A man wearing coveralls came in from outside through another door. He was huge and greasy. He faced the woman behind the plexiglass.

It took her a few minutes to locate the keys, then she slid them through the opening to Cleveland. "Show this young man to his daddy's car and let him get his medicine. Nothing else."

The man nodded and then looked at Niven. "Let's go."

They took a golf cart and drove past hundreds of cars, rusted out pieces of junk—Cadillacs, Chevys, Mercedes, Datsuns, Ramblers—every kind imaginable. Niven recognized an old yellow Yugo with its tailpipe hanging against the pavement. They stopped in front of the Jetta.

Cleveland said, "Go get your medicine."

Niven had thought through this delicate situation. From his pocket, he pulled out the remaining bills—if it worked once, it would work again. "Can you give me some privacy?" He handed the money to Cleveland.

The man slowly counted the bills with his very fat and greasy fingers. It looked like around ninety dollars. Niven could see the dirt under the man's nails, which were long and needed trimming. He said, "Five minutes."

Both stepped from the golf cart, and Cleveland opened the door to the Jetta. He got back into the cart and drove off.

The deposit envelope was where he'd stashed it under the seat. The uncut diamonds, the diamond wedding ring, and the cash from the Tramps' deposit envelope were in the trunk under the spare tire in a plastic shopping bag from Albertsons. All the stuff was in the Albertsons bag by the time Cleveland came around with the golf cart.

Back at the Ewing Bros. office, he used the pay phone to call for a cab. The office was now busier, and the woman behind the plexiglass took no notice of him or his supposed medicine. Fifteen minutes later, he was driven south to his apartment.

He could buy any car he wanted with what he now had in the bag. Fuck the Jetta and fuck Walter Niven Sr.—it was *his* problem now.

From the cab, he took the stairs to his apartment. He had his key out but right away noticed the lock and jam had been broken. He pushed open the door and peeked inside. The one-room place was trashed—his bed turned over, the carpet ripped, his trophies smashed, food and dishes on the floor. Niven listened for anyone still in the apartment, then walked in. The refrigerator had been left open, and a pound of ground beef stunk up the place worse than the shit he'd taken after leaving jail. The bathroom was empty, and all his bathroom stuff was scattered across the floor. Somebody had been looking for his money and diamonds. It had to be Skinny who'd talked, and it had to be just the diamonds they were looking for. Not cops—they would have known exactly where to find him. It had to be that jewelry store owner on Sahara who was probably connected.

Niven couldn't stay at the apartment. But he had cash to go wherever he wanted and immediately thought about the newest hotel and casino in town, the Mirage. He'd get a cab there and then call Tina to party. Call Kitchen and score some coke.

CHAPTER 18 – CORY
Monday

Cory had bought a cassette player and recorder at the Dog Pawn on Main St., then some blank tapes at the White Cross Drugs on Charleston. The player came with a small microphone that, back in his apartment, he held up to his mouth. He pushed play and record simultaneously and then into the microphone said, "Test, test, test." He pressed stop, then rewind, then play. "Test, test, test," it said back. He pushed the two buttons again to record a bit he'd been thinking about.

"I started dating this girl at my high school. Actually, she started dating me. As you can see, I'm not really a hunky specimen of a man and not really a cool jock. I tried, though. I went out for the football team my junior year. That lasted all of one week when, after going out for a pass, I missed the ball with my hands but caught it with my teeth. See these two front ones here? They're seriously falsies. Then, in the winter, I tried out for the wrestling team. They had weight classes, so I figured I'd only be attacked by someone my own size. That first tryout match, a skinny kid just taller than me, but apparently trained and skilled, lifted me up like a sack of potatoes and slammed me face-first into the mat. That was the second time my front teeth were broken, and now my mom was getting pissed at the growing stack of dental bills. So, as you can see, I'm not really the cool man-candy around school. Anyway, this girl was sitting in front of me in Social Studies class. She turns suddenly and, with a hollowed-out BIC pen, shoots a spitball right between my false front teeth and down my throat. So, it's—you guessed it—love at first *bite*. Seriously.

"Now, she's kind of strange. She'd have to be, well, off her nut to go out with the likes of me. When we first met, she was all goth, you know, all dressed in black with zippers everywhere. She acted all dark and mysterious and talked about a band called Sex Gang Children before shifting into the subject of suicide. Kinda creepy, but we got along. I've tried to commit suicide by football and wrestling, so we have that in common. Then, a week later, she changes costumes and is now preppy. She acts all coquettish. (Looked it up, *Coquettish*, 'behaving in such a way to suggest playful sexual attraction.') Instead of suicide, she's into bad boys and now asks me all these questions about if I'd ever 'done it' before and if I have a cool motorcycle. Well, bingo! Turns out I have this dirtbike, and though it's not exactly a Harley-Davidson, it works just fine to satisfy this girl's bad boy fantasy. So, we skip school one Friday afternoon and drive down to Lake Mead, where I know of this private beach where we can show each other our privates. I come back with a string of hickeys on my neck like I'd just had it out with Dracula. Seriously.

"But then the next week, she changes costumes again.

This time, she's a cheerleader, all dressed in one of those pleated skirts and a V-neck shirt with the logo of some other school's mascot—I guess that's all she could find at the Goodwill. And guess what? Turns out cheerleaders like jocks, and she starts saddling up to all the football players and wrestlers. So I'm out. I'm a total jock failure, so I'm seriously out. She won't talk to me or acknowledge me in any way. Totally ghosted. I know, boo hoo hoo.

"But wait! The story's not over yet. There's always next week or the week after. I'm thinking hot-sexy nerd with glasses who wants to go to my place and study biology. Or hot-sexy hippy chick who wants to get back on my dirtbike, drive out to Lake Mead again, get high, and swap saliva. Or a hot-sexy, playful dropout who wants to hit me in the mouth again with a juicy spitball. So what I'm saying here is, there's still hope. No shit, I think there's still hope."

Cory hit stop on the recorder, then rewind, then play. He listened to the bit. He thought it was pretty good, with places to laugh throughout. But to be honest, it was a little too close to home. Tanya had ghosted him, and he was hoping she'd get around to changing costumes again. In his heart of hearts, he favored a hot-sexy nerd.

CHAPTER 19 – EMMY
That Same Monday

Emmy had been able to bust open the apartment door with a simple shoulder bump—the door was cheap and hollow, the jam made of pine and about as strong as a popsicle stick. He walked in first, Swede behind him with the shotgun partially covered by a light jacket—you'd have to be blind not to notice the blued steel barrel. Emmy had asked him to leave the thing behind, but Swede was not the listening type.

No one was inside.

They saw the safe first, sitting conspicuously on the floor in the middle of the room. It was an old Mosler, and the open door swung wide with nothing inside. Next to it lay a notepad of graph paper with squiggly lines. Back in the neighborhood lived a guy named Fingers who could crack safes, and both Emmy and Swede knew the tools. To Emmy, it was sure evidence that the guy had robbed the Tramps' safe.

He said to Swede, "This is our guy."

The place was neat and clean, but strange things were everywhere. On a table at the head of his bed was a collection of trophies ranging from ten inches to upwards of twenty. A few were for track, a few for baseball, and one was for playing hockey that said, MOST VALUABLE PLAYER. They still didn't know if Niven was the guy's first name or last, but none of the trophies had engraved names. Emmy figured they were all fake and some weird ploy to impress a girl—or guy. Swede pulled apart the bed, and under the bottom sheet, in the middle of the mattress, was a hole the width of a golf ball. It looked like a stash, and Swede told Emmy to check it out. He did, reaching down about six inches with four fingers to find the bottom. Nothing but encrusted ticking, and now he felt grossed out and dirty with the thought of what the hole could possibly be used for. He found the kitchen sink and washed vigorously. In the meantime, Swede flipped the bed and then started in on the bathroom.

Emmy stayed in the kitchen and now looked through the cabinets. He searched each cup and bowl and looked at the cans of Dinty Moore Beef Stew and Campbell's Chunky Soup to see if any had been opened. He checked the refrigerator. The guy had a sealed pound of hamburger, a package of buns, and ketchup. Emmy pulled everything out and started going through each item, pulling apart the hamburger, ripping up the buns, and spilling the ketchup. Diamonds were small and could be hidden anywhere. The freezer held a quart tub of chocolate ice cream, and he placed the container under hot water. Then, both worked together to rip up the carpet. By the time they'd finished and found nothing, Emmy was sweating like a pig. Swede was bone-dry, cool as a cucumber.

They stood in the middle of the apartment, surveying the mess and wondering where else the guy could have hidden diamonds. They'd ripped apart everything except the walls. Then they unscrewed the electric outlets using the points of kitchen knives. Nothing.

Swede said, "Go over everything again."

"What do you mean?"

"From the beginning. Who took the package from the shop?"

"Skinny. That kid in the tunnels."

"Then what?"

They'd already gone over this twice, but Emmy knew Swede wouldn't let up. "The kid lost the diamonds at the nightclub, Tramps. The lady manager I know there, Deedee, called me up to say she had them. Then the guy here, Niven, robbed the place."

"Yeah, but who found the diamonds at the nightclub and handed them over to the manager?"

"This kid found them, a porter who sweeps up."

"Who's this kid?"

"His name is Cory."

"You know him?"

"Kinda, not really. He goes to school with Tanya."

"Who's Tanya?"

Emmy looked at him, exasperated. "My stepdaughter."

"Oh." The Swede paused for a moment, thinking. "What if the diamonds were never in the safe? What if this kid, Cory, hung onto them? Finders keepers."

"I don't think so."

"But you don't know?"

"No, not for sure." He added, "I think we should focus on finding where this Niven is hiding."

Swede stepped out of the apartment. "I think we can walk and chew gum at the same time."

Emmy closed the apartment door as well as he could. They returned to the Cadillac and drove south on Las Vegas

Boulevard to the Mirage. Before Swede stepped from the car, he asked, "Do you know where this Cory lives?"

Emmy did not like where this was going. And it felt personal. "No."

◆ ◆ ◆

Five years earlier, Emmy had been asked by Joey Aiuppa to take over The Gold Rush in Vegas after his cousin Tony was murdered. He knew no one in town, all the old Outfit guys who'd operated the skim were gone, and he had no business running a jewelry store. Stuff lined the cases with prices, but he had no idea where any of it came from or how to get more. He slowly figured it out, and the jewelry wholesalers found him. Then he bought stuff off the street from losers like Skinny who robbed people on the Strip, but also from gamblers down on their luck, and those wanting to get married … or divorced. Vivian, his future wife, came in one day wanting to sell a wedding ring.

Emmy was a smart-ass and said, "Who's the lucky guy?"

She looked up at him, something like anger and sadness all there in the same face. It took her a few moments to speak. "What kind of guy just decides to walk out on a marriage and a kid?" She started to cry.

He'd already figured out Vegas was this transient town with a revolving door for very fucked up people who'd left a fucked-up life back home only to repeat their hardwired mistakes in Vegas. It certainly wasn't a good place if you'd left home with a drinking problem. Then there were the wannabe gamblers. Some made it in cards or horse handicapping, but most were chronics who would lose a dollar as soon as they earned one. Men and women both. He'd seen ladies at the supermarket playing the slots that lined the entrance and exit while their babies cried and melted ice cream dripped to the linoleum. The town attracted the obsessed, deranged, and flawed. She'd probably made the mistake of getting pregnant and then marrying the guy.

He said, "I'm sorry." Then, he told a story. "My friend's sister married this loser when she was nineteen and just out of high school. The guy ran a dice game out of his parents' garage; that's how he supported his wife and the child they were gonna have. She had the kid, but as you can guess, the so-called husband rarely came home, rarely gave her money, and was constantly screwing around. The final straw was when he gave her the clap. She left him, or more accurately, he just never came home. She got zip from the divorce and became one of those single mothers on welfare. But then, one day, she met someone else. Long story short, the new husband was a great guy, and the last time I seen them, they were happy as clams."

She'd stopped crying and now stared at him with the anger side taking over. "What's your point?"

"Second time's a charm. Now, maybe you know what you don't want, and maybe you know what you do?"

He could sense his little story did not go over well. It wasn't like she was in any emotionally stable place to absorb the likely naïve words. Emmy had no idea what she was going through and realized he was being a jerk.

She said, "How much you going to give me for the ring? That's all I need from you."

He shelled out for the ring, probably too much. But in the transaction, he also got her name and phone number. A week later, he called and asked her out. A year later, they were married, both on their second. He thought they were happy in their own way with her late-night hours at the casino, his seedy jewelry business, and his weird stepdaughter.

Two years later, she died. Nothing gruesome like a head-on, robbery gone bad, or airplane explosion. Vivian was at work dealing cards at the Sam's Town Hotel on Boulder Highway. She was working swing and almost to the end of her shift at midnight, a boring Tuesday with no one at her blackjack table. She was just standing there watching the clock. Then she just fell over, a cerebral aneurysm. A thin spot in a brain artery just gave out, and she died before ever knowing she was dying, without ever saying goodbye to Tanya or him.

He never adopted Tanya but became her legal guardian. She was fifteen then and fiercely independent. She'd never warmed up to him before the death, and afterward could barely look him in the eye. He didn't push it. He made sure dinner was on the table every night at 6, kept a clean house, and provided Tanya with a bedroom for privacy. He had one rule, that she sleep in it every night, which she did. Another year passed, and they came to a kind of truce.

He guessed, like any parent of a teenager, he hadn't a clue what went through her mind day to day. He liked her, though—all of her eccentricities included. She might even turn out to be someone who did the extraordinary, moved past the trauma of her upbringing and maybe found something creative like writing or journalism—anything but the jewelry business.

He encouraged it. The previous year, he bought her a whole camera and darkroom set from some compulsive gambler who needed a couple hundred bucks. The camera was the best, a 35mm Nikon F2, the enlarger a Beseler. Since then, she'd never been without that camera. Emmy had bought her film by the gross and built her a darkroom in the basement.

The day after rifling through the kid Niven's apartment, he went down into the darkroom to see what she'd been up to.

He turned on the lights. Inside was a clothesline where her six-by-nine black and white photos were hung to dry. He looked at one of Hoover Dam's concrete deco towers that drained water from Lake Mead into the base of the dam, where it turned the massive turbines that electrified Las Vegas. One photo of the spillway looked futuristic and scary, like a set for that *Alien* movie. Then, a photo of the kid, Cory, standing next to his minibike motorcycle. Then, the kid standing in the same place, now with his shirt off, trying to look cool. Then, the kid sitting naked on a rock with a considerable hard-on.

His first thought was that he should never have entered the darkroom.

His second thought was that he'd let Karol know where to find this kid.

◆ ◆ ◆

That night, Emmy made dinner for Tanya and himself, a pasta with sausage, tomatoes, peppers, heavy cream, and parmesan cheese. She was now wearing some cheerleader costume, and Emmy made the mistake of asking about it, "What, did you join the cheer squad?"

Tanya had that Nikon camera strapped around her neck and shoulder like a purse, the one used to snap photos of the nude boy whom she'd no doubt just fucked. He could only hope she was smart enough to have some sort of protection.

She replied, "Nope." No elaboration, nothing. Just, "Nope."

Emmy couldn't help himself. "What kind of photos you working on now?" He looked up from his pasta and stared at her innocently. He added, "Down in the basement."

Tanya met his stare, a look that said, *Don't fuck with me.*

"You know, photos of stuff."

"Stuff?"

"Yeah, just stuff."

He wanted to ask, "Stiff stuff, hard stuff?" but let it go. Maybe she'd take the hint and keep the porno out of the house.

And that was the extent of their dinner conversation before they heard the doorbell ring and a knock at the front door. Emmy excused himself.

He assumed it'd be someone selling something, like religion, like a Mormon or Jehovah's Witness, but when he opened the door, Swede stood there with a grin on his face.

Emmy asked, "What's up, Karol?"

"Hope I didn't interrupt anything."

The man had balls showing up at his house uninvited. "Just dinner."

"You finished? You want me to come back?"

He asked again, "What's up?"

"I want to show you something. I can drive."

"Now?"

"You want me to come back?"

He knew Karol wouldn't give it a rest. Emmy could go with him now or go with him later, but he'd have to go. And he was finished with his dinner and finished with his dialogue with Tanya, which had gone nowhere.

He said to Karol, "Just a second," then closed the door without asking him in. Emmy made it a point to always keep his business and private lives separate, and he did not want Swede anywhere near Tanya, who might just decide to ask questions—or take his photo.

He walked back into the kitchen. "I got to go."

Tanya didn't say a word. The pasta was mostly gone, and Tanya had already pushed her chair back, ready to escape to her bedroom or down into the darkroom.

Emmy left the house and slid into the passenger seat of the Ford Taurus rental.

Right away, Emmy said, "That kid, Cory, the one who found the diamonds at the Tramps nightclub, is a porter there and walks around all night, cleaning up the floor. He works Friday and Saturday nights."

"Okay."

Then, for some unknown reason, probably because he felt guilty about giving up the kid, he added, "But I don't think he has the diamonds. I think that other kid, Niven, stole them when he cracked the safe."

"Sure."

"So where we going?"

"This museum."

"What museum?"

"The Liberace Museum."

"The queer?"

"I don't think he was queer."

"I think so. He died of AIDS."

Karol was quiet then and drove slower than the speed of traffic down Maryland Parkway, turning off on Tropicana. They pulled into the strip mall of the museum. He said, "Let's check it out."

No use asking why—he would illuminate at the appropriate time.

Emmy followed Karol through the front entrance. A woman at the counter looked up from behind a magazine. She was older with an elaborate beehive hairdo that reminded Emmy of his mother. Her nametag said DORIS LIBERACE. Some relative, he guessed.

She said, "We close in twenty minutes."

Karol had already pulled out his wallet and placed seven dollars on the counter. "That's fine, we'll be quick."

Doris looked closely at Swede, remembering. "You're back?"

"Yes, wanted to show my friend one of the items in the collection."

She wore reading glasses to take the money and ring up tickets. She handed Karol a receipt. Then, with a phony smile etched into her makeup-encrusted face, she said, "Nothing in the collection is for sale."

Emmy hadn't a clue why she said that.

Karol ignored the woman and walked into the museum. Emmy followed. The museum opened up into a lot of glittery shit that might have been interesting if he was into that sort of thing, and he wondered why Swede had an interest. They continued past rows of sequined costumes, candelabras, and other props. They passed a piano completely covered in little squares of mirror. Swede stopped at a cabinet filled with the kind of porcelain figurines dads brought home after fighting the Nazis in Germany—Hummels. Emmy remembered Karol collected those things—collected them while other guys collected motorcycles, beer cans, or bar signs. He guessed they were valuable.

Karol said, "I'll need some boxes, newspaper for packing, and boxing tape."

Emmy whispered, "You want to rob this place?"

"It's a two-man job. I'll cut and jump the alarm wires in back. Later, you drop me off with the boxes, then pick me up afterward. We pack up and leave."

Emmy looked around. The place was empty. "Karol, I don't do robberies anymore."

Karol touched his lips, an old gesture Emmy

remembered from when they were kids. He never knew what it meant, but soon afterward, they were always in some kind of trouble.

"If a window of opportunity appears, don't pull down the shade," Karol said.

"It's an opportunity for me to go to prison, and I've got a family now."

"Yes, but you still owe me."

Nothing he could say. Swede was completely out of control, and Emmy did owe him for taking the fall for a robbery committed over twenty years ago. He knew he had to agree but wondered when it would end.

CHAPTER 20 – NIVEN
Tuesday

The bed at the Mirage was as big as a pontoon boat, and he desperately wanted sleep after spending Sunday and Monday nights mostly nervous and awake in the Las Vegas holding cell with ten and sometimes thirty predators. But, before going to sleep, he wanted to count the loot he'd retrieved from his car at the Ewing Bros. impound lot. He emptied the cash from both the Tramps and Fridays deposit bags onto the bed, placing the handwritten checks into a small trash can liner he'd later throw into a dumpster. The cash was already bundled, and he put all the full bundles together in one pile, counting the bills in each just to make sure. Then, he combined the partial bundles. In all, he had $24,760. On top of that, a sack of rough diamonds and a cut-diamond wedding ring that had to be a couple of carats at least. Niven smiled to himself. The most cash he'd ever held before was just after high school graduation, and those envelopes only added up to a little over two thousand. He'd used that money to make a new life in Vegas. It was just so overwhelming. Now, what he wanted was a drink or a beer to calm down so he could sleep, but when he went to open the minibar, it was locked. And without a credit card, which he didn't have, they wouldn't unlock it. Well, fuck.

He slept regardless. When he woke up three hours later, Niven remembered the vivid dream that must have rippled through his unconscious mind right before his eyes opened. His father was there, and it was as though he'd never discovered the Percocet Niven stole from his dying grandmother. He and his father were hiking through the hills near a summer vacation cabin in the Poconos. Both carried those collapsible shovels that GIs or Boy Scouts use to dig foxholes or pit toilets or whatever. First, they were climbing high up on a hilltop, all light and airy. But then they were transported underground and it was dark and they were shoveling dirt. His father said, "In the hole, you'll find treasure." They kept digging until Niven finally hit something hard. They scraped around the box that had an old lock like on a pirate's chest, and Niven was able to open it with a skeleton key he now had in his pocket. Inside was a woman. Then his dad was gone, and now he was back outside in the daylight, and the woman led him by the hand through a grove of trees that opened up to a wide grassy meadow. Then she was naked with full breasts and wax-candy lips, and she was kissing his body. And Niven wanted the sex so bad and wanted her wax-candy lips on his cock. Then his cock was in her mouth. That's when he woke up, hard as a stick of firewood and right on the edge of a wet dream.

The clock on the nightstand read 10:05pm. Niven rolled over onto his back and thought about what the dream meant. His father had not kicked him out of the house, and they found the treasure together. Niven thought that part was linked to the money now stashed deep under the mattress. He thought it was a sign of good fortune and possibly redemption once he finally returned home. Then the woman part was easy to figure out—Niven was alone and horny as hell. For a second, he thought of finishing the job, his cock still mostly stiff. But then he remembered Tina back at Fridays. Tina would have that Tuesday night off and probably little to do other than watch *Designing Women* or *Full House*. He'd give her a call, get some coke, go gambling, and get laid.

She answered on the second ring, then said she'd be over in an hour. He told her to meet him at the bar closest to the front doors.

Niven then realized that in the equation of coke, gambling, and sex, he'd omitted the obvious fact that he did not have a change of clothes. Obvious because he could smell his own stench, ripe like roadkill. But he had money, and money could solve many, many problems.

After taking a shower and reluctantly pulling on his old clothes, Niven grabbed a wad of hundred-dollar bills from under the mattress. He walked the long hallway from his room to the bank of elevators, then stood waiting. A floor-to-ceiling mirror was at the far end, and he looked at himself in his black waiter pants, Puma running shoes, and the white T-shirt he'd worn under the red and white striped polo shirt that passed for a uniform at Fridays. He'd heard that hotels hung mirrors in elevator lobbies because some study proved that if a person could look at themselves while waiting, then the perception of time would be shortened—they wouldn't complain about the late elevator. And the funny thing was, just as Niven was looking in the mirror and wondering if he needed a fresh haircut, the elevator dinged, and the doors slid open. His perception was that he hadn't waited more than a minute. But had it, in fact, been two?

Niven found a men's clothing store in the shopping mall of the casino. He knew the store, The Chess King, that specialized in fashionable stuff for younger men. Inside, he picked out chestnut-brown, baggy linen pants by a designer called WilliWear, a white linen shirt to match, a silky T-shirt that'd look good beneath, and soft tan loafers with leather braided like a pie crust, which fashionable dudes seemed to wear without socks. He put on the whole ensemble, then stepped in front of yet one more mirror, appraising the result. He looked like Crockett from *Miami Vice*. All he needed were the Ray-Ban Wayfarer sunglasses to complete the look, and those he could buy right across the hall at a Sunglass Hut. He flipped out five hundred-dollar bills and, after receiving some change back, told the clerk to discard the old clothes he'd left in the dressing room. Then he bought the sunglasses.

The gram of coke was easy enough. Niven tipped the concierge a twenty, and while he was casually sipping a Stoli Cranberry at the bar nearest the entrance, a guy wearing a European motorcycle jacket and clear-framed glasses with slightly tinted pink lenses came over and palmed him the blow in exchange for a hundred. Then, only minutes later, Tina was standing at the bar entrance, looking around. Niven took off the sunglasses, so she'd recognize him.

He ordered more drinks.

Tina was cute and petite, like barely five feet tall, with disproportionately large tits. Her nose was slightly upturned and piggish, but he liked the way she wore her hair shorter and feathered like Joey Heatherton in that *Happy Hooker* movie. And she was fun, always up for something, always laughing at something. Right away, he told her that he had a gram of coke and a room upstairs, and right away, she said, "Let's go." He paid the bar bill, and they took their drinks and headed toward the elevators.

In the room, Niven splashed out a small pile on top of the desk and then pushed the coke into lines with the edge of the plastic keycard. He rolled up a hundred-dollar bill and passed it to Tina. She bent over, snorted a line, and then giggled. They passed the rolled bill back and forth until they'd both done two lines. He turned then and kissed her hard on the mouth. They rolled onto the bed, still necking like teenagers.

He asked, "Want to watch some TV?"

"TV? Like *Full House*? It's over already."

"No, like …" He had to think, and he thought of Joey Heatherton. "*The Happy Hooker*?"

That giggle again. She took her time, looking up with her head bent low, the whites of her eyes like cueballs. She answered slowly, "Sure," spreading out the 'r' in sure, like a kitten, "purr."

Niven pointed the remote at the TV and scrolled through channels until he found *Adult Entertainment*. He couldn't find *The Happy Hooker* but found a title that seemed to scream hardcore porn, *Taboo*, with the subtitle, "A Story of Family Incest!" Already, his dick was hard.

Tina giggled, "You're bad."

Niven clicked on the title. Then the TV began to think. But instead of copyrights and credits, a message came up: PLEASE SEE THE FRONT DESK. There it was again, *No credit card, No drinkie, and No movie*. He wanted to throw the remote at the fucking TV. The world was moving quickly toward those with credit and those without. Soon, cash would be incidental, used only to distinguish the Have Nots from the Haves. Fuck 'em. He had over twenty grand under the bed and more coming. He'd buy his way into the Haves.

Tina looked at the message on the otherwise blank screen. She did not giggle. But she was still on top of his bed, and ultimately, Tina did not need the lubricants of the hardcore cinema.

They had sex. Niven peeled her blouse up over her head and then unlatched the bra from between both tits that then popped out like cans of soda from a machine. She went to work on his beltless WilliWear pants. Kissing moved to oral, which he really liked, and something about the coke made it so he could hold off for an eternity. Then she led him into the bathroom. This was something he'd done with her once before and guessed it was her thing—fucking her from behind, fondling her tits, both focused on their bodies reflected in the mirror. Mirrors again, and like the elevator, time collapsed, and he spilled his load quickly, though it might have seemed like a full-length porn movie for her—he didn't know or dare to ask.

Once done, he said, "I have some cash. Let's go down and play the tables."

Tina giggled, "Sure."

◆ ◆ ◆

His game of choice was roulette. He'd taken a bundle of twenties while Tina was still in the bathroom, and now the two of them sat at the roulette table. Tina played random numbers right up past the ball drop, up until the dealer said, "No more bets." Niven played the basket, spreading his bets out between 1, 2, 3, 0, and 00. His theory was that you couldn't chase luck by betting randomly; you had to let luck find you.

Funny thing, both started winning.

First, Tina hit on a 23, which she said was her age. Both were playing red five-dollar chips called nickels, so the hit was worth thirty-five times that, or one hundred seventy-five bucks. Her little winning scream was like the yip of a bitten dog, which then turned into a steady giggle. People nearby were delighted. Then Niven hit on a 3. He was playing two nickels a number, and the payout was over three hundred fifty. He screamed, "Yes!" and pumped his fist. In the next spin, he doubled the bet—once luck found you, it was time to double down. It went on like that, Tina hitting every four or five spins, Niven doing the same, but now with twenty on each number, then fifty. A pit boss in a dark suit with black hair combed back from his forehead, an Asian-looking dude, changed dealers, but that did not cool their winning. Within an hour, both sat in front of high stacks of roulette chips.

Luck was like a circus act, and their table attracted other players who copied their bets. The pit boss was sweating from his receding hairline, daubing it from time to time with squares of beverage napkins that he crumpled and tossed in a waste basket. Finally, he stepped up to the table. "The Sigfried and Roy show starts in fifteen minutes. Would you like comped front-row seats?"

Tina looked at Niven. She giggled. "I've never seen Sigfried and Roy."

Niven looked up to the pit boss. "Can we get tickets for another night?"

A dumb question. "I'm afraid not."

Tina now had that pleading face, the same face that'd wanted a few more lines of coke an hour earlier. Just that thought made him realize *he* wanted more coke and that the show could be fun. And also, that luck was unfaithful and could leave him a jilted lover at any moment.

He said, "Okay, let's go."

After cashing in, Niven had a pile of hundred-dollar bills

an inch thick that fit easily into his baggy linen pants. Tina had half that, and even though he'd given her the money to play, she did not offer him a cut.

He gave the theater concierge a hundred after being seated. He gave the cocktail waitress another hundred after she delivered a comped bottle of French champagne. Then the show started, Sigfried and Roy appearing on stage, each in a test tube-looking thing filled with smoke. The test tubes lifted, and each stepped forward—huge wavy hair, billows of shiny fabric on their shoulders, matching capes, and space-age costumes. They marched to the front of the stage and stood so close that Niven could have spit and hit their black patent leather boots.

He looked to the booth on his left and saw another couple, older, the man with a Rolex watch and the woman with pearls and diamonds—real big-shots. On his right sat a man alone in a booth watching the show almost too intently. He was tall with bleached blond hair parted neatly and combed over his balding head. He wore a black suit with a white shirt and black tie. His thick square glasses looked, well, *square*. Niven figured him for one of Siegfried and Roy's ravenous gay fans, probably wealthy enough to get a photo and autograph after the show. All Niven wanted to do afterward was snort another line, have more sex, and get back to the tables.

Magic. He always thought it was hokey, like a guy at a kid's birthday party who pulled scarves from his mouth, rabbits from a hat, an assistant sawed in half, and coin tricks. With Sigfried and Roy, it was so much bigger, grander, and more exciting—white tigers instead of bunnies, a huge ripsaw instead of a carpenter's toy. Tina touched his hand when an elephant—a *gigantic* elephant—disappeared from the stage. They were comped a second bottle of champagne with another hundred to the cocktail waitress. Niven looked over once at the bleached blond dude, and it looked as though his whole body was quivering.

In the end, when Sigfried and Roy came back on stage in probably their tenth costume change, the whole audience stood with an ovation, Niven and Tina among them. It was just so spectacular. And who could have imagined—two safes, cash beyond his wildest dreams, winning at the roulette table, getting laid at the Mirage, comped show tickets, and champagne. He thought of his mom and dad then, back in Baltimore in their suburban home, and probably just this past weekend playing stupid golf at the country club and drinking bootleggers with their fat friends. They thought their son was such a loser and had said so when Niven was kicked out of the house.

After more sex, after more coke, he and Tina were back at the same roulette table, the same pit boss looking over at them and now seemingly pleased. He motioned with his hand, and a minute later, a cocktail waitress was standing at the table. Both ordered Coronas with limes. Niven pulled out the wad of hundreds and passed twenty of the bills to the dealer. The man took the bills and fanned them out against the green felt. He called, "Changing two thousand."

The pit boss confirmed, "Changing two thousand."

The dealer looked at Niven then and asked, "Twenty-five-dollar chips?"

It was then that he really looked at the dealer. The man was older, like fifties, with stiff, graying hair that stood up in some military style. His lips looked thick and moist, and Niven expected to see spittle run down the edges after the wet tongue came out like a snail from its shell. But it was really the glasses that got him, horn-rimmed tortoiseshell with the rims resting against his plump cheeks. His father wore the exact same glasses. "Sure, quarters."

The dealer took eighty green chips from the stacks in front of him and slid them across the table. Niven bet the basket, one chip for each of the five numbers.

He asked Tina, "Aren't you playing?"

She sat in the seat next to him with her little purse tightly clutched on her lap. "I'm good. I'll just watch."

The dealer spun the ivory marble—the pill—in the opposite direction the wheel turned. The sound it made was unique and unmistakable, like the squeal of tires or glass breaking. Then, the bounce as the pill hit the rails and grooves of the wheel and finally settled on a number. The dealer, with his fatherly glasses and thick fingers, put the glass marker on top of his quarter chip and announced, "Number one, winner." Then, the payout of eight hundred seventy-five dollars. Tina gave her one-note yip, giggled, and touched his thigh under the table. Niven coolly stacked the chips next to the others, then played again, doubling his bet.

Then his luck changed.

He began to lose.

It took only another hour before his chips were gone, and he was back in his pocket for the remainder of the hundreds.

Then Tina was tired. "I got to work lunch tomorrow."

He tried, "Stay, I got the room."

She stood and kissed his cheek, the giggle gone. "It's nearly two in the morning. I didn't bring anything to stay the night." She added, "Hey, I had fun," then brushed her hand over his head, kissing him now with dry lips on his unexpecting mouth.

Her kiss interrupted his next line. "Fine, goodnight." He

knew it sounded petulant, like a little boy. To soften it, he said, "I don't work until Thursday night. Maybe I'll see you then." He pushed more chips onto the table.

In a way, losing was more addictive than winning. If you win, it's someone else's money, and it's something you didn't have before, a gift that had less value because another person paid the price. When you lost, it was your own, and the masochistic pain inflicted pressed you on to keep playing and get it all back. The harder you tried, the more you died. In pinball, if you nudge the edges of the flashing cabinet too hard, the machine tilts and shuts down with a sound like a record turntable gone bad. In a word, Niven tilted.

The pit boss never changed dealers, and the man with his father's mock tortoiseshell eyeglasses continued to spin the pill and drop his marker on numbers other than his. He played alone well into the morning, losing what he had in his pocket, then going back up to the room three times to lose what was left under the mattress. Each time he came down to see the same dealer with his big paws clasped in front of him like some mourner at a funeral, Niven's funeral. And he wanted so badly to beat the man who reminded him of his father.

Finally, in his frustration, in his dad-hate, Niven stomped from the roulette table.

He yelled, "Sure, take everything!" He walked in the direction of the elevators. Still in the casino, he ripped his new white linen shirt from his chest, buttons popping, yelling, "Here, take more, take my shirt." He kept walking, now pulling off his silky undershirt. "Take this too." He flipped off each sockless shoe. "Take my shoes." He unbuttoned his WilliWear pants and stood for a moment, pushing them down to his ankles and stepping from the limp fabric. "Take my pants."

Just as he was about to discard his boxer shorts and walk

naked through the casino, a security guard approached. The husky man with his uniform, pepper spray, and handcuffs blocked his way. Niven thought, *Great, end up in some holding cell again.* But what the guard said was more sympathetic. "Sorry, mister, you can't go streaking through the casino."

That was all, and Niven proceeded to walk quietly and somewhat still clothed past the guard and into the elevator lobby.

He pressed the up button and stood, now self-conscious; people were looking at him. He looked away and toward the lobby mirror. The reflection of a pathetic young man in his dirty white boxer shorts stared back at him. Seconds or minutes later, he stepped into the elevator. On his floor, he walked down the excruciatingly long hallway to his room.

Only then did he realize he needed the keycard in the front pocket of his linen pants.

He turned around and walked back toward the elevators. He moved slowly now, defeated, his actions coming back to him like a bad dream.

The ding and the doors finally slid open.

Thankfully, the guard was standing in the elevator, clothes in hand.

Then, back in his room, still in his underwear, he had one last thought before going to bed, before waking up to the stupidity of the long night. He still had the uncut diamonds and the wedding ring.

The ring he could sell.

CHAPTER 21 – TANYA
The Next Friday

Towards the end of her first year in high school, Tanya had been told by two teachers that she showed a lack of impulse control. In one instance, she raised her middle finger during a soccer team photo. It wasn't like she was the class clown; she wasn't a big jokester or prankster and, in fact, didn't know why she'd even done it. Only later did she look back and try to discover any rationale. It wouldn't have made her popular, and she didn't think it was a cry for help. Tanya thought it had more to do with a kind of denial, a rejection of what she was supposed to do and be. And maybe it worked because she *was* kicked off the team. In the other instance, she lifted her thigh-length tunic up over her head in the middle of Algebra class to reveal a white bra covering her growing breasts. She then pulled it back on, backwards. For that, she was sent to the principal, who became the second teacher to lecture her about impulse control. The principal knew that her mother had recently died, and he thought Tanya's behavior might be connected somehow. He suggested she see a therapist. But then he proceeded to explain what controlling impulses exactly meant, which was to regulate one's actions in response to urges or temptations. Tanya knew all that, but what she'd done with her tunic was not impulsive. Just the opposite—a very thought-through, premeditated act. She felt she needed to make a statement, one that rejected any expectations her teacher or other students had for her behavior. But rejection implied some alternative—what *she* expected of herself. Tanya had no clue what she expected or wanted, and *that* might have been connected to the loss of her mom.

It wasn't until the following year that she came up with *The Art of Being Impulsive*. There were the usual cliques at school—jocks, stoners, nerds, mean girls, cheerleaders, band geeks, and theater kids. She guessed it was natural; all part of growing up, and maybe healthy on some level. She was attractive, or so people said, and that one physical trait made her popular. She felt pulled into various clique orbits, invited to parties or asked to try out for cheer or a theater production, or, in one instance, because she'd been called upon in geometry class to diagram some problem on the chalkboard, asked to join a math group. It seemed so absurd to her to be a part of one group because a cheerleader could rarely be a band geek or a math nerd. What she wanted was not to be labeled as part of a clique, but also not labeled as a loner. She wanted to be everything and nothing all at the same time, which brought her to *The Art of Being Impulsive*.

She could decide anything, do anything, or be anyone on a whim. Of course, she knew the underlying hypocrisy. Her impulsivity needed to be driven—she had to consciously and purposefully drive herself to be impulsive. But then she thought about hypocrisy in general. People say they're this or that, believe in what they think is right but break their personal commitments all the time—a teacher who won't assign an essay because they'll have to read and grade it; masculine jocks who blow each other in the locker room; Jesus-loving kids who live by hating others. Being truly human was to be hypocritical; life was just too complicated to live by creed or ideal. So, Tanya thought hypocrisy was essential to being impulsive, especially if you *understand* the hypocrisy.

Then, there was a deeper meaning to *The Art of Being Impulsive*. She believed the world had currents of movement and behavior that drew people in and away from each other like driftwood or blowing desert sand. To be totally impulsive meant not only resisting the conformity of groups but also following the currents that would introduce her to new people and experiences. She'd gotten into a car with a stranger once who'd asked if she wanted a ride home. Of course, he was a freak, and what he really wanted was to talk about penises—size and the ones she'd seen. She'd seen a few, mostly in photos, and described them. The man then scientifically explained size differences based on race and distance from the equator. They drove around for an hour talking, and the description of penises did interest her, though not as much as it did the man. After that hour, he matter-of-factly dropped her off. Another time, she dressed up in some slutty outfit and walked the Strip. A tourist solicited her, and she followed him back to his room at the Desert Inn. She'd never had actual sex and subsequently lost her virginity to this man. She walked away with a hundred bucks. Then that Friday with Cory. She'd asked him to skip class and drive to Lake Mead on the back of his dirtbike. Why not? Tanya followed the life currents, and what the currents suggested then involved getting naked in the lake and having sex for the second time. Turned out she really liked sex.

Her photography became a part of *The Art of Being Impulsive*. Emmy had given her the camera and photo equipment, and she documented what she could, which turned out to be mostly people in their life current of experiences with expressions of shock, pleasure, hate, surprise, pain, and sometimes total apathy. Those expressions were the true form of impulsivity, contradicting their actions and conscious thoughts, and showing the hypocrisy of their lives. The photos gave her those connections.

The following Sunday, after she'd skipped school with Cory, an impulse told her to try the whole cheerleader thing. At Goodwill, she found a pleated skirt and a few shirts that looked slutty and vaguely like something someone in cheer would wear. On Monday, she wore the outfit and played around with the act of flirting—random flirting. She stuck around after Spanish class and approached the teacher at his desk. She asked him, a Hispanic guy who wasn't bad looking despite a hastily fixed harelip, what the translation of the word impulsive was. She said the word slowly with pouty lips, "Im..pul..sive." Tanya approached within touching distance, and he took a step back, slightly stunned. He said the word in Spanish, which she knew already but wanted him to pronounce. He used the feminine, *"Impulsiva."* She could see the confusion and uneasiness in the man's face—she'd never asked a question in class and rarely turned in homework. She lifted her camera then and took a photo—the focus, speed, and aperture already set. She smiled again and said, *"Gracias."* She later saw in his shocked image a slight smirk.

During lunch, she sat down uninvited with some of the girls on the cheer squad and a few of the football players. They looked at her, stunned. At first, they ignored the intrusion and continued talking amongst themselves. Tanya waited through half the lunch period before asking one of the cheerleaders, Tammy, when the next tryouts were. The girl was the prettiest with permed blond hair that spilled up and over her shoulders like a fountain of bubbles.

Tammy looked up with a sneer, "You want to try out for the cheerleading squad?"

"Yes." Tanya was sincere, at least at that moment. She thought cheer might be fun and cool, like roller skating.

"You're putting me on?" Tammy gave her that look, like *Come on, get off it.*

"No, seriously."

"Seriously?" Then, "It'll be posted in the fall. Like, the season's almost over."

Tammy went back to talking with her friends, ignoring Tanya. But one of the guys, whose name was Todd, looked interested and gave her a smile. She winked back. Then, right before everyone picked up their food trays to leave, Tanya asked the group, "Mind if I take your photo? Like for the school yearbook?" Her lie.

Tammy said, "Of course."

Tanya then stood up and focused her camera on the group at the table. Tammy gave a fakey fuck-you smile while Todd pursed his lips, like blowing a kiss.

Later, he approached her in the hallway between classes. He asked if she wanted to go out to the lake for a keg party on Saturday. She looked at him. Todd was like a quarterback or something and popular even among the populars. In a way, she was overwhelmed by the attention. She felt heat rush to her face, a blush turning to flush.

She stammered out, "I'd love to," then walked away before she full-on swooned.

Tanya didn't see Cory until Social Studies class, and

looking at him then was like viewing a past life from a dusty photo album.

She went to the keg party with Todd. He picked her up in front of the house after Emmy had gone out to do whatever he did. She wore what she thought a cheerleader would wear for a keg party at the beach, which not so coincidentally was the same costume she'd used months earlier to troll for tourists along the Strip—a tight-fitting pink minidress, black hi-top Chuck Taylors, and a faded Levi's jacket. She'd tied her hair up in a matching pink lace scarf and wore eye makeup that she copied from a magazine photo of Madonna. She thought the outfit would get her noticed, and when Todd rolled up in his tricked-out VW Baja Bug, he actually whistled. She jumped in the passenger seat, her Nikon camera slung over her shoulder in lieu of a purse.

They talked about stuff over the loud whine of the engine, Tanya mostly feeding the boy questions about football and his ambitions. Turned out, he wasn't so ambitious and simply wanted to get a job parking cars at Caesars Palace. He said valet attendants there made more in tips than anyone else on the Strip—dealers, waiters, and concierges included. Tanya thought for a moment and said, "I wouldn't mind slinging cocktails at Caesars," and when she said it, felt she meant it, walking around in those cool Roman costumes with the *I Dream of Jeannie* hair and meeting high rollers at the card tables.

The party was not far from where she'd gone with Cory a week before, a place called The Cove at the end of a dirt road that Todd took at a frightening, though exciting, speed. They parked among the other cars and then scrambled down the steep slope to where the kids were drinking beer around a huge bonfire with rising flames that could have cooked Joan of Arc. And because she arrived with Todd, the other kids talked to her.

She snapped two rolls of film. She'd come prepared for the darkness with high-speed ASA 400 Tri-X and shot with the camera's aperture wide open. She photographed kids drunk and dancing. She photographed Todd as he gave her some suggestive look, and Tammy as she reacted to some off-putting comment. A fight broke out between three guys, all throwing wild punches and tearing at each other's shirts. She documented the whole thing, knowing that much of the action would be blurred, and thinking that the blurred images would look interesting and cool against the stationary in-focus onlookers, the spectacle more about witnesses.

She and Todd split when the party dwindled, and he took her for a real thrill ride through the desert before stopping at the top of a ridge overlooking the lake. He shut off the engine, gave her one of those needy looks, and then leaned over with his lips parted, his tongue peeking out like a shy salamander. She kissed him, and his lips were all soft and wet, the salamander tongue now out of hiding to touch hers. He cupped her breasts through the fabric of the tight dress, then pulled down his loose board shorts, guiding her hand to his cock as though she were blind. They kissed, and she stroked his cock. He whispered, "Use your mouth." She thought about that—what a cheerleader would do. What she thought was that a Tammy would leave something on the table. Give it up too quickly, and Todd might not have any future interest—the conquest to the summit already reached. He'd probably brag back at school, and she'd be labeled a slut. A goody two-shoes cheerleader was no slut.

She said, "It's that time of the month," which had nothing to do with a blow job, but she guessed it sent the bad news without abruptly saying no. She stroked him until he finished, his semen splashing up to soil the front of his Guns N' Roses T-shirt.

He said, "Thanks, that was great."

Then Tanya raised her camera one-handed to capture his expression. She did not ask his permission and guessed that he wasn't surprised since she'd taken so many photos throughout the night. In fact, he might have expected it. One for the yearbook.

On Sunday morning, she searched impulsively for someone else to become. The Clark County Library was less than two miles from her home, and she walked in the cool of the morning past The Boulevard Mall and then the smaller strip malls that defined off-the-Strip Vegas. The library stood on the corner of Maryland and Flamingo in a mega-structure that looked like a cross between the Greek Acropolis and a Costco warehouse.

Inside, she browsed through old magazines, trying to catch a current, something that caught her eye and led to a new experience. She saw an article about Johnny Cash, The Man in Black, then photos of Yoko Ono in a newer *Rolling Stone*. John Lennon had been dead for almost ten years, but she was keeping his memory alive in a 50th birthday broadcast of "Imagine." What caught her eye first was a photo of Yoko in Central Park with a Nikon F2. What she liked then was her black suit, which somehow linked back to The Man in Black. And that's what she decided. Black. An artist thing, she thought, and that's what she felt about her photography. It was her art.

She went to her favorite Goodwill, back near The Boulevard Mall, and found an armful of black clothing—shirts, pants, a suit, ties, and shoes—all of which cost her around fifteen bucks. She tried on the suit that night and looked in the mirror. The lapels were wide and low cut, which seemed too feminine for the look she wanted. A plain white cotton shirt with a thin black tie from the sixties worked to shave off the feminine edge. Then she took scissors to her hair and cut it back just above her shoulders. She liked that the ends looked jagged as though she'd cut them herself, which, of course, she had. She decided to go without makeup and let people see the bare flesh behind the animal-tested mask.

Tanya thought of Cory then. He'd talked about being a comedian, and she wondered what kind. Cool like Lenny Bruce? Crazy like Robin Williams? Wise-cracking like Rodney Dangerfield? Impish like George Carlin? All were artists in their own way. Artists and actors. Like herself, she thought. She'd see Cory tomorrow and would have to ask him.

CHAPTER 22 – THE SWEDE
Saturday

Karol was back at the museum, a strange regular that Doris Liberace perhaps took for a superfan with a long-standing crush on her deceased brother-in-law. Whatever she thought, he didn't care and now stood in front of the glass case, eyeing the individual Hummels. Some were junk, but others had real value, and he thought, more than that, a certain aesthetic and compassion of their maker. Apple Tree Boy & Apple Tree Girl were the originals, copied so many times that they'd entered the world of kitsch. He knew they were originals because of the brown base of the two trees, the resting songbirds, the precise details of each apple, and the features of the figurines themselves. The Apple Tree Girl rested on a limb with her back to Karol, her right hand holding a pruned branch, her face turned to look over her shoulder. Her eyes seemed to avoid Karol's stare and rest just below his chin—shy and unwilling to make eye contact. He sensed she was unprepared to be looked at and admired, the first glimmer of self-consciousness, one that he could remember as a child of eight before that piano teacher's husband touched his cheek. The Apple Tree Boy sat on a tree limb, his bare knees thrust out as though on a swing. The boy looked down and away, unaware that Karol was watching him. Boys matured later than girls, and Karol could tell that, unlike the girl, he was not self-conscious, a time before that touch, when the world was small, wondrous, and non-threatening—a time before the apple was bitten. Karol didn't normally buy Hummels, but this one and others in the case were exquisite and worthy of his admiration.

He left the case of figurines and walked to the back of the museum, back to where a locked exit with an alarm sensor led to an alleyway. At six-foot-two, he easily reached the sensor and yanked off the wires that would complete the circuit once the alarm was set. He stripped the wire ends with a pocketknife and twisted them together. Doris would never know.

It was Saturday night, and he decided to retrace the path the diamonds had taken—go to Tramps and see the boy who'd found the velvet pouch. The manager woman may have called Emmy, but Karol had no reason to assume the boy hadn't held onto them, that they'd never entered the safe. What was the saying? A bird in the hand … No, possession is nine-tenths of the law. That was it. The boy would have wanted to possess the diamonds, hold them for as long as he could, hold them until cash was placed into his outstretched hand.

Karol knew the Vegas club would be going all night long, fueled by booze and cocaine. He decided to drive back to the Mirage, nap, and then shower. In the room, he turned on the television, undressed, hung up his suit coat in the closet, and draped his slacks over the desk chair to preserve their razor crease. He left the television channel playing the first program that appeared, which turned out to be an instructional show narrated by Telly Savalas on how to play the table games at the casino. Savalas, with his thick lips and bald head, talked like an Outfit wiseguy about the game's relative simplicity, the helpfulness of the dealers, and the fun of casino "action." Savalas reminded him of all the wiseguys back in Chicago with their overbearing approach and affected intimidation. Blah, blah, blah. He left the television on but turned off the sound. He called to get a wake-up call at 1 a.m., then closed his eyes to sleep. He woke up three hours later, two minutes before the phone rang. Telly Savalas was still pitching the ease of winning.

An hour later, he drove into the parking lot of the nightclub. The place was still busy with a line down the sidewalk and nearly around the wood-sided building, guys and gals dressed in their best going-out clothes and waiting to get in. To Karol, they were all hustlers and sluts, and he wasn't going to wait with that trash. He fished a twenty from his wallet to bribe the doorman, a good-looking kid with sharp features, pointy cheekbones, and a wispy hairdo that moved like Ken doll plastic as he turned his head. The kid took the twenty with a nod and said, "Welcome to Tramps."

Karol walked in and then looked around at the madness. He was overdressed in his dark suit, white shirt, and black tie, and probably an oddity to most of these kids. This was no place for adults. Karol twisted through the crowd as best he could. People bumped and touched, and all that touching bothered him, the sweat and germs. He stopped at the bar in the back by a booth where a DJ spun records. After waiting a few minutes, he ordered a glass of water with ice. The bartender, a guy with a 50s pompadour, replied quickly, almost before he finished pronouncing the word ice, "Perrier or LaCroix?"

The question confused Karol—all this business about Perrier or La Croix. What was unclear about water with ice? He started to repeat his order when the bartender said, "Bubbly or still?"

"Still."

A second later, the bartender was back with a bottle. He said, "A dollar and a half."

Karol pulled out his roll of bills and found two singles. He placed them on the bar and said in a more stern voice, "Glass." Then, "Ice."

Unoffended, the bartender delivered both and took the two bills. Karol walked away before the change arrived.

The easiest place to stand was right in front of the DJ booth, but then the DJ behind him reached over and poked him on the shoulder, "Mister, can you move? You're blocking my view." And before Karol could respond, the DJ added, "Thanks." He moved a step to the side and in front of a wooden beam, apparently one holding up the roof. He stood there with his half-full bottle of fancy water and the full glass with ice and watched the crowd. Some stood around like him, some sat at tables and booths, and others gyrated like fools on the dance floor. It wasn't long before he spotted the kid with his little broom and dustpan.

Karol could see the advantage—all these drunk and stoned idiots reaching into their pockets for cash, jumping up and down on the dance floor, and casting off their coins, bills, and jewelry. Just come along and sweep it up. The kid wore the same yellow polo shirt that all the other employees wore. His brown hair hung into his eyes, like he needed a haircut, and the kid's focus was always on the floor, looking, and sweeping. Then he moved off to a bus station where he sifted through the collected garbage. Karol could see him pocket a bill of some denomination. He made a mental note: the bangs, the yellow shirt, and one more thing, shorts. Most of the bartenders and security guys, the bouncers, wore long pants, while this kid wore shorts. Karol left his spot near the DJ booth and walked out to his car. He knew it would be a few hours before the kid punched out, so he drove off to a convenience store for coffee and gas for the Taurus.

The sun was just coming up behind the mountains when the kid finally walked out the back employee entrance. He still wore the yellow shirt and was easy to follow as he drove off down Flamingo on a small motorcycle. He zigzagged through streets north and east until he took a left into the parking lot of a cheap apartment that advertised studios for two hundred and fifty dollars per month. The kid walked into a street-level room.

Karol wouldn't need a gun or a knife; his six-foot-two presence would be enough. He stepped from his car and walked through the parking lot to the door. He knocked.

The kid asked from behind the door, "Who is it?"

"Truant Officer."

"I go to school. My mom knows where I am."

"Just need to talk. Open the door."

The door opened. In the fifteen minutes the kid had been inside, he'd already changed into pajamas, matching tops and bottoms a robin's egg blue. Cute. The kid swiped the bangs from his eyes. "What is it?"

Karol stepped inside and shut the door behind him. The apartment looked orderly with clothes off the floor and stashed somewhere. He guessed, folded. It smelled like talcum powder, like baby powder. A small kitchenette was in the back, the sink clear of dishes. The full-sized bed was made with a corner pulled back, the kid ready to be tucked in. Cute. And he wondered what kind of fucked up home life the kid survived to be out on his own like this. Karol had grown up with all sorts of kids with fucked up home lives—his was fucked up—but he didn't know anyone who left. Just the opposite; many stayed in their homes way past high school, possibly contributing to the fuckedupness.

The kid stepped back into the room and stood near the kitchen dinette table with two chairs. "So what's the deal? You taking me back to my mom? I don't think she wants me around. Just so you know. And I've been going to school every day."

Karol walked up to the kid, standing within arm's reach. The kid leaned back against the side of the table. "We just need to have a talk. I don't care about your mom or your school. I want to talk to you about the diamonds."

An instant look of recognition—Karol was sure of it. Then, the kid paused, undoubtedly thinking of a ready lie. "I have no idea what you're talking about."

"Yes, you do."

"No, I don't."

This was where Karol was supposed to tell the kid what he knew and convince him to tell the truth. But the reality was, he'd need to get rough sooner or later.

He said, "Sit down."

The kid did as he was told and sat in the chrome and vinyl dinette chair. Karol took the other chair and moved it in front of the kid, then sat facing him. "Give me your hand."

The kid sat on both hands. "No. Fuck you."

He said gently, "Come on, just give me your left hand." He motioned with his finger. "Come on." Karol forced a smile.

The kid then did what was asked and held out his left hand. Karol could smell the fear behind the dust of talcum.

Sweat, but not the jock odor kind, more sweet, salty, familiar. Karol held the hand and looked at the fingers, soft and uncalloused. Beautiful, really, almost porcelain. He bent over and took the kid's pinky in his mouth—gently, lovingly. His lips, then teeth, found the first knuckle, the gap between two bones.

He bit, letting the severed tip fall from his mouth and onto the floor between them.

Instantly, the kid pulled his hand back but without making a sound. And before he could make one, Karol was up and around him, with the kid's neck in the crook of his elbow. "Calm down."

The kid shook uncontrollably, trying now to scream but unable.

Karol said, "Tell me about the diamonds." He released the pressure on the kid's neck.

The kid plunged the bleeding hand under his opposite armpit. "I gave them to Deedee."

"Who is Deedee?"

"The manager, the lady who was shot when the safe was robbed. The diamonds were in the safe."

"You know I'll kill you if you're lying?"

The kid nodded.

"Do you know who Niven is?"

More pressure around the kid's neck. He garbled, "No!"

All of this, and the kid was telling the truth. Karol knew truth like he knew lying and fear. This was no street kid who lied for a living, and for lying, you needed practice. Karol thought he could even detect well-practiced lying. It had something to do with the confidence of it. Wiseguys were always lying and did it as though they believed it. Confidence and ego. The kid had neither. The diamonds had to be with this guy, Niven, or whatever his real or full name was. Sooner or later, he'd find him. Take more than a fingertip.

Karol released the pressure from the kid's neck and stepped back. He lifted off his squarish eyeglasses and slowly cleaned the lenses—no spots of blood that he could see. He walked toward the door and didn't look back when saying, "Get that finger fixed. Tell them that it was caught in your bike chain. You know better than to say anything about me."

Karol was near the door when he looked back to make sure he was understood.

The kid was looking at the severed pinky, the part still attached to his hand. It'd mostly stopped bleeding but left a trail of blood from beneath the one armpit and down the side of his soft blue pajamas. The kid then looked up, and the fright Karol had seen before now dissipated.

The kid said, "I understand." Then, right before Karol was out the door, he added, "And thanks for not taking this other one." The gutsy kid held up his middle finger—the fuck you.

The gesture made him smile.

CHAPTER 23 – KING
That Same Saturday

His penis was what bothered him most. It stung every time he had to take a piss, and that was often, sometimes just a dribble that hardly relieved the urge. He remembered growing up back in West Virginia when he could cross swords and out-piss the other kids in the neighborhood. Now it was like crossing butter knives. He'd tried the penicillin, but that only gave him diarrhea. He consulted a guy named Woodford who was once a nurse at Sunrise Hospital before stealing from the medicine chest. Woodford stuck his finger up his ass and proclaimed his prostate the size of a lemon when it should have been more like a lime. His enlarged prostate was cutting off the flow. But that didn't explain the burning. Then other symptoms came and went: a debilitating fatigue, more diarrhea, sores on his dick. Woodford took a look at his sores and said he likely had AIDS. It could have been the needles they passed around like joints. It wasn't sex. There was a time he liked sex, and it didn't seem to matter if it was with a woman or a man. But he hadn't really been interested in years, like way before he landed in

Vegas. It had to be the needles. Since then, he'd drastically cut back, and the habit was nearly gone. It was just a matter of time until he was also gone.

He played dominoes that night with the kid, Skinny. Funny kid. He was like a little brother or what King imagined having a son would be like. Skinny looked up to him, hung on his every word. What King had to offer wasn't much: how to make a living without provoking the authorities; a few rules to live by in the rat-filled tunnels beneath the city; how to navigate that world above if you didn't really want that world to begin with. That, or maybe this place beneath the Strip was the world, and the people up top were the rats. It didn't really matter; King didn't want the world up top, no matter what. He wanted to be underground.

Skinny had asked about that. "When was the last time you were on the street?"

It had been a year, forced out when the rains flooded the tunnels. Five had died.

Then, "Why have you stayed down so long?"

King knew why, and it was all fucked up. When the tunnels flooded that one time, the memories came streaming back. He'd been a miner in West Virginia. His daddy was a miner, and his grandfather before him. His older brother was one too. King guessed it was preordained or some genetic peculiarity, like trout swimming upriver. He never finished high school and began working at the age of seventeen as a miner's assistant, also called a "worm." His job was to play fetch for the real miners who worked the equipment. He wouldn't play fetch for his dad or brother, so he found another crew to work with.

Hollingsworth #5 was bored into the side of a mountain with seams of coal no more than three feet tall—called low coal. They'd take an electric car nearly a mile in, following the conveyor belt that transported the coal out. They all wore helmets with carbide lamps and knee pads. The last hundred yards or so to the continuous mining machines were just the height of the seams, and they crawled. He spent most of each day on his knees filling the belts with loose coal, fetching water or tools, helping set charges, and then other odds and ends the four miners on his crew could think of. As far as he knew, low coal mining was the worst kind of mining there was. And being a worm was the worst of the worst.

The day was Friday, April 12, at 3:26 in the afternoon, almost quitting time for the weekend. His dad and brother were on another crew further down in the mine when their boring machine broke through to an old, abandoned shaft that wasn't on any charts. It must have started as just a trickle—and there was always some water in the mines—but then the trickle turned into a flood as the crack widened and then burst. The old mine was filled to the top with tainted water. His daddy, brother, and three other miners instantly drowned.

Though he wouldn't find that out until ten days later, and for those ten days, he and the others were stuck.

They saw the water coming at them, rising around their boot tops, rising up to their bellies. They crawled against the tide of water and almost made it to the main tunnel, but the water kept rising, forcing the five into another room, another shaft that had been played out. That shaft ran upward, and the five moved ahead of the rising water. They reached a shelf near the end, and that's where they were trapped. The water continued to rise, almost to the shelf, but then stopped. It seemed a miracle at the time, an answer to the prayers.

It never seemed like a miracle to him. A panic set in, hard breathing, heart pumping, and all he could think about was slowly drowning, taking that last gulp of air, and then holding it for as long as possible. Then the realization that he couldn't hold his breath forever, and that he'd have to suck in the tainted, poisonous mine water, breathe it in so that his lungs filled and stopped. Then minutes more as the realization of death was like that first step off the electric cart, that first knee on the floor of the pitch-black darkness. When the water stopped its gradual ascent, he hardly believed it.

Ten days. He found out later that fifteen others had been rescued from a room closer to the entrance after eight pumps had run nonstop for three days. He learned that the other miners running the pumps and drilling air holes into the shafts had assumed that the others further down were dead. During that time, the water receded by only five inches.

What they had for those ten days was a quart of fresh water, a thermos of milk, and four sandwiches. They switched off their headlamps, knowing that the fuel wouldn't last, and that they might need light for an escape if that chance ever arrived. The milk, fresh water, and sandwiches were gone in two days. They drank the mine water after that—breakfast, lunch, and dinner. With some, the stomach cramps were all-consuming, and they lay groaning and lethargic. The tainted water did not affect King in any way. He guessed, luck of the draw.

One of the miners, Lemore Rawlings, was a lay preacher, and twice a day he led prayers. None of them could see him in the pitch black of the flooded mine, but King remembered his pointy nose, his big eyes that poked from his skull like a Fowler's toad, and the bangs of his black hair that swept across his forehead. Funny-looking guy. But King had to admit, Lemore held them together for those ten days without food or clean water. He even convinced most of the others that the foul water was there by God's hand, and that it would nourish them throughout the ordeal. It was a given that they would survive.

The pumps continued day and night, and though the five couldn't hear them, they measured the depth each day and could see the water recede. Hope was all there in the inches lost. Before they could finally walk out, the rescue team of miners walked in, chins barely above the water, helmets scraping the mine's ceiling.

They recovered the bodies of the other crew a few days later. There'd never been any hope for his daddy and brother.

The company closed down the mine then, and King stayed home with the unemployment insurance that would last him six months. His daddy and brother, along with the other three crew members, were buried with a ceremony that brought out hundreds of miners wearing their work overalls and helmets. Lemore gave the eulogy, quoting from the Bible, "And people shall enter the caves of the rocks and the holes of the ground, from before the terror of the LORD, and from the splendor of his majesty, when he rises to terrify the earth." Then, "For all have sinned and fall short of the glory of God." Then a prayer, "Dear God, I come to you with a humble heart, acknowledging my sin and asking for your forgiveness. Please wash away my guilt and grant me the grace to resist temptation and live a life pleasing to you. Guide my steps and help me to follow your will. In Jesus' name, Amen." What King guessed the preacher was trying to say was that we all sin and should ask for the Lord's forgiveness. But he took it to mean that his brother and daddy had strayed from the Lord, fled underground, and that's why they died. If King was on the fence then about God and the Bible, he was an atheist now.

At home, his mother would not look him in the eye. He

guessed he stood as a reminder of what had happened. Or maybe the shame that he survived when others didn't. Most days, King loitered at the local tavern, eating his meals there, and drinking. He wanted to go back into the mines, but jobs were scarce.

Then Vietnam. As a miner, King was considered essential to the war effort. As an eighteen-year-old boy on unemployment, he was considered ripe for military service. His draft notice came, and a month later, he was at Fort Leonard Wood for basic training. A few months after that, because of his experience as a miner with explosives, they sent him to Australia to learn demolition. Then King was back underground, blowing tunnels used by the Viet Cong. Being in those tight tunnels, sometimes no more than two feet tall, was almost a comfort.

After the war, he drifted. He stayed in Southeast Asia and worked odd jobs. In Borneo, he cut and hauled trees alongside aboriginals. Like himself, they loathed direct sunlight, and all worked for pennies logging beneath the protective canopy of the tropical forest. He worked on a fishing boat off the northern coast of Australia, preferring to tend the nets at night. He drifted back to the United States. He wandered, hopping freight trains and picking fruit with the migrants or just hitchhiking aimlessly from town to town. He ended up in Vegas one hot summer and found the tunnels. He'd been in the tunnels for over ten years.

Skinny had asked why he'd stayed down so long.

Maybe, deep down, he thought he deserved it. Regardless, he now had a taste for being underground.

King said just that. "I don't know. Just developed a taste for it."

CHAPTER 24 – SKINNY
Sunday

Skinny emerged from the tunnels, the Underground, in the early afternoon when the sun was at its zenith, furnace-hot, and blinding. He wore soiled khaki pants and a shirt with a button-down collar. He had a dog with him, a mongrel, some German shepherd but with the longer and lighter hair of a golden retriever, then with ears that flopped over like a hound. The dog was docile and dragged slowly behind him from a piece of hemp rope. He carried a small red backpack containing a liter-sized Coke bottle filled with water and a few granola bars that locals had passed out from their cars at street corners—Skinny guessed to alleviate their guilt in the face of destitution. The idea was to look like a pathetic college boy who needed to get back to his family. His cardboard sign, neatly legible, read NEED BUS FARE TO GET BACK HOME. Rat King had assigned him the same place between Caesars and the Mirage. He reached the spot by early afternoon and sat on an Army-looking olive-green blanket in an unshaded spot exposed to the blinding sun. He had a baseball cap with a Cubs logo that he pulled down as far as possible to hide his face from the Metro or mafia dudes searching for him. He hoped no one would ask him about Chicago—all he knew was that it was somewhere between Las Vegas and New York and that the weather sucked.

By late afternoon, he'd collected close to forty dollars. He thought the college boy getup was really working. It was moms he did best with, middle-aged or older, with children likely out of the house and on their own. Give to this kid and be right with the world, a kind of prayer or offering for their own child's safety. At least, that's what he thought.

Much of the time, he spaced out, bored and hot. He thought about his own mom back in Huntington Beach. She'd had him when she was still in high school, knocked up by some Marine asshole off to fight Communists or whoever in Vietnam. The guy, his supposed father, had died over there, rotting in some shithole. He grew up calling his mom by her first name, Monika, which sounded a lot like mommy. They lived in a two-bedroom apartment close enough to the beach that once he had a bike, he could ride there whenever he wanted. He was her little man, and they were more friends than son and mother. Later, more like husband and wife, and once he started getting high, she wanted some of that too, and they'd sit around at night getting high and watching whatever came on the tube. It was Monika who turned him onto smack, and it was the smack that came between them. She'd been a waitress at the Denny's on Main Street before getting fired.

She started bringing boyfriends home. He liked one guy who'd take them swimming at Patriot Point. Once that guy was gone, some biker dude moved in. Then it seemed the whole biker gang moved in. Monika was then passed around like a stubby roach. Skinny spent more time on the streets by himself, returning to the apartment now and then to score more dope from the bikers.

What made him move to Vegas? A group of kids he was hanging out with were driving there for the weekend, and they asked him to come along. They stayed at the Oasis, getting high and then cruising the Strip. Later, he was out on the Strip alone after scoring some cheap crystal. He didn't have gambling money and, regardless, was too young to enter a casino. But he could buy a Budweiser in one of the little stores that advertised tall boys for a dollar. Then the Strip was so cool with all the lights and action, and he just walked and walked. When he finally returned to the Oasis, his friends were gone. Left him stranded. That's how he landed in Vegas, stranded. He tried to call Monika, but the line had been disconnected. He met Niven soon afterward, and that's when he learned the snatch and dash.

He was in his spot between the Mirage and Caesars, eating a slice of leftover sausage pizza from a delivery box someone had dropped off, when, right in front of him, stood Niven dressed in some cool nightclub outfit.

He said, "Skinny?"

"Bro, like everyone is looking for you, cops and heavy mafia-like dudes."

"Yeah, I know."

That's when he told Niven about the flood channels, Rat King, and protection. "You need to go underground. That's where we'll be."

Before Niven left, Skinny asked, "Dude, can you spare some weed?"

CHAPTER 25 – CORY
Monday

"So, I work at this nightclub called Tramps. The place is kinda cool, and it's definitely the place to be in Las Vegas, the hot night spot, with dancing, booze, coke sold in the parking lot, and, well, tramps. You know, sluts. Seriously. The funny thing is, the place was not initially designed with sluts in mind. There are no photos of sexy chicks on the walls; it's not all neon and mirrors like some porno shop or nudie bar. It's not like the Crazy Horse Saloon or even the Crazy Horse Too, which, for those of you who don't know, are the two nudie strip bars in town, and *they* have nothing in common with Indians or the American West. Which is funny or ironic because Tramps does. The original owner was a guy named Frank who was shot and killed during a robbery, as was his wife ten years later, just last week. Seriously. But more of that later.

"When Frank built Tramps, he had in mind a family restaurant with maybe some music at night. The theme envisioned was the American West with freight trains. And— you guessed it—the name Tramps was not intended to conjure up hot women and sluts, but those guys that rode the freights. You know, hobos, bums. Irony. Let me define it for you: a state of affairs or an event that seems deliberately contrary to what one expects and is often amusing as a result. See?

"So, my job is to carry around one of those little brooms and dust pans with the long handle, like something an old lady would use to pick up sidewalk dogshit. This is actually the best part of my job because of what people drop and lose. Of course, it's mostly coins and dollar bills, which adds to my measly five-dollar-an-hour wages, but I also find little vials of cocaine, which I can turn around and sell to the bartenders. A week ago, I found not only an open condom wrapper but the used condom itself. Disgusting. Seriously. Now, I'm sure you're wondering if it's possible to fornicate in tight and crowded spaces? On the dance floor? I've seen it done. No shit. Then, just the other day, I found a little velvet pouch. It was right after the DJ played that *Animal House* song, "Shout," where everyone is jumping up and then squirming on the floor. That song is a gold mine for me, with everything flying from pockets. So, I take the pouch into the back and look inside. Diamonds. I shit you not. A sack full of uncut diamonds. I'm seriously rich, right?

"Back to Frank's wife, whose name is Deedee. I'd given her the sack of diamonds so she could sell them and cut me in on the cash. It's an arrangement we had. So, she puts the diamonds in the safe with the intention of calling her connection the following week. The next Tuesday, she's opening up the place and walks in on a robbery in progress, the safe open, money and diamonds in hand. The robber or robbers shoot her dead. Now I realize nothing in this particular part of my story is funny on any level. So be it.

"Of course, those diamonds I found were worth

thousands. I don't know how many thousands, but I bet if I'd been able to cash in, my cut would buy a sex change with fantastic new titties down at Chuckle's House of Organ Reconstruction just off East Fremont. And I'd be tempted to do just that. I don't know about you guys, but male genitals are freakish in a way, all wobbly flesh that just hangs there like some mutant appendage. The thing is useless; it can't even pick up a pencil. Maybe once aroused, it can depress an elevator button. But I'm getting off track here. The point is that someone lost those diamonds and would do anything to get them back. Seriously.

"See this pinky finger? Let me unwrap the bandage for you. Now, look closely. The end of my little pinky is gone. The way it happened, someone who wanted those diamonds back found me. This guy was a true freak. Way over six feet tall, bleached blond hair pasted to his head in that very unfashionable wet look, dark suit, white shirt, and tie. This guy was the spitting image of Lurch on that *Addams Family* show, a slightly more presentable Frankenstein. The guy must have followed me home from Tramps after my shift ended at five in the morning. Came into my tidy apartment and then proceeded to ask me questions. Now, I was more than happy to answer each and every question to the best of my knowledge, but he didn't give me the chance. Just slipped my little pinky finger through his moist lips and then bit down hard. Seriously. I know, I know. Then he let me spill the beans, of which there were few. The last thing he asked was if I knew a Niven or Navel or something. I'm a smart-ass by trade, and what I said was, 'I have one, a navel, but I call it a belly button.' Lurch actually smiled. Not quite a laugh, but I got a smile out of this guy. Best you could do with that audience. Then he left. My pinky finger was there on the floor where he'd spit it out.

So now I don't know who this Niven or Navel guy is, but if I were him, I'd find a rock to crawl under. If he's found, I'm sure Lurch will have a nice finger salad. Seriously.

"So, I go to the emergency room and tell the doctor that I lost my fingertip in a motorcycle accident. I'm perceived as a dumb kid, so he found this story entirely plausible. But then what he said cracked me up. He said I should have kept the end of my finger, wrapped it in cellophane, and put it on ice—that he could have sewn it back on. And I'm thinking the end of my pinky is about as useful as a limp dick. Seriously. Sew on the stump so that I can use it like a more useful stiff dick to at least depress an elevator button. For real."

Cory played back the routine on his cassette recorder. It was mostly comedy gold, he thought, though maybe too real and close to home in parts, and he wasn't quite sure about the bit where he considers a sex change. He had work to do.

CHAPTER 26 – EMMY
Tuesday

Stupid. Ripping off the Liberace Museum was just stupid, but he felt obliged to help. He owed Swede for the rap he took back in Chicago. When was that? Over twenty years ago. He guessed he also felt responsible for the stolen diamonds. They were out there, somewhere, and they should've been focusing on finding those. Stupid.

Emmy sat behind the wheel of a worn, tired, and rusty Dodge van that he'd bought off a guy on the North Side. It hadn't been hard to find—he just drove around until spotting one in a driveway with a cardboard sign that simply said $500!!. He parked his Cadillac a few blocks away and then paid the guy what he wanted, no questions asked. Later, he topped off the gas tank and added a quart of oil. The van blew a little black smoke but would do the job.

When he picked up Swede at the Mirage later that night, the freak said, "It better not break down."

Emmy did not respond to the crack about the van. What

did he expect, a manufacturer's warranty? Instead, Emmy asked about gloves. No special outfit was needed, but you didn't want to leave prints behind.

The Swede was wearing his usual dark mortician's suit with a white shirt and black tie, and he sat up in the front seat of the Dodge van with the doghouse between them that covered the eight-cylinder Mopar engine. For a quick second, Emmy thought it might not be the appropriate outfit to wear for a robbery. In the old days, they wore jeans and black T-shirts, but that's what they wore every day, regardless. Now, they dressed in suits like grown-ups. Emmy was also wearing a suit and guessed they really didn't need special outfits—robberywear—to break in and steal some expensive pottery. The goal was not to be seen, period.

Swede did not respond to the question about the gloves.

Emmy had already turned onto Las Vegas Boulevard, but he could feel Swede watching him. "You fill up the tank with petrol?"

Emmy didn't respond. It seemed neither was going to answer questions.

He turned on the radio and clicked a few buttons. Heavy metal guitar solo, Coke the real thing, some Mexican shit, a rap song with the line, "Daddy's little girl, what daddy don't know won't hurt him." He thought briefly of Tanya. *What he didn't know won't hurt him*, but something told him he did know. A station he liked, smooth jazz, lived somewhere on the top of the dial, but he wasn't going to take the time to find it. Something weak or vulnerable in that gesture, trying to find something lost. He switched off the radio.

Swede said, "You find anything out about the diamonds?"

A question he *would* answer. "The detective I know, Pete,

is looking around for that guy, Niven. He checked with the apartment manager and got his real name, Walter Niven Kolchek. Funny thing is, Walter Kolchek was in the city lockup over the weekend, something about a stolen vehicle registration. He was released on Tuesday morning. He didn't go back to the apartment. They had him but let him go."

"What's so funny about that?"

Emmy turned off on Flamingo Road. He didn't look over at Swede—could feel his eyes feasting on the pulsing jugular running the length of his neck. "I guess funny, like ironical. Not funny, ha-ha."

"Ironical."

"Well, anyway, there's nothing to say this guy Niven even has the diamonds. We know he broke into the safe, but who's to say the diamonds were even in there?"

"They were there."

Emmy looked over. Both Swede's eyes behind his square glasses closed slowly, then blinked open, no doubt deep in thoughts of the violence that warped the tall man's mind. "You know something I don't?"

"I had a chat with the kid who found the diamonds on the floor of that discotheque."

"Cory?"

"He confirmed that he gave the diamonds to the manager, who put them in the safe. This kid, Niven, has the diamonds, and he wouldn't have had the time or connections to find a fence. He still has them. Maybe not for long."

Now they were off the Strip and heading down Flamingo toward where The Home Depot stayed open twenty-four hours and sold the stuff they needed: boxes and packing materials.

So, Swede had talked to Cory, the kid who'd brought

Tanya home from school on his minibike. At Deedee's funeral, the kid said it was over between him and Tanya. But a few days later, he showed up again, again with Tanya on the back of his minibike. She wore all black, some new thing he couldn't quite figure out. Emmy noticed then that the kid's little finger had been bandaged up, which looked shorter, odd, like a three-legged dog. He was too pissed off at Tanya to ask the kid what'd happened. Now he figured he knew.

What he didn't know won't hurt him.

He said nothing to Swede, but all that violence now seemed to be getting closer to his home and family. The man would have no boundaries when getting what was owed to him.

Emmy said what he thought Swede would want to hear. "We'll find him. Pete's on it. Won't take long."

He looked over to see the freak's eyes slowly close and then open again. "Tick tock."

They stopped at The Home Depot, and Swede returned with six folded boxes, a roll of brown packing paper, a handheld tape gun, and a box of latex gloves. He guessed Swede was going to grab everything but the pianos. This was no smash-and-grab. Packing boxes, carting them out, and loading the van would feel like an eternity.

Back in the old days, they'd done a job like this—jump the security wires on the door, then drill out the lock pins. Emmy had a Makita drill for that purpose with new bits and an extra, charged battery. What he remembered about the past job was that it was the one where Swede was caught and then sent to Joliet for five years.

The museum was one of a dozen storefronts in a strip mall on Tropicana. Emmy pulled the van into the mall's parking lot and then drove around to the back. Most of the other stores were long closed, and the only business still open was a bar called Top of the Trop, which he knew would be slow this time of night with just a few retirees spending their Social Security money on nickel slots and seventy-five-cent draft beers. They might have to worry about some mook taking out garbage, but Emmy parked the van close to the museum's back door, blocking any view.

Swede said, "What time you got?"

"One twenty-two."

"Give me an hour, so do two-thirty."

"Over an hour?"

Swede looked at him with those eyes—wide open, white all around. Shark's eyes behind an eyeglass aquarium. "Just open the door."

Emmy gloved up and then stepped from the van with the drill and bits. He approached the steel-sheathed door, then used the smallest bit to put a pilot hole just below the key slot where he knew the pins were positioned in a line like little pistons. He used the second bit to go through the metal and into the pin chambers, then used the largest bit to drill out the pins, all without needing the second battery. He fitted a screwdriver into the key slot and turned until the bolt slipped back from the door jam. He opened the door slowly, nervous that Swede hadn't jumped the wires correctly.

No alarm sounded.

Swede came from the van with the packing materials and quickly slipped through the open museum door. Emmy eased the door closed and then drove off in the van.

He drove east to Maryland Parkway and then north to a quiet bar he knew called Rueben's. He knew the place from back before he moved to Las Vegas, back when his cousin Tony worked out of The Gold Rush and, along with the Outfit, ran the town. At least, that's what Tony thought. He'd taken Emmy to Rueben's back in the seventies. The place was open twenty-four hours and seemed swanky at the time with dark green booths, green lampshades on wall sconces, which kept the place in dim smoky light. A saltwater aquarium stretched the length of the back bar with a real shark. The bar was owned by a Jew named Rueben who presided over the place from a corner booth where he mostly read the Daily Racing Form and drank coffee. On Wednesday nights, he'd have White Castle hamburgers flown in from Chicago. All the waitresses were dead gorgeous and wore tight-fitting tuxedo things, like Playboy bunny outfits but without the cotton tails and ears. The music was disco. The old days. Now you could buy frozen White Castle burgers from Safeway and heat 'em up in your microwave back home. He'd done that.

The outside hadn't changed—Rueben's name spelled out in scripted gold leaf across windows blacked out against the daylight. The inside hadn't changed—the green booths, sconces, a small shark swimming back and forth like a dog at a fence—he thought of Swede's shark eyes. The smell was different, or so he thought. Beer. Back in the day, no wiseguy would be caught dead with a beer. Now, it was all cheap glasses of light beer. The dance floor was still there with the rotating, colored lights. Michael Jackson was playing, but no one was dancing. The place was half full. Reuben's booth was empty.

Emmy sat at the bar and ordered a cup of coffee. The bartender was back seconds later with a mug, a Domino sugar packet, and two single-serve cups of half and half. He left the side stuff alone and drank his coffee black. He checked his watch, ten minutes to two.

The Outfit guys had pretty much been gone since he moved to Vegas five years ago. No one told him what to do, but habits were hard to break, and his past had followed him. He'd done muscle jobs for Pete and moved stolen property through the shop. But all that had slowed in the last year. He guessed the town was growing up. Churches, schools, and shopping malls signaled a place where families wanted to raise their kids. Emmy was all for it.

Habits. He really didn't need to buy junk stolen from junkies like Skinny. What did it make him, like an extra five hundred a month? Then he had to pay off Pete or do his bidding just so the cops would look the other way. It seemed so obvious that he didn't need to do all that, just buy and sell jewelry like anyone else. Another guy in town advertised cash on the barrelhead for unwanted gold jewelry, and Emmy had heard he bought it by the ounce and then turned around and sold it on the open gold market. He probably paid the ladies two hundred an ounce, then sold it for four. Bad habits—Swede would be the last. He finished the coffee and paid when the bartender came around for a refill. Quarter after two.

He pulled the van alongside the museum exit, then sat and watched while the minutes clicked down to two-thirty. No one drove down the alley or exited from the back of the bar. At the agreed time, Emmy slipped through the two front seats and opened the van's side door. He stepped out and opened the door to the museum.

Swede stood stone-still with his arms hanging down like dead weights. Behind him were six boxes, each the size of a motel mini fridge. Emmy said, "You remember to pack up the medicine cabinet?" A joke.

It took the freak a second to answer, obviously not getting it. "What are you waiting for?"

Emmy moved around the man and lifted the first box. It wasn't so heavy. Swede followed.

Then the back door of the bar, the Top of the Trop, opened and a large man in kitchen whites stepped out with a loaded garbage bag. Emmy and Swede stood silently just outside the van and watched. The man walked to the dumpster, opened it, and then tossed the bag in.

On his way back, he looked over and stopped. He said, "Hey, what's going on?"

They said nothing. Swede put his box down on the alley pavement.

The man slowly walked toward them. The distance between was about as far as Emmy could throw a baseball in his youth. "You guys shouldn't be back there."

Just a cook in a white T-shirt, a soiled apron tied around his bulging gut, and thick black shoes that glimmered with grease under the alley lamp. Emmy guessed it would be hard to keep a check on weight gain while staring at fries and chicken wings all day.

He whispered to Swede, "Let's just get in the van and go. This clown will never get close to us."

"There are still two boxes."

"Forget the boxes."

"I can't." Swede then pulled a gun from somewhere inside his suit coat.

Emmy whispered adamantly, "Don't." He said it but knew Swede wouldn't listen. When did he ever listen?

Swede lifted the gun with a straight right arm and sighted down the barrel. The cook was stepping closer, but still a hundred feet away.

Emmy tried again, "He can't make us at this distance, in this light. Let's just go."

Swede fired. The cook tipped over like a grazed bowling pin. Emmy guessed a clean headshot. At that distance, it was hard to tell. Swede put two more rounds in the large man's torso.

They quickly packed up the other boxes. In that time, no one else came from the bar—the music and clamor of slot machines drowning out any noise from the outside world. The beer would flow, but the fries and chicken wings would come out late, or not at all.

Emmy drove and Swede sat beside him like nothing had happened.

Out of control. First stupid and now out of control. Nothing was said—no question as to why Swede had to shoot down a cook. None that the freak would answer. Then, when was it? Only last week, he'd killed an innocent bum lying down against the concrete wall of the flood channel. It was all senseless. He'd also done something to that kid, Cory, Tanya's maybe-boyfriend. The shit was getting close to home and beginning to rub off. The stink was all over him. The fucking Outfit, a bunch of loser hoodlums back in Chicago who still thought they ruled the world; old school Italian shit like they were all Ceasars, running things with their tribunes, prefects, and centurions. He was done with it.

Swede said, "Dump these boxes off at The Gold Rush, then drop me at the Mirage. Ship the boxes to my address in Chicago."

An order from Caesar himself. Emmy knew the tyrant had to die.

Emmy read about the killing and robbery the next day in the Review-Journal. The assailants were unknown, and no one had heard the shots. He read the article twice, looking for any detail that might suggest the stink was still on him. That was just before a kid walked in with a smart-alecky look on his face. He said, "My wife said no," then pulled from the breast pocket of his rumpled linen shirt a diamond wedding ring—Pete's ring. "How much you give me?"

CHAPTER 27 – NIVEN
Wednesday

The ring was worth way more than that, like three thousand, but this goombah was only offering him three hundred. "Six hundred." He said it as a statement, though, of course, it was a question. Six hundred would buy him a gram, another night at the Mirage, and a stake to get his money back from the casino. The man didn't reply, and Niven said again, "Six hundred. I paid five times that for the ring back in California."

"Did you keep the receipt? You wouldn't be the first lover boy to ask for his money back. If you'd bought it here, I'd have given you a refund."

Receipt? What an asshole. "Okay, five hundred." Niven stood to his full five-foot-eleven height and cocked his head sideways. "Take it or leave it."

The old mobster gave him a sly smile, just the edges turned up. He'd heard this shit a million times. Guys must come in here night and day with watches and rings, hoping for another crack at the tables. "I'll give you four hundred. That's a hundred more than I first offered. Only because I feel for you. Hell, you get on your knee with a rock like that, and even I'd marry you."

Funny guy. Four hundred would buy him a gram, a little gambling money, and a week at the Oasis—he couldn't return to his apartment. "Okay, four hundred."

"I'll just need to see some ID."

"Four hundred cash. That's what you said. Why do you care who you pay it to?"

"Sorry, I gotta keep a record of every payout. I got audited last year, and that cost me a small fortune in fines because I didn't keep proper records. It's an IRS thing."

"Fucking IRS. But it's not like I have to declare this on taxes or anything?"

"No, only if it's over ten thousand. Four hundred, they don't care. Just need the ID for the books. You know, to avoid any fines."

He could taste the cash. And for some reason, he thought of those gold-wrapped chocolate coins his parents had given him at Christmas. At the time, they seemed even more exotic than the real thing. It was all funny money, but now the coins would have a cocaine center, and he could almost feel the drug in the back of his throat. His mouth watered with the thought. Mouth sweat. Niven reached into his back pocket and pulled out his wallet and Maryland ID. Walter Niven Kolchek Jr.

The man looked at the ID and wrote the info on a notepad beside the cash register. He said, "Walter, I'll be right back with your cash."

He gulped. "Yeah, four hundred dollars. Cash."

"Sure, just a moment." The guy walked into the back room, came out a few minutes later, laid four hundred-dollar bills on the glass countertop, fanned out like fingers.

Coke, cheap hotel room, win-back. Maybe a cheese burrito. Niven walked from the jewelry store without another word to the slimy goombah in his suit and slicked-back hair.

He walked the two blocks to Las Vegas Boulevard, then north toward downtown and the Oasis. He'd lived there for three months after getting kicked out of the home he'd grown up in. He did smack for the first time right there in room twelve, smoking it laced in a joint. A month later, he was shooting up right into a vein. Then his money ran out, and he started doing the snatch and dash with Skinny, making enough to get high each night. They shared a room at the Oasis, and in the mornings, they'd shoot up with whatever was left over, nod out for a few hours, then hit the Strip in the afternoon. One day, he just decided to quit, and for Niven, it was like a bad case of the flu, nothing he couldn't handle. Skinny was there helping him through the dopesick, but also continually asking him if he wanted to shoot up for the relief.

In the end, after those first few days, he did take a hit of coke, and that relieved the overwhelming dread he'd been feeling—wondering what the fuck he was doing in Vegas to begin with, what he'd given up back in Baltimore. Made him decide to get a job. Then, he filled out an application at TGI Fridays with fake work histories and references. One reference was Kitchen, who duly said that Niven was a great employee and was sorry he'd been laid off after the business closed. Waiting on tables was actually fun, and he was good at it, especially after a hit of cocaine. And that's what he wanted now, a hit of coke and a chance to win his money back at the tables.

What was that urge? He'd never been much of a gambler and now wanted to win it all back. It was the feeling of hitting a number with a thirty-five to one payout; all those chips slid across the table to reside in front of him, tasty like the gold chocolate Christmas coins. And then another voice inside his head told him otherwise. Tilt. He'd tilted like a pinball machine bumped too hard. He was like that pinball, just a tumbling piece of nothingness, manically popping around the playing field that was Vegas. He guessed that he had an addictive personality.

Fuck it, *Viva Las Vegas*.

He knocked on Kitchen's door, number five, the Jungle Room. Kitchen peeked through the curtain and then opened the door a few inches, the length of the nickel-plated door guard. He said, "Niven, you need to get the fuck out of here."

"Dude, just let me in for a second. I'm flush."

"You don't understand. There are cops and like Mafia guys looking all over for you. Scary motherfuckers. I don't need that kind of heat. Now … Get … The Fuck … Outta … Here." And at "Here," the door closed in his face.

Fucking Kitchen. How much had he spent with the guy over the last year? Like thousands, five thousand maybe. The guy owed him the courtesy of an exchange. Niven wrapped on the window. The curtains parted just an inch, and Niven slapped a hundy against the glass. There, motherfucker. No words were spoken, but a minute later, the door opened with the door guard latched. The hundy slipped into Kitchen's hand, and a second later, a clear plastic baggy was thrown out and onto the stoop. A gram, and Niven picked it up. The door closed, and to the closed door, Niven verbalized what he'd just thought, "Motherfucker."

He turned around, baggy in hand, and walked toward the Oasis office to get a room for a couple nights. That's when he saw it, the Caddy idling out in front of the motel, and he was sure it was that goombah from the jewelry store sitting behind the wheel.

◆ ◆ ◆

He'd go back to Baltimore when he could. His dad had thrown him out for what happened, which was taking a bottle of Percocet from the medicine cabinet of his dying grandmother. He'd been stupid to leave the bottle out on the little desk in his bedroom. Then things got out of hand, his dad accusing him of the theft, Niven creating an obvious lie and saying something he later regretted. "Your mom won't need those pills anymore." His parents kicked him out. He took his graduation money and what clothes he could fit into a duffel and left, driving west until he hit Las Vegas. It seemed so right at the time, a new town on the fringes of America, a place to start all over. But he hadn't started all over, just picked up where he left off.

Time had passed, and maybe the wounds had healed. His mother would want him back, maybe his father too. If he could find a fence for the rough diamonds, he'd go back more honorably, with money in his pocket. Let them see that he *could* make it on his own.

But for now, Niven needed to slip the guy in the Caddy. The back corner of the Oasis funneled into a narrow passage, a back exit that led to an alley. He took that and then walked the alley across Paradise to another alley that went to Sahara. Then he headed west. Skinny had mentioned the flood channels, and that's where he planned to hide until things cooled. He crossed over the Strip, looking both ways for any sign of the Caddy, then past the Bonanza Gift and Souvenir Shop where a year ago he'd bought an inconspicuous tourist T-shirt that said LAS VEGAS NEVADA with crisscrossing palms. It was a shirt he could ditch as soon as he grabbed a purse.

He thought of what he might need in the tunnels and went into the gift shop to find a flashlight and some food. The flashlight had a Space Boy logo and a button above the on/off switch that could be used for sending Secret Codes. The food he bought, candy bars, were all his favorite Reese's Peanut Butter Cups.

Niven was back outside with his plastic shopping bag, walking past the Golden Steer Steakhouse. Then, the Mint casino, where some of the Oasis regulars hung out late at night playing slot machines, and where the Oasis hookers found their tricks when not standing on the corner displaying their outrageously slutty outfits. Then, over the interstate. He knew of an entrance to the flood channels just on the other side, near the railroad tracks. He'd heard about the flooding way over a year ago. He thought it was October. A few bums died. This time of year, rain was like a lie made up to scare little children.

Niven found a cut in the chain-link fence and passed through. The entrance was right there, five-foot-tall rectangular concrete tubes that he knew opened up into a maze of cavernous tunnels that he guessed could protect half the population from a nuclear blast; the others vaporized like plebs at Pompeii. Before walking in, Niven looked around once more at the neon-lit Las Vegas he'd be leaving—the Stratosphere, the Palace Station Casino, and the line of high-rise casinos and condos.

Then he saw it again, the Caddy. He figured the old goombah would not follow him into the underground darkness.

◆ ◆ ◆

The flashlight illuminated only a small cone of the detritus and concrete surrounding him. He swung it back and forth at any real or imagined sound, cockroaches scattering or just a click that might have been the sound of the gravel beneath his sockless loafers.

He heard rustling, like maybe a rat trapped in a cardboard box. His light caught a mound of rags that moved, then above, a winter cap and whiskers. The man smiled, showing a pink tongue and one long tooth. He said, "Got any spare change?" A hand appeared from beneath the rag pile, open with fingers wriggling like fat worms.

Niven reached into the pocket of his WilliWear pants and fished out the change from the Bonanza Gift and Souvenir Shop. He dropped the coins into the man's hand. It wouldn't do well to start making enemies now.

Niven asked, "You know this kid named Skinny?"

"Oh yes. Skinny. Keep walking and find The Rat King."

Then the old bum was gone beneath his rag pile before Niven could ask what a Rat King was or if the Skinny the man referred to was really Skinny or just prophetic-sounding gibberish. He kept walking, and now he could see that the beam from the Space Boy flashlight was beginning to dim and that soon he'd be walking in complete darkness, exposed to lurking bums or some Rat King that might eat him like some bone-in-the-nose cannibal. He turned off the flashlight and used the Secret Code function to pulse a beam at intervals to conserve battery life. He should have thought to buy back-ups. He passed graffiti tags that said UDRGRD, but not all in the same script, so he thought it more of a statement of sorts, like DISCO SUCKS and not an artist's self-important signature. Then he got it, UNDERGROUND. Obviously.

He saw lights ahead and kept his flashlight Secret Code off. He passed small groups of bums clustered around candles and old-timey lanterns, the kind bad guys in Westerns threw into barns to set the hay on fire and incinerate the farm animals within. He asked each group the whereabouts of the Rat King, and all just pointed further down into the tunnels, and he guessed, like a spider web, they joined at a central hub where the predator lay in wait. Great—from the grip of one into the grip of another.

But Skinny said he'd be safe.

He thought he was like a mile in when the tunnel opened up into a huge cavern lit with candles and lanterns like at one of his parents' late-night summer parties back in Baltimore, their garden trellises strung with twinkly lights. He wished he were there now, sipping a G and T on the patio, regaling neighborhood friends with tales of Vegas. He hoped this would become one of the stories with, hopefully, an amusing ending. He imagined a part of what he'd say, "The cavern smelled like wood smoke and piss …"

He asked another bum about the Rat King, and the man pointed toward a shack made of construction throw-offs: bits of plywood, sheets of asphalt shingles, planks of wood, and roofing tar paper.

He spotted Skinny right off, sitting at an upside-down storage bin across from a large man with a graying lumberjack beard and a puffy stocking hat. As Niven walked closer, he could see the tiles of dominoes. He shouted before coming closer, "Skinny!"

Skinny looked up and then stood. "Niven!" He was still dressed in the grubby college boy outfit. "You on the run?"

"I guess." He stood awkwardly above the makeshift game board. Niven knew he looked out of place, his dance club outfit among rags. He added, "Cops and this gangster-looking dude."

"Then you gotta have the diamonds, right?"

Lying, it was just so easy. "No, I told you I never had them. Though I guess these guys think I do."

The lumberjack dude looked up at him, silent, un-introduced. Possibly The Rat King. He didn't look too nimble to be the king of all these rats. It was something else he had.

The dude spoke. "You got 'em. What else you got?"

"What?"

"Y'all lying about the diamonds, and I'll eventually shake them outta you like a Cracker Jack prize. Snatch them right from your bunghole if you got 'em stuffed there. But what else you got?"

Skinny jumped in, Niven guessed to ease the tension. "This is King, also around here, Rat King."

Niven looked into the plastic bag from the Bonanza Souvenir Shop and pulled out two peanut butter cups, holding them out like offerings. Both took a candy bar.

The Rat King said, "I do enjoy buttercups, but what else you got?"

Skinny elaborated, "You holding?"

Caught between a rock and a hard place. This guy was going to take everything, nothing he could do. "I got a gram of coke." He pulled the plastic baggie from his front pocket. The diamonds were in the same pocket and now likely, noticeably, bulging out.

Rat King snatched the coke from his hand. He opened the baggy and dipped a long pinky nail into the powder. He lifted the coke to his nose and made an inhaling snort. He said, "Thanks," now seemingly less threatening. He handed the baggy to Skinny who didn't have a long pinky nail. Niven reached into his back pocket, pulled out his wallet, and handed Skinny a credit card. He dipped the edge into the powder and took a hit. The credit card was linked to his father's account at Chase Manhattan Bank—useless ever since he left home. He thought maybe one day it would work again.

Skinny said, "Nice," then handed the baggie and credit card back to Niven.

Rat King stood and then jumped behind Niven, holding him in a bear hug. So quick and nimble for such a large man. Quick as a rat.

Niven said only, "Fuck," then squirmed uselessly.

Skinny whispered, "Chill, man."

Rat King said, "Let's find those diamonds." He held Niven tightly but was still able to grab his crotch, searching with his fingers. A second later, he found them in his front pocket. "There they are."

Niven tried to think of something to say. *Sorry that he'd lied? Can we split whatever you get for the gems? Can I have them back?* He was underground, maybe a mile from any entrance, probably right under the Strip. He guessed he was safe from the cops and gangsters but at the mercy of the Rat King and his kingdom of bums.

All Niven wanted was to go home to his parents. He just said, "Okay." Okay, King could keep the diamonds.

Rat King said, "They'll be back."

"Back?"

"The cops, the Mafia guys. They've been here before; they'll be here again. Anyone see you enter the tunnels?"

Niven paused. A lie? The pause already told Rat King what he knew. No use. "Yes."

"They'll be here soon, tomorrow, and they'll be ready for a fight."

Niven thought about rats. "Scatter?"

"No, fuck 'em. We'll eat them alive."

Niven was still thinking of cannibals and rats. "Seriously?"

CHAPTER 28 – PETE
Thursday

Pete got the phone call right before he sat down to eat a frozen Totino's pepperoni pizza. That Thursday night, he planned to watch *Top Cops*, *Cheers*, and *L.A. Law*. He had a special interest in *Top Cops*. Over a year ago, an intern from the show called him, looking for someone on the force who'd received a commendation for doing something above and beyond the call of duty. She had that annoying valley girl accent and kept saying the word "like"— "Like, do you know any cop … Like, is there like someone who was involved in a gang shootout …"

Pete definitely had stories above and beyond, but the good ones he couldn't tell. One story involved a local hood and cab driver named Martin Shumate. Before joining Metro, Pete worked security for Benny Binion at his Horseshoe casino downtown. Pete was more of a private investigator than floor muscle, and his job was tracking down deadbeat gamblers, thieves, and rumors of possible thefts. He heard on the street that someone planned to kidnap Binion's son and hold him for ransom. Pete did solid detective work, originally finding out from a hooker that it was Shumate who hatched the scheme. Then he got the full details by threatening one of Shumate's associates.

He went to Benny. His nickname was Cowboy, a big man from Texas who sat smoking a fat Cuban behind a mahogany desk that must have weighed half a ton. Binion was an old criminal and gangster, starting off in the moonshine business and then gravitating to illegal gambling in Dallas. He'd killed people in Texas he shouldn't have, then, after almost being assassinated himself, fled to Las Vegas. He started up another gambling racket, this time supposedly legal. Benny or Cowboy did things his way, which was not to trust the slow grinding of the judicial system. He wanted Shumate dead.

Pete did the killing, one in the chest and one in the head, leaving the body high up on a mountain ridge overlooking the city. The lights of Glitter Gulch were the cabbie's last memory.

None of this could be told to the *Top Cops* intern, but what he did talk about was a commendation he'd received for saving a few tourists at the MGM Grand fire in 1980.

The valley girl asked, "Did you, like, run into a burning building and get, like, burn scars?"

He'd gone to the hospital for smoke inhalation and had a chronic cough and headaches for the next year, but no burns. He said, "No," without telling her about the smoke issues. He never did receive a callback from the show, but enjoyed watching it each Thursday, nonetheless.

The call he received just before turning on that night's episode was from Emmy, who knew never to call him at home except in an extreme emergency.

The old Outfit guy said, "That Niven kid showed up today and hawked Deedee's engagement ring. I bought it back and then followed him to a flood channel entrance."

Deedee. Her death was still fresh in his mind. He'd spend much of that day tracking down Walter Niven Kolchek Jr. through the Sheriff's department. Anyone who wanted to work in Vegas needed a Sheriff's Card, the idea being to keep gangsters and felons out of town. Then, anyone hiring a new employee also needed to let the Sheriff's department know. So it was easy to track the kid down to the TGI Fridays on Flamingo. The General Manager there said the kid was supposed to work that day but never showed or called. Niven, if he ever did show, was terminated.

That kid had killed Deedee, probably the only person he'd loved since his first marriage ended in divorce fifteen years before, his ex-wife taking their two kids back to Duluth in Minnesota. Deedee was his ticket back to some kind of real relationship. He had plans to leave his sparse and depressing apartment and move in with her. They'd talked about it. He remembered that her townhome smelled like perfume with those little bowls of fragrant dried flowers spread around like candy dishes. Man and wife. That was all gone now.

"Why didn't you hold him?"

"Just me, and I'm not the tough guy I once was. Followed the kid. You got the muscle to go down there and get him."

This was personal, like Benny-Binion's-son personal. Personal, like he wouldn't bring the job into this. "You and I go down there. And bring that Swede guy along. Chances are, the kid has the diamonds he's looking for. Bring whatever you can carry, automatics if you got 'em, scatter guns if you don't. Handguns."

"Okay, tomorrow morning?"

"Tonight … And Emmy?"

"Yes?"

"You still got those two lemons?" The M26 grenades, called lemons, were from a job three years ago. They were never used.

A pause. "Yes."

"Bring 'em."

♦ ♦ ♦

A couple of blocks into the channels, the temperature turned cold, like fifty degrees. Pete hated the cold, first growing up in Duluth, where even on a balmy summer day elsewhere in Minnesota, the big lake kept temperatures ten degrees colder. Then, the winters were unbearable with all the snow and the constant wind, which seeped through any cracks in the old house sheathed in asbestos shingles. He remembered the Armistice Day Blizzard in 1940 when he had just turned ten. It had been a mild November day, and his dad and two brothers were out shooting ducks at a camp on Island Lake. First wind, then rain, then snow. The wind uprooted trees, and the snow clogged every road in and out of the city with drifts twenty feet high. The temperature dropped to nearly zero. Pete was hunkered down in the house, but his dad and brothers were exposed out on the lake in a rowboat. They couldn't cross the lake back to the camp and were stuck on the opposite shore for two days, hiding beneath the overturned boat. The youngest of his two brothers, Will, died from the cold.

Then Korea. He'd signed up the day war was declared. He was part of the 7th Infantry Division stuck on the east side of the Chosin Reservoir when over a hundred thousand Chinese invaded. They fled in trucks loaded with dead and wounded. It was Duluth-cold, twenty degrees below zero, with that wind off the reservoir. Pete was part of an MP unit whose only job was to keep the trucks moving. But then the convoy stalled after another attack. The trucks were abandoned, and the dead and wounded were neglectfully left behind. He survived.

After the war, the thought of returning to Duluth and settling down in that cold was tantamount to going back into battle. Then, maybe the guilt of what he'd done, the abandonment of others, and the fact that he survived intact would always follow him in the small Duluth community. He persuaded his then-girlfriend to move somewhere warm. Vegas.

The fifty degrees brought up all those tortured memories. And part of remembering the cold was a hatred. A hatred now focused on one thing, killing Niven.

He'd been in the cold flood tunnels before, and they always creeped him out. They were a separate place, unconnected to aboveground Las Vegas. He could control the aboveground, but the underground was someone else's, and he knew about The Rat King. As far as he or Metro cared, The Rat King could have it—the cold and filth and zombie bums who lived there. They could come out and beg for coins, then get the fuck out of sight. But they weren't supposed to cause problems, and The Rat King had to know that harboring the kid who killed Deedee, robbed a nightclub, and stole diamonds would be a problem. Why The Rat King would do it was a mystery, and maybe once confronted, he'd hand over the kid. No questions. But it could go either way. The three of them were armed to the teeth and ready for any eventuality.

Pete carried a flashlight with a battery the size of a lunchbox and a headlight the size of a car's. Slung from his shoulder was a fully automatic M16 rifle, and stuffed into the cargo pockets of his black dungarees were three twenty-round magazines. His Smith & Wesson 38 Special was holstered near his left armpit and hidden behind his tan Members Only jacket. He didn't think he'd need the 38, but it went with his outfit like socks and boxer shorts. Emmy carried a pump-action shotgun that held five shells. His suit pockets bulged with more shells and the two grenades. Swede, the weird fucker, had a second pump-action shotgun, this one sawed off.

They had no plan, or the plan was simple—demand that Niven be handed over along with the diamonds. If The Rat King refused, take him.

The bums knew they were coming, a few scurrying ahead to relay the intrusion. They passed the same graffiti, UDRGRD, then another message, PIGS DIE. Swede chambered a round, then Pete and Emmy did the same. The smell was there—smoke and piss. The way these people lived…

The channel tunnel opened up and ahead was a lit chamber the size of a basketball court. Pete had never seen the Rat King but knew him to be large with a graying beard. And there he was, posing in front of a tar-paper shack with a Colt automatic held at his side. They walked closer, and The Rat King smiled, teeth the size of pumpkin seeds and splayed out like headstones. Weird eyes. The kid he knew to be Skinny stood just off to the side, and next to him was Walter Niven Kolchek.

The Rat King spoke first. "What have y'all come for?"

Pete motioned his M16 toward Niven. "Him and the diamonds, then we'll leave."

"Why should I do something like that? Everyone here is under my protection. You see, that's all I can offer these people who you kick around on the surface. Just yesterday, my good buddy here," and The Rat King pointed at a filthy rag of a man who looked eighty, though Pete figured from the man's thick hands and the way he stood that he was not much older than forty. That man's mouth contorted into a toothless grin.

The Rat King continued, "His name, which no one above in the light would ever ask, is Joseph Kerr—Joker. Yesterday, Joker was attacked by three drunk college boys, kicked, mocked, and then robbed. These kids stole the small plastic cup that contained maybe twenty dollars in coins." The man, Joker, turned his head to show a purplish swollen eye, dried blood still staining his cheek. "Joker didn't bother reporting the assault; a police report that would go completely ignored by y'all. And we could not take our revenge, or there would be Metro consequences. No, we take your abuse on the streets. But not here. This is our place, and if I let one be taken, everyone could be taken, and then what use do they have for me?"

Pete barely paid attention to the big man's rant and couldn't have cared less about Joker's swollen eye and their troubles on the street—just one more sad story any cop in Vegas witnessed every day.

What he did care about and pay attention to was the way the kid, Niven, stood behind The Rat King, looking all casual and cocky, like he was protected, like Pete couldn't touch him. Then the kid took a bite of what looked to be a peanut butter cup, just a rabbit nibble at the chocolate edge. It pissed him off, then enraged him—the indifference and arrogance.

Pete lifted his M16. The selector level was set to SEMI.

The first bullet caught the kid in the shoulder and spun him to the ground. The second bullet hit the spot where the edge of the peanut butter cup had, a split second before, been pressed against the kid's teeth.

CHAPTER 29 – SKINNY
That Same Thursday

Skinny was dope-high when he witnessed Niven twist and then fall to the concrete floor of the flood channel. It reminded him of that night at Tramps, the Animal House song, *Shout*. He'd been so lost in the moment—dancing, jumping, twisting, and then, *Get a little bit softer now, get a little bit softer now*, so that he was squirming on the floor like a butterfly trying to emerge from its chrysalis. Niven was squirming. He looked up, stunned, just as the second bullet hit him in the mouth. Skinny assumed it hit there because what he actually saw was the flesh ripped from the side of his face. Beautiful in a way, the explosion of red like a small fireworks show. He smiled.

Then, slow motion. King lifted the black handgun and, with his arm outstretched, pointed. The bang, louder than the rifle shots that downed Niven. The cop doubled over, dropping the rifle as he hit the pavement. How did he know it was a cop? They all stood funny, all stiff posture, like they knew everyone was watching them for some sign of trouble or whatever. But they gave nothing away, except the way they stood, so that you knew they were cops and would give you a beating if you didn't do exactly as they said. The cop went down and twisted up like a pretzel, then reached inside his Members Only jacket for his hidden piece. Undercover cop.

Another bang, now way louder, this time from the tall dude dressed in a suit with a smart tie. Bleached blond hair. Skinny knew a sawed-off shotgun from a million TV shows and movies. He didn't really know why they bothered to shorten the thing, other than it fit better when hidden under an overcoat. That guy in the movie *Bullet* with Steve McQueen—the hitman in the muscle car—had a sawed-off under his tan raincoat. Scary cool. King was knocked back like he'd been hit by a truck. King was kind and gentle. Considerate in a way, almost fatherly, though what would Skinny know about fatherly?

Hide, he should hide, but he just stood there watching as the tall man's smoking gun turned toward Joker with the busted eye. Joker once said he'd worked on ships and had sailed around the world five times. Just imagine that—leaving under the Golden Gate Bridge in San Francisco, seeing the volcanoes of Hawaii, sushi in Japan, millions of Chinamen, Africans with bare tits, Mexican hookers, then what? All Joker had to show for his travels were stupid tattoos. One showed an anchor wrapped in a red ribbon with the words, LET THE GENTLE ROCKING OF THE OCEAN CARRY YOU AWAY. That's when he heard it, the ocean, like the faint sound from a seashell held close to his ear. When was that? Probably in school when he was itty-bitty. Then, the blast, and Joker was dead inside his shroud of old rags that held in the blood and gore like a sandwich in wax paper.

He watched as the tall dude's shotgun barrel swung back toward *him*. He stood there like an idiot when his core animal-self wanted to run or hide. He still wore his college boy outfit—the alligator shirt and khaki pants that had been a good money maker out on the Strip. Over the preppy shit he wore a long olive-green coat that looked like one from a World War II movie. The coat smelled like smoke and piss, like everything Underground. In a way, the smell was comforting, like a home-cooked meal. He closed his eyes right before the bang and waited for the explosion of flesh, his flesh. In that split millisecond, time crawled like a caterpillar. And he wondered what it would feel like to explode from within, and would it hurt, or would it just send him into a different world, a different body that would rise above the world and look down on all that was, all the bullshit his life once was? A butterfly, he guessed, that would dance in the wind and just fly free and know that it was above it all, resolved to be unresolved. But he didn't explode after the bang, and he wasn't set free.

He opened his eyes.

The tall dude with the hair was on the damp concrete floor, the sawed-off shotgun still clutched in his fingers which tried to move but couldn't. The dude squirmed to the side but couldn't hold onto the shotgun, and he looked up at Emmy, the Chicago Outfit guy from the jewelry store on Sahara. Emmy, but everyone on the street called him Nuts. He watched as Nuts moved the barrel of his shotgun so that it pointed at the face of the tall dude. The two were so close, Nuts could have spit and hit him in the eye. Bang. The head and hair were gone in a spray of flesh and red blood. Like fireworks.

He heard the noise again, the sound of the ocean in a seashell. Louder now so that it drowned out the shouts of the other guys who had moved closer to take their vengeance on the only intruder left standing, Emmy, Nuts, who now walked backward in the direction he'd come. From his pocket, Nuts pulled out something the size of a tennis ball, held it tight, and then pulled a small ring with a dangling pin. Everyone knew what a hand grenade was from all those war movies, and everyone stepped back. Nuts dropped the grenade at his feet and then ran in the direction he'd come. The guys who'd moved in now moved back. Explosion. The blast to his ears felt like being slapped, and he knew what it was to be slapped. Then ringing, but he could still hear through the ringing, and the sound of the blast was replaced by the seashell sound that overwhelmed it like a curtain shutting out light.

The flood started—just a trickle of water at first that sent them scurrying. When the trickle became a gush, they all ran.

Others were around him as the water level climbed to his ankles. He'd run about a block from the shack when the water rushed around his knees and slowed him to one careful step after another. The woman who handed out the rags and costumes lost her footing and was swept past him. King called her Rags, and Skinny had seen she had no teeth—her lips collapsed around pink gums that moved like a mouthful of Dubble Bubble. He'd never asked her where she was from, and the woman had few words for him. She disappeared in the rush of water and blended in with the garbage washed from the streets aboveground. Other bodies passed him, some struggling, some not. The water crept past his knees, and he became afraid that one off-step would send him into the current with the others. Then a gush like a wave hit him thigh-high, and he was thrown into the water, now moving roller coaster fast.

He thrashed to keep his head above water.

The channel diverted, and Skinny was swept to the right, where he knew it would eventually spill into the desert on the far side of the interstate. But that was a mile away, and the water continued to rise. Then, he could see a man on the rungs of a rebar ladder that rose to a street-level manhole cover. Closer, the man was Nuts. He was looking upstream. Skinny swam as best he could to get closer to the ladder. He held out his hand at the last moment, trying to grab a steel rung. But it was Emmy's hand he found, and Emmy who pulled him up onto the ladder.

He stood two rungs above him, Skinny's feet still beneath water.

He yelled down, "Where are the diamonds?"

One quick release of fingers, and Skinny knew he'd be swept back into the flood. He didn't care about the diamonds. The fact was, he'd completely forgotten about the diamonds until Niven showed up. Then King had quickly found them. "King has them."

"Who's King?"

"Rat King. He had them in his coat pocket." King was probably dead now and being swept toward the desert.

Skinny was pulled further up so that he could stand on the ladder and hold onto the rungs. Emmy climbed ahead to the manhole cover.

He yelled, "Get up here and help."

Skinny climbed until both were side-by-side, their heads nearly touching the round cast-iron manhole cover. Both pushed, and the heavy cover moved just an inch, then settled back. Emmy climbed up another rung and now had his shoulder against the cast iron. Skinny moved up too, their faces so close that Emmy's hard breathing hit his cheeks like a hot wind.

Emmy said, "One, two, three," and then both pushed with all their strength. The manhole cover moved up, and they pushed an edge over the ring that had held it in place. Light streamed through the crack. Slowly, they inched the cover to the side so they could climb through.

Above, any clouds that might have darkened the sky and let loose the rain that flooded the tunnels were now gone. Just sunlight. And in some strange way, Skinny had the feeling that he'd been reborn.

CHAPTER 30 – EMMY
Friday

That Skinny ran off as soon as they were up top. Emmy had worn his nice suede desert shoes into the tunnel. Now, one was gone, and the other was destroyed. He slipped off the destroyed shoe and started walking in his socked feet toward Flamingo Road. He continued up and over the Interstate to where his Cadillac was parked, near where the underground flood channel spilled into an open cement wash that ran clear out of town to what he guessed was some kind of reservoir. He didn't know; he'd never been that far west.

Three bodies were scattered at the exit to the flood channel tunnel. Emmy watched as two firemen on ropes rappelled down the twenty-foot wall and checked pulses. One at a time, the bodies were secured in harnesses and pulled up and over the edge to where they were examined by cops. He recognized the bum Joseph or Joker by his swollen eye and Niven by his lack of a face altogether. He wondered what the cops would make of that.

Pete drifted out, a fireman catching him by the arm and

again checking for any sign of life. Pete was harnessed and hauled up. One cop instantly recognized the body, making a special call on his handheld radio. Another covered Pete's white and puckered face with a coarse gray blanket from the trunk of a squad car—cops had to think of all eventualities.

Other bodies floated out. Emmy waited until the firemen fished out each one, three more. He waited until the water receded, and it was apparent that no more would emerge. The sun had dried the clothes on his body. He did not see Swede or the Rat King. Part of him still wanted those diamonds back, and he still had connections with Metro despite the absence of Detective Pete Askoff.

Emmy didn't know how he felt about Pete's death. The detective had hounded him from the first month he'd set foot in Vegas, extracting payments that allowed Emmy to keep The Gold Rush open, then strong-arming him to do side jobs. But they'd become closer over the years, sometimes taking coffee together and talking about personal stuff. Pete had talked about Deedee, and Emmy was sad about how that turned out. He guessed, for now, he was out from under. Maybe someone else would nose around for the extortion, but he didn't know who, and Metro had changed over time. Bad cops and Outfit guys were becoming a thing of the past. Or so he thought.

Emmy walked back to the Caddy and drove further west. He pulled over every few blocks to see if other bodies had washed up on the spillway edges. A mile further, he saw the flashing lights of another fire crew and stopped to see them beside two retrieved bodies. Their faces were covered, but Emmy saw that one was tall and wore dark slacks from a men's suit. Swede, for sure. Instead of sadness, Emmy felt relief. Part of his violent past was behind him, and good riddance. The other body was much smaller, Emmy thought a woman. He drove on until he found the end. A grating of crisscrossed rebar sieved the water coming from the spillway before it splashed out onto the open desert of the reservoir. No bodies were caught in the grating, and the water had already soaked into the dirt, revealing nothing.

The Rat King was nowhere to be found.

◆ ◆ ◆

He didn't know what he was waiting for as he sat with his coffee and read the *Review-Journal*. He guessed he wanted to know if the Rat King was found. He wanted to read in black and white copy that Swede and Pete were both dead; he wanted to know what that would mean. The headline on the front page of the Local section read:

Channel Flooding Kills Homeless

Fourteen bodies washed from the flood channels after Thursday's rain in what Mayor Ron Lurie called, "Sad, a shame, an outright preventable loss of human life." Eight of the bodies were found near Flamingo and Interstate 15, where the underground channels emerge into the South Spring Valley Wash. The bodies have yet to be identified.

Sheriff John Moran, who was at the scene where the eight bodies were found, said, "The homeless have little or no identification. It will take some time to find out who these unfortunate people were. It's as though they hardly existed." Three bodies were found further down the South Spring Valley Wash, and three more were found on a search deep into the tunnels of the flood channels. Sheriff Moran added, "This is a warning to anyone who seeks shelter underground. Though we live in a desert climate, these floods do happen." When asked what could be done to prevent such a disaster, Sheriff Moran said, "I plan to approach the City Council with a request for warning signs."

The supporting black and white photo showed the channel exits and flooding water but no bodies. Emmy guessed it was a lazy stock photo shot a year or three before.

He stayed at home that day after driving Tanya to school. She now wore only black. Overall, he thought her appearance better than the cheerleader, hooker, hippy, and preppy outfits she'd worn in the past. He could live with black. He stayed home again the next day and wondered what he would do with The Gold Rush. On Sahara, near the Strip and Naked City, the shop would never be anything but a place to buy and sell cheap chains and rings, much of it stolen. And without Pete to keep the heat off, the beat cops would be down on him like dogs on a stray cat. He could sell the business—he owned it outright— but knew the value was only in what little inventory he had, and that value was based on wholesale prices. Fuck it, he'd run a going-out-of-business sale. Then maybe he'd get a regular job. He heard that other people just worked regular jobs for a living. It had to be less hassle.

Two days later, he read another headline:

Detective Dies in Channel Flooding

One of the sixteen victims of last week's channel flooding has now been identified as Detective Peter Askoff of the Las Vegas Metropolitan Police Department. In addition to injuries sustained during the flood, Detective Askoff had gunshot wounds to his abdomen.

Asked about the eventual cause of death, Sheriff John Moran said at his press conference, "The cause has yet to be determined." Asked why the detective was down in the tunnels in the first place, Moran tersely replied, "His job." Asked what his job was down in the tunnels, Moran said, "We do not discuss ongoing police investigations."

The article went on to list others identified in the flood. One was Karol Bergstrom, aka The Swede, from Chicago, and another was Walter Niven Kolchek Jr., formerly a waiter at TGI Fridays on Flamingo. The article did not mention their gunshot wounds, and no one named King was listed—if that was, in fact, his real name.

Tanya was dropped off that afternoon by the kid Cory, riding again on the back of his minibike. She wasn't wearing a helmet, and, besides being unsafe, it was against the law. Her black outfit looked skintight, and on her feet were black slippers like ballerina shoes, about as good against the bike's sprocket and chain as banana peels. Emmy stood inside the door when she walked in. She stopped and looked up—he guessed, expecting a tongue-lashing.

What could he do? He remembered his own mom standing at the door late one night after he'd been out with the neighborhood hoodlums. She asked, "Where have you been?" He spared her the details, "Over at Mancini's having a soda." They had an unwritten understanding—she'd play the concerned mom, and he'd play the good son.

Tanya was smart. Smarter than any report card could show him. If she wanted to play whatever she was playing now, beatnik or ballerina, then so be it. He'd done what he could as a stepfather, more than most. The more he pushed, the more she'd just be pushed away. You think you have control, but what it really amounts to is betting against the house.

He just said, "So, you like this kid Cory?"

She looked at him, maybe wondering what the new angle was. "He's trying to be a stand-up comedian. I'm going to watch him in a couple of weeks at Tramps nightclub."

"What, like Eddie Murphy?" He'd seen his stand-up routine on TV somewhere. Funny but disturbing when it came to sex.

"More like George Carlin." Her arms had been folded across her chest, but now each hand retreated into the pockets of her tight black jeans.

"Okay if I come?" He thought, *Why not make her squirm a little?*

She called his bluff. "Sure, that would be nice."

"Okay." Then he asked again, "So you like this kid, Cory?"

She tipped her head sideways, and then the tip of her tongue just barely pierced her lips, like it was the first time she'd thought about it one way or another. "Yeah, and he's funny. You'll see."

The next day, another headline:

Gun Fight in the Flood Channels Leaves Four Dead

Unnamed sources, survivors of the channel flooding, reported a gun battle prior to the rising waters. Detective Peter Askoff is said to have gunned down the former TGI Fridays employee, Walter Niven Kolchek Jr., who was said to be unarmed. Detective Askoff was then shot by a man survivors referred to as The Rat King. Following that exchange, a man, described as tall and wearing a dark suit, shot The Rat King. The tall man has since been identified as Karol Bergstrom, aka The Swede, from Chicago, Illinois. Mr. Bergstrom then turned his gun on an inhabitant of the channels, Joseph Kerr, a homeless man often seen on Las Vegas Boulevard panhandling for change. Another man, described as being of medium height with black hair, then shot and killed Mr. Bergstrom. The bodies of Mr. Kolchek Jr., Detective Askoff, Mr. Bergstrom, and Mr. Kerr were all recovered in the flood waters. The black-haired man along with the man referred to as The Rat King have yet to be identified or located.

Asked why the Detective shot down an unarmed former employee of TGI Fridays, Sheriff John Moran replied, "Detective Askoff has a long and distinguished career with the LVMPD, and when the truth comes out, Pete Askoff will be shown to be a true hero of the department." Asked about the tunnel resident referred to as The Rat King, Sheriff Moran replied, "I have no idea who this man is, and we have not found a body that matches his description." He added, "In all honesty, I'm not sure he existed at all, and the survivor stories of homeless men living in the flood channels are not to be trusted."

One week after the flood, Emmy returned to The Gold Rush and opened the doors. The place now had a dusty look to it, like he'd been gone a year or more. Nothing had changed after he took it over from his murdered cousin ten years before. On the walls still hung a few watercolor paintings. One showed two old-timey guys in floppy felt hats sitting on their haunches and panning for gold. Another showed a saloon scene of three women high-stepping in frilly dresses, revealing the skin of their knees and calves to the whooping and hollering miners. He guessed he'd never really looked at the paintings, all part of the place like windows and electrical outlets. The cheap jewelry was left out in the display cases, and the few good pieces were locked in the safe.

He'd take the safe with him when he closed the place, bolt it to the concrete pad of the ranch house, which he never planned to sell. All in all, a good place to live out his remaining years. He'd keep Tanya's room just the way it was left when she finally moved out and hopefully married. If it was that Cory kid, so be it. Keep the big place around for his grandchildren to visit.

The eight boxes of Liberace's porcelain figurines were neatly stacked in the back corner by the rear exit where he and Karol had left them ten days before. The psychopath wouldn't have gone through all the trouble if the things weren't worth a fortune. Emmy would put them on a high shelf in his garage and wait until the figurines were all but forgotten, then sell them to collectors through a trade magazine. There had to be one, like *Antique Week* or *Old Lady Collectibles Today*. It could be a nice side income to supplement what would likely be shitty working-for-the-man wages.

Emmy sat in his cracked vinyl office chair and thought about what it would take for a going-out-of-business sale. A big outdoor banner for sure, and then maybe an ad in the *Journal*. Normally, little of the merchandise was marked. A guy or gal would come through the door and just ask, "How much for this?" and Emmy would come up with a price. He knew the value of the stuff, like he knew where to wipe his ass. But if he was going to do the sale, pricing had to be marked and then marked down so they'd know the savings. And that was a huge hassle.

Emmy remembered the other jewelry store that bought anything gold by the ounce. He knew the stuff he sold was worth only slightly more than its value as melted-down bullion. The price of gold was going up. That was it, put all the shit in one big bucket and hold onto it. He didn't need the cash right then, and gold investing was as good as the stock market. He'd tell his landlord he was moving out—they hadn't had a real signed lease in years. It seemed too simple. But maybe that's what he'd missed all these years while trying to steal and hustle for a few bucks. Maybe those straight law-abiding motherfuckers had it right the whole time. Get a job, cash your paycheck, watch sitcoms, play with grandkids, and sleep soundly.

It might not be that simple, but it was definitely simpler.

CHAPTER 31 – CORY
Monday, Two Weeks Later

Cory sat at a cocktail table near the makeshift stage with Gabby and the three other comedians hired for the show that night. He sat listening to their banter as they passed the time before going on stage. One guy described a tour he took that day of Hoover Dam, standing below the massive concrete wall and looking up. He had a punchline, "Sure puts your dick into perspective." They all laughed. Cory didn't contribute a word, and no one needled him with questions. He guessed they knew he was nervous and didn't want to give the newbie any grief. He guessed they also didn't consider him part of the group. He wasn't paid to be there, didn't work the circuit, and was probably just some dumb local kid thrown a favor, like the owner's son, or he knew Steve Wynn, or had given Gabby a blow job. Whatever they thought or assumed, he was ignored.

He'd seen Tanya come through the club's front doors wearing black, her face done up with heavy dark mascara and contrasting red lipstick, the camera around her neck like an accessory to her new costume—if this *was* just another costume. Trailing behind was the stepdad, Emmy. Threw him off—why the guy was there. The two had never acted as though they maintained a father-daughter relationship, whatever that might be. To Cory, the relationship seemed more like cop and convict. Then, what bothered him more was that some of his material was about Tanya. He thought she would think it funny and cool and possibly be impressed. The stepdad might just be pissed. And it wasn't as though Cory had a margin of trust with this guy to begin with. Then he wondered if fathers knew, or assumed, that their late-teen daughters were fucking the guys they went out with. Or did they just do an ostrich routine, stick their heads in the sand?

Finally, Gabby took the stage and introduced the line-up for the show, letting everyone know that a local boy, an employee of Tramps, would come on first. He said, "Let's give a big, warm Tramps welcome to Cory Fresh."

Hand clapping and a few shouts as he walked up the two stairs to the stage. He stood before the microphone that pointed to a spot just above his nose. He'd seen people adjust the mic stand but hadn't a clue how it was actually done. Gabby walked back on stage and took control. "I can make it go up, and I can make it go down," which was a crass Gabby joke that got a laugh. Cory smiled nervously, stood silent for an uncomfortable three seconds, then began.

He looked over at Gabby and said, "Seriously?" That got a laugh.

"Okay, so I'm still a high school student, all of seventeen years old. Of course, like all high schoolers, I hate school, and really, all I want to do is get laid. For real. Like, I was in social studies class a couple weeks ago listening to blah, blah, blah, Red Coats and Indians, and muskets, and I'm like half asleep. Then I notice this girl two desks in front turn around to look at me. She turns around twice, and I'm thinking maybe she has a crush on me. Seriously. I know the girl; her name is something like "banana," maybe Briana or Hannah. She's goth, all dressed in black with these pants with enough zippers to close the fly on Paul Bunyan's trousers. But she's definitely hot. She turns around a third time, and now she has one of those clear BIC pens in her mouth, though I can see there's, like, no ballpoint to it. She quickly spits into the thing, and a little wad of chewed notebook paper shoots out. Hits me right in the face. A spitball. Seriously, a spitball like some twelve-year-old delinquent. Hit's me right below my eye and sticks there. She turns around just as quickly, and I peel the spitball off my face, a gob of her saliva dripping down to my lips. Then I taste it. And now I imagine a whole mouthful. Then, like, I get a hard on. Seriously. Oh, right, her name's Savannah. Rhymes with banana."

He heard laughter from the fifty or so people who sat in the darkness of the club. He heard the laughter but couldn't see who. Hopefully, Tanya and her Stepdad.

Cory continued. "Now Savannah—and everyone calls her Vana—is kind of strange; she'd have to be to go out with the likes of me. When we first met, like I said, she was goth. She acted all dark and mysterious and talked about suicide and eating bat meat. Kinda creepy, but we got along. Then, a week later, she changes costumes and is now all preppy. She acts all coquettish. I know, I had to look that word up myself. 'Behaving in such a way to suggest playful sexual attraction.' Now, instead of suicide, she's into bad boys, maybe thinking *I'm* a bad boy. She asks me all these questions about whether I've ever 'done it' before and if I have a cool motorcycle. Well, fuck me! Turns out I do have a motorcycle, this dirtbike, and though it's not exactly a chopper with ape-hanger handlebars, it's passable to satisfy this girl's bad boy fantasy. So, we skip school one Friday afternoon and drive down to Lake Mead, where I know of this private beach where we can show each other our privates. I come back with a string of hickeys on my neck like I'd just had it out with Dracula. Seriously.

"But then the next week, Vana changes costumes again. This time, she's a cheerleader all dressed up in one of those pleated skirts and a V-neck shirt with the logo of some other school's mascot—I assume that's all she could find at the Goodwill. And guess what? Turns out cheerleaders like jocks, and she starts saddling up to all the football players and wrestlers. So I'm out. I'm a total jock failure, so I'm definitely out. She won't talk to me or acknowledge me in any way. Totally ghosted. I know, boo hoo hoo.

"But wait! This story is not over yet. I figure there's always next week or the week after. I'm thinking hot-sexy nerd with glasses who wants to go to my place and study biology. Or hot-sexy hippy chick that wants to get back on my dirtbike, drive out to Lake Mead again, get high, and swap saliva. Or a hot-sexy-playful dropout who wants to hit me in the mouth again with a juicy spitball. So, what I'm saying here is that there's still hope. Seriously, I think there's still hope. In the meantime, it's just me, my imagination, and my hand."

Big laugh, and he paused to set up his second bit.

"So I work at this nightclub here, you know, called Tramps. My job is to carry around one of those little brooms and dust pans with the long handle, like something an old lady would use to pick up dog poop from the gutter. Lots of people come through here, drunk or otherwise, and I see some strange shit. Last week, I was standing next to the bar, the one right behind me, drinking a Coke and watching the customers. One guy was dressed really nicely in a suit and tie, with his hair combed perfectly across his scalp. Like the Gordon Gekko creep in Wall Street. He was alone and not talking to anyone. Then I notice his hand slowly rise from beneath the bar top and move to his chin. He nonchalantly scratches his chin, then ever so casually moves in for a nose pick. He must have known there was a nugget because it didn't take long for him to scrape it out. But then here's the really disgusting part. He ate it. Seriously!

"But actually, the best part of my job is picking up what people drop and lose. Of course, it's mostly coins and dollar bills that embellish my below-the-poverty-line wages. But I also find little vials of cocaine, which I can turn around and sell to the bartenders. A week ago, I found not only an open condom wrapper but the used condom itself. And you probably want to know if it's possible to fornicate right here on the dance floor? Yes. I've seen it done. Helps if the people are packed together like sardines in a can; a casual penetration can then go relatively unnoticed.

"But back to sweeping shit up. Just the other day, I found a little velvet pouch. It was right after the DJ had played that *Animal House* song, "Shout," where everyone is jumping up and then squirming on the ground, humping the dance floor. That song is a gold mine with everything flying from the dancer's pockets. I take the velvet pouch into the back and look inside. Diamonds. I kid you not. A sack full of uncut diamonds. I'm rich, right?"

"So the manager here is, or was, an older woman named Deedee. I gave her the sack of diamonds so she could sell them and cut me in on the cash—assuming no one showed up to make a claim. It's an arrangement we'd made. So she puts the diamonds in the safe with the intention of calling her connection the following week. The next Tuesday, she's opening up the club and walks in on a robbery as it's taking place—the safe open, with money and diamonds in hand. The robber shoots her dead. Now I realize nothing in this particular part of my story is on any level funny. But it's true. Seriously.

"Of course, those diamonds that I found were worth thousands. I don't know how many thousands, but I bet enough to fulfill an expensive fantasy. Okay, question, what would some of you guys do?"

Cory held his hand up to shield the spotlight so that he could see the crowd. One guy said, "A three-some." The crowd laughed.

Cory asked, "Is that your wife or girlfriend next to you? What does she think about bringing another woman into your bedroom?"

A laugh, and he could see the girl shake her head, "How about another man?" Another laugh.

"I'm sure Gabby is up for it." Laughs.

Then Cory asked, "How many of you idiots would buy a Ferrari?"

Clapping, then someone said, "Lamborghini."

Corry jumped in. "You know what I'd buy? A hot tub. No, seriously. I'd put a big hot tub right in the middle of my one-room apartment. I'd watch TV in that thing, eat frozen pizza, and maybe do some laundry. I really think that would be cool. Then I'd ask Vana if she wanted to come over to my place and take a hot tub. And if she did, guess what? She'd have to strip down to a small bikini or, better yet, get fully naked. That hot tub would for sure get me laid. Then afterward, we could sit there, eat pizza, and watch *Two's Company*.

"But getting back to what I was saying—someone lost those diamonds, and I'm guessing that someone would do anything to get them back.

"See this pinky finger here? Look closely; the end of my little pinky is gone. The way that happened, the someone who wanted those diamonds back, found me. This guy was a true freak. Way over six feet tall, bleached-blond hair pasted to his head in that very unfashionable wet look, dark suit, white shirt, and tie. This guy was the spitting image of Lurch on that *Addams Family* show, a slightly more presentable Frankenstein. The guy followed me home from Tramps after my shift ended at five in the morning, came into my tidy apartment, and then proceeded to ask questions. Now, I was more than happy to answer all his questions to the best of my knowledge, but he didn't give me the chance. He just slipped my little pinky finger through his moist lips and then bit down hard. I know, I know. Then he let me spill the beans, of which there were few. The last thing he asked was if I knew a guy named Filbert. I'm a smartass by trade, and all I know about Filberts is that they're nuts, and that's what I said, 'I know a nut named Filbert.' Lurch actually smiled. Not quite a laugh, but I got a smile out of this freak. Best you could do with that audience. Then he left, my pinky finger lying there on the floor where he'd spit it out. Dead serious.

"So I go to the emergency room and tell the doctor there that I lost my fingertip in a motorcycle accident. I'm perceived as a dumb kid, so he found it entirely plausible. But then what he said cracked me up. He said I should have kept the end of my finger, wrapped it in cellophane, and put it on ice—that he could've sewn it back on. And I'm thinking that the end of my pinky is about as useful as a limp dick. I said, 'Not sure I'd need it.' Then *he* said, 'It would for sure throw off my golf swing.' Seriously, he said that.

"Now about this guy, Filbert. Heard about him from Harvey Swarthy on KTNV Action News the other week.

Turns out he was one of the guys shot and killed in the flood channels during the shootout you all probably heard about. There are over three hundred miles of tunnels under the city that keep us dry when we get hit with a percentage of the four annual inches this desert town collects. From what I've heard, these tunnels are, in reality, one big homeless shelter, the perfect place for the indigent to be out of sight, out of mind. The city planners who devised these elaborate plans plan to build another two hundred miles of homeless shelter. I know Vegas has flooded before, but come on, seriously, we get four inches of rain per year. Seattle gets *forty*. *They* need tunnels.

"But I'm getting off track. I assume this Filbert guy stole the diamonds out of the safe that's right behind all of you and then shot poor Deedee. Harvey Swarthy on KTNV Action News said nothing about diamonds. So here's what I think. Filbert didn't have the diamonds when he was shot; that someone in the tunnels took the stones from him. Now I'm going to find them—I have as much claim as anyone. Seriously, finders keepers.

"I have zero idea how this story ends; it's what's called a cliff-hanger. Hopefully, Gabby here will have me back again to let you know how it turns out.

"Okay, I know my routine ended on a seriously serious note, so I'll provide some amusing facts. Did you know that Las Vegas is the brightest spot on Earth? Brighter than Times Square or Hong Kong. It'll be the first place an alien aims for when descending through our atmosphere, drawn here to plug in and troll for their sex-periments. Then, did you know that in Las Vegas, we have over three hundred weddings per day? Graceland Wedding Chapel is the most popular, with a cast of fifteen rotating Elvis's to bless the consummation. And for another fifty each, five will watch and rate your performance.

Finally, there are more than one hundred thousand hotel rooms in Las Vegas, and if every honest politician in the country decided to stay here, there'd still be a hundred thousand left.

"Seriously, folks, thank you. That's all I got."

Applause. A two-fingered whistle. Someone shouted, "Seriously?" More laughs.

And what did that feel like? An adrenaline rush for sure, unlike any before. He'd done something he'd wanted to do for a long time—wanted to do for a living. He now felt part of a group, like he'd arrived, fit in like he guessed an artist selling their first painting, or some race car driver advancing to the Mint 500.

Then it was over, and the other comedians took the stage. Before Gabby went up and finished the show, he whispered to Cory, "You got it, kid." Then added, "But you went over your fifteen minutes."

Cory whispered back, "Sorry," then sat silently through the rest of the show. He waited until the end when Tanya walked up from the back of the room.

She kissed him on the mouth. Behind her was the stepdad, Emmy, looking around like he didn't want to witness all the kissing business. Cory smiled at Tanya, who smiled back. He then focused on the red of her lipstick. He imagined the red smeared over his mouth, and instinctively wiped it with his shirt sleeve.

She said, "You were great."

His smile widened, stretched, almost painfully. "Thanks." He added, "Didn't expect you to be here. Sorry about the bit about us. Thought it was funny, but maybe I should have asked your permission. And I really didn't expect you to bring your stepdad."

The stepdad, Emmy, stepped forward. Cory had always seen him in a suit, but now he wore jeans, an open-collared shirt, and a Cubs baseball cap. And the baseball cap—about as natural on this guy as earrings. Cory's first thought was that the stepdad was in disguise, a costume, maybe taking after his stepdaughter.

Emmy said, "Nice routine."

"Thanks." It was all he could think to say, not wanting to step into uncomfortable territory.

The stepdad tipped up the baseball cap visor and gave Cory a look, more quizzical than threatening. "So, you think you know where those diamonds are?"

He shirked. "I don't know. Just part of the bit, I guess. Probably buried under a couple feet of washed-away desert sand and garbage."

Tanya stood back and began taking photos. It made him uncomfortable, and he unconsciously squinted and turned his head.

Emmy turned his back to Tanya and the camera. He said directly to Cory, "You really want to go around telling crowds of people how you screwed my stepdaughter?"

There it was, and it took him by surprise. "I didn't use her name."

"I know who you were talking about, and that's all that matters."

Tanya had stopped taking photos but stood a few feet away, smiling. He guessed she couldn't hear the actual words and was just pleased that the two men in her life were speaking. And what did it really matter? Lives were there to be lived in the open. Like stars and galaxies, Cory wanted to be recognized and seen. He wasn't going to live like a bum in the flood tunnels. And fuck it if the stepdad couldn't take a joke. "She could do worse, probably has. If you got a chastity belt, you'd better strap it on and throw away the key."

Emmy looked up like he'd been slapped. Cory could see this was the kind of man who could literally kill. But then something changed, some kind of epiphany, and the lines around his jaw noticeably relaxed. Then his arm came up with an open hand, and in slow motion, the stepdad gave Cory a gentle slap. He stood there, nervous, expecting anything. Emmy smiled and said, "Never do that to her hard. Don't break her heart, though I realize that might be impossible. Don't get her pregnant. And let her be herself … like you even have a say."

Cory relaxed, "Save it for the wedding toast."

Emmy laughed.

Tanya stepped over then. "What are you bozos laughing about?"

Emmy said, "I guess I just gave away the bride."

Tanya did that look, wide eyes and a tight-lipped smile, "Not so fast … Nuts."

CHAPTER 32 – TANYA
September, Three Months Later

What did she see? A middle-aged woman sitting at a bus stop with her small pug dog. She wore a flip hairdo from the sixties, silver pumps that shimmered under the bright sunlight, a red dress that flared at the knees, and black cat-eye sunglasses with diamond rhinestones on the hinge. Her finger wagged in front of the pug's face, giving the dog a lecture Tanya couldn't hear. The woman looked up unafraid when Tanya approached. She asked to take her photo. The woman said, "Of course," and then smiled, lips spread to show a narrow front-tooth gap. Tanya took six quick shots at different angles.

Further down Las Vegas Boulevard from Charleston, she passed The Little White Wedding Chapel. On a July Tuesday, early afternoon, the temperature was close to one hundred, and no one was getting married. The bright green imitation grass out front looked as though it could melt.

A homeless man lay in the shade of the Howard Johnson Inn sign. He wore Adidas running shoes soiled nearly black, stained gray sweatpants with a white stripe up each leg, and a black sleeveless T-shirt with an imprint of the iconic "Welcome to Fabulous Las Vegas" sign. The skin showing had tanned to the color and texture of chestnut belt leather. He looked dead, but Tanya could see the man's open mouth and a slight rocking movement in his chest. He had no blankets or bags or food cartons. Nothing. She didn't take that photo—maybe too easy.

Tanya kept walking to where the boulevard merged with 4th Street, forming a pie wedge. At the tip of the wedge stood another homeless man, this one younger and working each side for handouts. She crossed the boulevard to stand near the man. Closer up, he was more a boy, not much older than herself. His sockless feet fit inside checkered slip-on Vans. He wore cargo shorts, the kind found at Old Navy, and a long-sleeved T-shirt with a Corona logo. On his back was tied what looked like a kite, the leading edges shaped and silk-screened to be butterfly wings. The boy's unwashed and snarled blond hair was held in place with a woman's plastic headband. Two six-inch lengths of hanger wire sprouted from the headband and held up old radio antenna balls from a 76 gas station. The Styrofoam balls had faded from orange to a soft peach. She stepped in front of the boy, still twenty feet away, and read his cardboard sign, SAVE THE RAT KING. He held a child's yellow plastic sand bucket. He walked from one side of the wedge to the other as clusters of cars drove by. In the five minutes she watched, the boy collected a dollar bill and some change. Tanya reached into her pocket. She had a ten, a five, and a few singles. She peeled off a single and walked up to the boy, who stood still, looking at her. He held out his bucket, and she dropped in a dollar.

She asked, "Can I take your photo?"

The boy smiled. "Take all the photos you want."

Tanya started clicking and moving. She finished one roll

of film and reloaded. She moved in closer and captured his face, the tips of the butterfly wings, and the coat-hanger antennas. She asked him, "Who's The Rat King?"

He looked at her, bewildered, "King of the rats."

She didn't pursue it.

◆ ◆ ◆

Tanya worked in the darkroom late into the evening. She'd developed the film used that day, and the three strips of negatives hung from a clothesline to dry. Earlier developed rolls were in eight-inch cut lengths held in transparent protective covers that fit in a thick three-ring binder. She pulled out one length with the negatives of Cory before his last performance at Tramps. He sat with three of the other comedians, drinking a Coke, quiet but listening. One of the comedians, an older woman, said something funny, and the photos caught Cory laughing at her joke. Tanya could tell his laugh was forced and that his mind was on the performance he'd have to deliver shortly. And there it was, the thing she liked most about Cory, his intensity and passion. The following photo was taken just before he went on stage. That close-up told the story of raw fear.

She chose shots that captured all that—intensity, passion, and fear. One by one, Tanya placed the negatives in the carriage of the Beseler enlarger, focused the image on eight-by-ten sheets of matte photo paper, and made the exposures. One by one, they were splashed through the chemicals: developer, stop, and fixer. The images came to life like an appearing ghost—just an aura first, then a discernible image. She'd never gotten over that magic. The wet photos were hung alongside the strips of negatives, and she looked closely. The contrast and sharpness were there—photos she might show to others one day.

An hour later, the negatives had dried, and she cut the three long strips into manageable lengths. She looked at each length on a light table using a magnifying glass, not unlike the loupe Emmy used to see inside diamonds.

The woman on the park bench. Tanya could tell she was—at least at that moment—happy, that whatever world or decade she was locked in, contained memories that put a smile on her face—wrongs since then overshadowed. Tanya wondered at what time in her life that would be—where she'd lock into what felt good. She knew, though, that she'd never lock in. Change was the only thing that interested her. Impulsive change.

She felt sorry for Cory in that regard.

Then, the Butterfly Boy. He smiled in every shot, though not the sincere smile of the Bus Bench Woman. He was acting for the camera, which pissed her off. SAVE THE RAT KING. What did that mean? Who was this boy? If he was still out the next day, she'd follow him, get to know him. Tanya knew something was there for her to discover. Butterfly wings and rat kings.

Two days later, the boy was back out at the intersection early in the morning, catching the rush hour traffic into downtown. Same wings, antennas, sign, and yellow bucket. Tanya stayed in the shadow of a cinder block wall below a neon sign that said STAR HOTEL, DAILY WEEKLY RATES. She was dressed in black and wore a plain black bucket hat—no one misjudged her for one of the street hookers who passed. She did not bother the boy or retake his photo. He must have seen her but did not make eye contact. The boy solicited the cars for handouts and occasionally stopped to drink water and eat what he had.

The Butterfly Boy finished in the early afternoon before the evening rush hour. He began walking north on 4th Street, then jumped over to 3rd. Tanya followed at a distance. At Charleston, the boy walked west and crossed the interstate. A few blocks further, just past the University Medical Center, he entered an office building. He came out with a full grocery bag and then walked back toward the interstate.

Tanya stood where she was and waited for him to pass. When he did, she walked alongside him. She asked, "What do you have there?"

"None of your beeswax." The kid clung to the bag, looking at her now like she was some thief. His butterfly wings were still attached along with the headband with the antennas and faded Styrofoam balls.

She kept walking beside him. "You remember me? I took your photo the other day over on Vegas Boulevard and 4th."

"Yeah, I remember."

As they walked, Tanya pointed toward the butterfly kite. "Why the wings?"

"I'm invisible otherwise."

Somehow, that made sense. The costumes she'd worn had been an act of appearing or presenting; she was invisible without. She guessed the camera was her costume now, and she was okay with being hidden behind a lens.

Tanya asked again, "So, what's in the bag?"

And maybe because they'd talked and she'd introduced herself in a way, he answered, "Medicine for The Rat King."

"Can I see?"

He stopped, and she stopped. He looked at her. "You wanna help?"

"Maybe."

He put the bag down on the sidewalk and then opened the top. What she saw first was a sky-blue box of Trojan condoms, lubricated, one-hundred count. Then a roll of flesh-colored bandages, six inches wide, then another hundred-count box, this one generic-white with a forest green label that said DISPOSABLE SYRINGES. Lastly, a brown-tinted pill container the size of a juice glass.

She asked him, "What are the pills?"

He mumbled each syllable slowly, "Azi-dothy-midine. For The Rat King." The boy closed the top of the bag and continued walking.

Again, Tanya walked beside him. "What's the matter with The Rat King?"

"He's hurt," the kid paused, "Then he's got the AIDS."

She understood. She knew from TV news that the AZT drug was fucking expensive. She stopped when the boy stepped through a hole cut in a chain-link fence. She photographed him walking away, the butterfly wings bouncing like a child's backpack. She yelled after him, "What's your name?"

The boy stooped into a concrete tunnel, a sewer drain, but Tanya could swear she heard him yell back, "Leopold."

◆ ◆ ◆

Photography. It had to tell a story. Arthur Rothstein's *Girl at Gee's Bend*, 1937, in one of the Time-Life books. The black girl stands in the window of a log cabin. Her age is difficult to determine; she could be ten or twenty. The logs are chinked with mud and grass. The chinking is sloppy, with blades of grass sticking from the mud, which appears hastily stuffed by hand. It's a cheap fix by people who are literally dirt poor, but there are no gaps, which suggests a functional necessity. The girl wears a hand-stitched shirt over a white undershirt. She looks away from the camera with a blank expression. Tanya thinks, a face relaxed, which reveals not a present frame of mind but what life has ingrained, averaged out—not happy but not sad, more a contempt, like 'who's stealing my chickens?' Hinged to the window case is a door that can be closed against the cold. The door is covered in newspaper used for insulation. The newspaper itself shows an advertisement of an affluent white woman serving two plates of food—pies, Tanya thinks—to a family not in the image. The black girl looks toward the advertisement but not at the white lady. Tanya thinks she's been around white advertising her whole life, and what she's really doing is looking to see who might be stealing her chickens.

Tanya wonders about Arthur Rothstein. Did he pose her that way to show the social and economic contrast between the girl and the white lady? If so, he missed the story.

That afternoon, she walked the mile or so to the Boulevard Mall. Inside on the second level was a Claire's Boutique that sold earrings, makeup, and kitschy stuff to young teens. Tanya hadn't been there in years but remembered they had costumes. Inside, she walked through the few aisles and found what she was looking for, a Monarch butterfly cape. The next day, she stood out on the corner with Leopold, the cape strapped to her shoulders, and held a cardboard sign, SAVE THE RAT KING. She stood in front of a one-gallon white bucket with a wire handle, and in her hands held the Nikon F2 loaded with high-definition ASA100 T-Max.

A week later, more people had joined. Cory was there with butterfly wings he'd made himself from a bed sheet. Emmy came out on his day off from the Starbucks inside the Mirage. He helped collect money but did not flaunt wings. A network TV news show ran a story about the butterfly people at the junction of 4th and Las Vegas Boulevard. Leopold had been too distracted to answer the newslady's questions, so Tanya stepped in for the interview. They were collecting money to purchase the AZT drug for the homeless in Las Vegas with AIDS. She did not mention the prophylactics or needles.

The next day, more joined, all dressed in their butterfly costumes. They were now officially The Butterfly People. A backstage employee from one of the Vegas shows that still featured showgirls delivered a new costume to Leopold, The Butterfly Boy. He now stood at the tip of the wedge in high-heeled boots, a rhinestone bodice with attached wings, and a headdress of orange ostrich feathers. He wore the costume proudly, and the whole assemblage on the boulevard looked like a parade of burlesque dancers. Cars now drove out of their way to donate.

A month later, the throng of Butterfly People thinned, but money was still collected. Leopold still stood at the front with his original sign, now tattered and almost illegible.

Then, one day, he stepped from the tunnels, donned his wings and ostrich feather headdress, walked to the boulevard wedge, and stood with a fresh cardboard sign.

THE RAT KING IS SAVED.

279

Kurt Johnson
Burntside Lake, Ely, Minnesota

FIND MORE FROM AUTHOR KURT JOHNSON

www.KurtJohnsonBooks.com

KurtJohnsonBooks.substack.com